MW01147507

# TIN CANS

*Family, friendship, loyalty, and consternation is at the heart of Tin Cans.*

Lana must decide what to do with her mobile home business, which is always teetering in the red. Exhausted from the process of keeping the business afloat, what will happen if she closes?

Will her family think its just one more failure?

Will her friends stand by her?

And what about her employees? They are such a wacky bunch, who would possibly hire them.

*All in all, its good old fashioned dysfunctional fun.*

# ABOUT THE AUTHOR

**Lise Freeman** grew up in the Metropolitan Washington, DC area, allowing her to experience a myriad of people and politics. She has dipped her toes into many careers since including real estate, but her passion remains her writing – with her style of humor coming from her mother, one of the funniest persons she has ever known.

Currently her life revolves around two wonderful children, in awe of them every day.

Tin Cans was born of the author's experience of owning several mobile home businesses and is her debut novel.

F
FREEMAN

**oveletta** IMPRINT
**CUSTOM BOOK PUBLICATIONS**

*Asia's Global Print & Digital Publisher*

3/17 17.95

# TIN CANS

A Novel
by
LISE FREEMAN

*Dedicated to my family and friends, all of whom in one way or another, are part of this book.*

*Special dedication to my mother, the original Evita, still the funniest person I have ever known.*

# Chapter 1

Anxiously, I push the 'up' button on the elevator, the door slides open, gingerly I step inside. *Whoooooosh!* Off we rocket, not up but sideways, ever faster, now reverse and plummet into the garage, then burst outside into the daylight. Where the hell are we going! What the H E double hockey sticks is going on? I just want to go the fifth floor; lingerie, pajamas, swimsuits. Oh My God! Shooting out through the roof, we peak then start to fall, plummeting faster and faster… Jolting upright in bed, now fully awake, I wipe the sweat dripping off my forehead. *Crapola,* not again. Unfortunately, I have this crazy elevator dream on a too regular basis.

Of course there is a deep, inner, soul searching meaning to my dream but as usual, I choose to put blinders on and ignore it. On with my day, I bounce out of bed, do my morning get-ready-for-work routine, throw on my Florida Manufactured Home Shirt, finish by putting enough product in my chocolate brown hair so it will break if anyone touches it. Added bonus; the spiky hair adds the final touch of height to my already six foot frame.

Not even out of the neighborhood, my cousin Tedi – short for Theodora but if you call her that she will give you the stink eye – calls to shoot the shit.

'I had that dream again,' I start.

'Cripes,' Tedi replies. 'You know what it means doncha, your life is out of control.' Tedi is our family lesbian, not a dyke, but not exactly a lipstick lesbo either, maybe a lip gloss lesbo. We have been attached at the hip forever, growing up only four houses apart. She is also my business partner.

'Tell me something I don't know. Are you coming in today?' I ask, thinking I really wish our business would take two steps forward, and stay there instead of always equally going two steps back.

'Yep, I am on my way to the Hollywood office now. We need to go out tonight I could use an adult beverage… or ten.'

'Maybe,' I sigh. 'I could use some brain down time. We'll catch up tonight; I'll see you at the office shortly.'

My name is Lana Turner – thanks Mom -- my life seems to mirror Frank Sinatra's *That's Life*. Right now its somewhere between April and May, I'm not riding high, but I'm not shot down either. Of course it may have to do with the fact that my business attention span is usually two years max. For my latest venture, I have opened two manufactured home offices, aptly named Florida Manufactured Home Store. For you layman, I sell manufactured homes, aka mobile homes aka trailers. I have one office in Hollywood, not California, but in Florida, and another in West Palm Beach. I know people hear Palm Beach and think of the *Rich and Famous*, but the people that buy homes from me are neither. And unfortunately, I am in a quandary regarding my business, its borderline going into the red, and I am not sure if I have the energy to save it.

Racing down the turnpike my mind goes faster than the car. Okay, I ponder, what is on my plate today? What's closest to the money? That's my mantra, work the deals that are closest to paying, and work my way through the deals, next closest to the money. It's driven my success so far. I started this business on a shoe string, and last year we sold over four million dollars in homes, not bad. Now I just need to figure out how to sell six million this year so we can outpace our bills.

Yet another possible opportunity has presented itself, and hopefully this will be the one that propels the business substantially into the black. Hurricane Lisa recently hit

Puerto Rico and created an unfortunate housing shortage via its savage winds and rain. Bringing in manufactured housing is quick and inexpensive, and if I can be the supplier, it could be the answer for me as well. Win, win.

Tedi is standing outside the office as I pull up, having her monthly smoke. I know, right, in this day and age? But it's only a once in a while thing. Annoyed, the guy in the office next door comes out just as I get out of the car, and yells, 'Why don't you just smoke in the office instead of polluting the air out here?'

Tedi yells back at him simply, 'It's a *Non Smoking Office!*' while blowing out smoke in his direction. Tedi is slightly height challenged, but more than makes up for it in attitude. Her eyes are so dark they are almost black and send an unmistakable message not to 'F' with her.

'But you all...' he begins, until he locks eyes with Tedi, and instead decides to make a hasty retreat into his store. Enough said. Tedi stomps out her cigarette and follows me into the office.

The office is not exactly in the high rent district, but it's certainly welcoming. Situated in a small strip mall, the large windows look out onto the traffic zipping up and down one of Fort Lauderdale's main drags. Inside, the office is wide open, with desks for my staff, a small private office for me, plus a comfortable conference room for privacy. The indoor-outdoor carpeting has seen better days, but haven't we all. And conveniently, there is a liquor store right next door.

As soon as I walk in the door, I am verbally accosted by my Lauderdale assistant, June. We actually inherited her when we sold her a mobile home, still not sure how that worked.

'Uncle Larry called'. She sounds anxious. 'He wanted to remind you he is coming in soon, very soon.'

Uncle Larry is of course not really my uncle, but an investor that we work with from Texas. He has been described as resembling a dead baby bird which I can live with since he is a cash-infusing sugardaddy to my business. Larry puts up the cash to buy fixer uppers, we rehab, then sell them and split the profits, plus he finances almost anyone with a pulse and a cash down payment, sweet deal.

'He also asked if I could reserve a rental car for him, can I?' she pleads.

'That's fine,' thinking I hope she gets one with a big back seat. Consensus is she is having an affair with him. I try not to think about it for two reasons; one – ew, two – I would probably have to fire her.

'So gang, what is on tap for today?' I glance around the room at my two sales people, Mike and Diane, hoping to hear tales of sales.

Diane is an old friend of Tedi's, and Mike is an ex of Diane's. Sounds like a soap opera, right? Diane actually has many exes. When she walks into her favorite watering hole, everyone shouts her name, kinda like Norm on *Cheers*. And I am not saying she is loose, but no one is a stranger in that bar if you catch my drift.

Diane waves me over to her desk. 'I am going to need your help getting my buyer into Vista Community. She has a felony, but I think justified.'

'What's the felony?' I am almost afraid to ask.

'Arson, she burnt down the house she was living in with her boyfriend. She worked, he stayed home and spent her money; she was clueless, thought the mortgage and all the bills were getting paid. Bottom line, the bank foreclosed, she burnt it down. She should have burnt it down with him in it. I've given her the nickname, *Blaze*.'

Alrighty then.

'Okay, I'll call the community manager at Vista and see what I can do.' I know what I can do, it'll cost me an expensive lunch and a plain white envelope causally left on the table. I wonder what the going rate for arson is these days? Don't get the wrong idea, most people that buy manufactured homes are your typical home buyers. Those buyers just don't seem to come through our doors.

'And you Mike, what have you got for me today?'

Mike has a wooden leg. No one has ever questioned why he does not take advantage of modern medicine. Maybe he can't afford a new prosthetic leg, maybe he wants to be a pirate, I do not judge. I hear he is a good dancer though – go figure.

'Well, nothing to compete with that, but the day is young.'

Swell.

'I think I found a good deal on a rental car for Uncle Larry,' June chimes in, hoping to get a brownie point, her glasses falling down her nose. 'But I am not really sure what kind it is. The rental company is called Royal, and I think the guy said the car is a *fuckus*?'

'Sounds perfect June, you just got Uncle Larry a Royal Fuckus,' I respond laughing. I don't care that no one else laughs, I crack myself up.

'And Evita is on the phone for you,' June says hesitantly.

Evita is my mother, her real name is Isabel, and drama rules her life. I love my mother, but she really is a nut job. She also happens to be the funniest person I have ever known. She never talks much about my father, and I don't really have any memories of one. She was a working single mom before it was chic. 'Hey Mom, what's shaking?'

'Just want to make sure you will be at the family reunion, Leebee.' *Leebee* is somehow being short for Lana. It's better than *Moose* which is what my older brother Max somehow got out of Lana.

'Yes, Mom, Tedi and I are flying up together.'

I can hear her eyes roll, she knows Tedi and I have a tendency to get into, well, situations we'll call them. Our family reunion, first of its kind, is in Boston, a mystery since no one in the family actually lives there. I am already having anxiety attacks; most certainly I will need a shrink tune up before we go. Part of the stress is due to the fact that my mother and Tedi's mother do not always get along; in fact they are polar opposites. Tedi's mom, Sylvia, has been married to my mom's brother, John, for forty-five years, look up the word stable and you will see their picture. My mom, well, she is more of the Harper Valley PTA type. I should probably pack my black and white striped shirt.

'I'll call you this weekend Mom; gotta go, things to do, places to go, people to see.' I quickly hang up, avoiding any nuggets of knowledge she may want to share. Some of her nuggets are inspiring, like 'be *a leader, not a follower,*' and then there's '*we are all the same height in bed.*' Good to know, just not from your mother.

'I think we should go a day early, a cousins' day with our sisters,' Tedi suggests. 'Make it our mission to scout out the perfect bar, one with Harpoon Ale on tap, Boston Clam Chowder and those little oyster crackers.'

'Hmmm, how long have you been pondering that one? Well, I would think that shouldn't be too hard to accomplish,' I reply. Ohh, what wishful thinking. The fearsome foursome on the loose in Boston; good thing the city is small enough to navigate on foot.

The day is spent working with the sales people, locking down deals and finishing ones with loose ends. Tedi and I, along with our manager Toby, put our heads together on advertising strategies, and look at ways to cut the budget. Toby is not only my lovable manager – not in everyone's opinion – but best bud, who does everything but sales, suggests cutting commission percentages to the sales people. Tempting but we agree that will go over like a lead balloon, not that Toby cares.

'Okay, I am spent,' sighs Tedi, '…and ready for an adult beverage. What time are we meeting tonight?'

'I have a few things to wrap up, maybe seven?'

'Works for me, see you there with bells on.'

Toby sighs, 'And the sad part is she will really have bells on; it's a requirement at the bar so all the single women will be warned she is on the prowl. If she could dial back her moves a notch or three, she might actually get a date.'

'Now be nice, she is not as skilled at dating as you are, and certainly not as practiced.' Zing.

'Well, I guess at least she tries to date, unlike someone else we know.' Zing back.

'And with that, I am out, I'll give you the scoop on tonight, tomorrow.'

♦ ♦ ♦

# Chapter 2

It's karaoke night, meaning the parking lot of *Comfortable Shoes*, the local lesbian hangout, is packed. We have the usual assortment of vehicles from sedans to trucks, okay, maybe a few too many trucks. Ah, there it is, Tedi's 1965 Mustang convertible, how she loves that car. She is convinced it's a babe magnet, it's certainly an improvement over the Taurus wagon she used to drive.

It's a relief she is already here. Even though I know a lot of the women at the bar, I am still a bit uncomfortable going in by myself. Straight women present a special challenge to lesbians, like they only need to convert one more to get that free toaster.

Right now, I don't prefer either sex and I'm okay with that. I'm sure my inability to romantically commit has to do with my dysfunctional upbringing. Isn't it wonderful that we can blame our parents for all of our emotional baggage? Anyway, I have no desire to find a soul mate at this point in my life. I have no time, I have other priorities, or so I keep telling myself.

Darkness and smoke attack my eyes the instant I walk through the door, my eyes adjusting before I can begin scanning for Tedi. There she is at the bar, talking to Teresa who has never met a glass of wine she did not like. As I walk up, I hear Teresa saying to the bartender, 'What happened? Did you trip on the way over here? My glass is only three quarters full!' Yikes, she should be a treat tonight.

'Hey Cuz!' Tedi yells. She has to yell, it's very loud in here, it is always loud, lesbians are a loud group. Wonder why that is?

'Hey Tedi, hey Teresa, looks like we have a full house tonight.'

'Yeah,' Tedi says. 'We have all of our K.D. Langs, Melissa Etheridges, and Sophie B. Hawkins lining up to croon.'

It's pretty much the same thing every karaoke night, just like any other bar — mostly inebriated bad singers. The good thing is if you actually get up and sing, there is usually someone worse that you. Signing up to sing is always a fleeting thought of mine, very fleeting. But just maybe one day, never say never.

'You want the usual, Lana?' The bartender is waiting with a martini glass in hand; it's scary that I have a *usual.*

'Sure Candy,' and boom, Candy promptly delivers a Grey Goose martini. I'm positive Candy is not her real name, but in my humble opinion it's preferable to Butch. Very attractive, she smartly keeps the girls in plain view to encourage bigger tips. In fact, her T-shirt says 'Tips make my boobs get bigger'.

I turn to talk to Tedi, who just tipped Candy for me. 'So what's the latest on the family reunion activities?'

'Well, Aunt Rita is running the show so it should be a real hoot, and I don't mean that in a good way. She sent my dad a preliminary list of songs we can all sing around the campfire.' Aunt Rita is the glue of the family. She lost her husband a few years back and now it is her self-proclaimed mission to keep the family close, she even writes the semi-annual Turner Times newsletter.

'Ugh,' I groan. 'I am going to have to have therapy before *and after* this reunion.'

Tedi shoots me a look, 'Warning! Warning! Sherri at ten o'clock and moving in fast.'

Oh crap. Sherri is a striking red head that, for whatever reason, has quite the thing for me. She is my height, six feet, and has a figure that is will make most humans with a pulse do a double take. If she has a fault, it's her extravagant make up, like Kim Kardashian or a drag queen.

'Lana,' she says in a tone that unfortunately makes my knees somewhat buckle. If I were ever to switch teams, she would be the one.

'Sherri,' is the only word I can manage.

'Are you singing tonight?'

'Not tonight, but maybe one of these nights, are you singing?'

'Of course Lana, and I think you will like my selection.' With that she sashays off.

Tedi was glued to the exchange. 'Why don't you go for it, and wipe the sweat off your forehead.'

'Stop trying to convert me,' I say, annoyed. Turning to Teresa and conveniently changing the subject, 'So how's the shed business, Teresa? Sales booming?'

'My boss is an asshole,' she replies and takes another gulp of wine. I nod knowingly, bosses can be that way.

From the stool behind me, a gravely male voice threatens, 'Lisa, you need to stay away from Sherri, she's with me now.'

Spinning around, I look into the eyes of a beautiful woman. Craning to see behind her, there are just more women. I'm confused, did that voice come out of her?

Tedi whispers behind me, 'Transgender in progress.'

With that clarification, I say, 'You must be thinking of someone else, my name is Lana, and I barely know Sherri.'

'You are not fooling anyone Lisa, you know what I am talking about.'

'No worries, I get this all the time,' I explain, 'I just have one of those familiar faces that everyone thinks they recognize.'

She stands up, an imposing figure, glaring at me, 'You need to heed my warning Lisa.' Then walks away.

'Your face gets you in more trouble,' Tedi observes.

'So is that Sherri's…?' I ask.

'Ask her yourself, here she comes.' Tedi is getting a big kick out of this.

Sherri sidles up to me, too close, 'Don't let her scare you off Lana, she has a crush on me but the feeling is not mutual. There is no connection, not like you and I have.'

Wait… what? What connection? I don't even bother to respond as I am now thoroughly flummoxed. Teresa is watching all of this through the bottom of her now empty wine glass while Tedi looks like she is going to explode. I simply order another martini. Seems like the best course of action.

And so the night went. Tedi and I dissed our families, gossiped about the employees, laughed about Toby's choice in dates, and generally had a therapeutic evening. Tedi and I have the kind of relationship that we don't even have to finish our sentences before we start laughing, our humor is totally in sync. It's not unusual for one of us to fall off our bar stool laughing anytime we are together.

The evening is wrapping up when Sherri takes her turn at the microphone. *'Damn, I wish I was your lover,'* she belts out, *'I'll rock you till the daylight comes,'* her eyes like a high tech laser directly on me.

Oh boy, this evening is now over. I say a quick adios to Tedi, who does not want this entertainment to end, and head for the door. Doing my best not to make eye contact with Sherri, I can feel her stare searing into back of my head. It's all I can do not to break into a full out sprint.

As soon as I am in the parking lot, I stop and breathe in the glorious tropical night air. Of course the top goes down on my convertible and Cher goes on full blast. Cher clears my head, stops my brain from hurting itself with too many thoughts. Bless you, Cher.

♦♦♦

# Chapter 3

Pulling up to the West Palm Beach office, I see that Toby is already there, which means the employees will not be happy. They cringe when Toby and I are in the same office; we have a way of irritating everyone with our special brand of humor.

The West Palm office is a smaller version of the Fort Lauderdale office, down to the thread worn indoor-outdoor carpet. This strip mall also has a liquor store, which I am sure was a factor in me signing the lease.

'Good morning all!' Cheeriness oozes from my voice. Penny and Mable, my sales gals, look up briefly from their desks with a nod of acknowledgment. Sandy, our admin gal, always with a smile, returns my *good morning* with one of her own.

'Where's Toby?' Looking around he is nowhere in sight. 'We need to get our reservations and get our game plan for the Puerto Rico trip.'

'He's at the liquor store, I think buying lottery tickets,' Sandy answers. Mable's eyes light up, she is hoping he's bring back vodka even though its only nine am. Mable is a sweet as syrup sales person; everyone instantly loves her and trusts her. She is also rail thin, wears bright orange lipstick, and lives in what we call 'the compound,' a heavily gated mostly senior community even though she is only forty-two. Mable was born old. Oh yeah, and she is lily white like a freshly bleached sheet, the lipstick definitely helps make her visible.

'Why are you both in this office today?' demands Penny. 'Doesn't Mr. Sunshine need to be watching the goings on in the Lauderdale office?'

'Well Miz Sunshine, I need him here to go over our Puerto Rico trip, and if you are nice to him he might even bring you back a bottle of rum,' I answer, hoping to placate her.

'Whatever.' Penny has a real way with words. Translated, her response means, yes please, I will take the bottle of rum.

'Well, send him into my office when he gets back.' I plop my behind into my big girl office chair and start to finalize our presentation for our trip. Sorting through my notes, I am thinking, geez, I hope these people are open-minded, this could really solve their housing problems ... and my own financial ones.

Our presentation is simple, cheap housing, built well, delivered fast, that's the Evelyn Woods version. I hear the front door open, knowing it's Toby as he sends his first zinger at Penny without missing a beat.

'Well Liz, headed for the Black and White Ball *again* today? Isn't that the third one this week?' Toby quips.

We affectionately call Penny, 'Liz,' since she has been married seven times, and has admitted to wanting to beat Liz Taylor's marriage record. As far as the Black and White Ball comment, everyday Penny wears a white polo shirt and black leggings, not the most flattering for her ample figure. She is also pale, like a Kabuki dancer, the only color she sports is a bright red lipstick also known as 'the target'.

'Nice Toby,' Penny retorts, knowing she is not equipped to win this battle of wits, but is willing to give it a valiant try.

Thinking I should put her out of her misery quickly, I say, 'Oh Penny, always quick with the wit, should we come back in an hour?' Toby and I exchange smirks.

Shooting me the evil eye, Penny gathers momentum and fires, 'You know Toby, there is a tasteful way to display your assets without wearing hooker shorts.'

'As Miss Piggy says, '*Style comes in all shapes and sizes, therefore the bigger you are, the more style you have*' and these shorts showcase my big style,' retorts Toby. 'And thanks for noticing my assets.'

'I'm not your type, I'm not inflatable,' Penny fires.

'Well done, Penny!' I exclaim, 'And with that we bid you adieu, back to work all; you've been a fine audience.'

Nothing like starting the day with a juicy sarcastic exchange, and it's all in good fun, really, it is. Toby does wear his shorts a bit short, but in his defense, he is gay and he has nice legs. He is not a flaming queen, in fact your *gaydar* – gay radar – would not go off if you were to meet him, except, yeah, okay, the shorty shorts.

Toby joins me in the office and we refine our presentation, hoping it makes as much sense to the powers that be as it does to us. He cringes as we look up flight schedules and realizes it's a four hour flight, mostly over water. Adverse to flying is putting it mildly, Toby absolutely hates to fly, nothing about it makes sense to him, two hundred tons of metal floating in the air.

'Oh my God,' he whines, 'do I really have to go? And can I have cocktails on board?'

'Yes and yes, and I think we should take the eight am flight, I'm sure you can get a Bloody Mary on board, and maybe one at the airport bar.' His wheels are visibly turning, most likely thinking about garnishes he'll want.

'Why don't you take Penny; because she is boring?'

'First off,' I explain. 'She has that steel plate in her head and won't make it past the metal detector, really delays the security check. And second, she would be too busy looking for husband number eight.'

'Our little Penny sure has a colorful past,' Toby giggles. 'I forgot husband number two mistakenly shot her as she was sneaking in their bedroom window from a long night out. Wasn't he also in trying on her dresses at the time?'

'Who knows, I need a husband map to keep them all straight.'

'Fine, so where are we staying?'

'Ritz Carlton.'

'Wow! Fancy Schmancy! Ritzy titzy, Mama. That makes this much less painful.'

'Less painful for you,' My brow furrows thinking about finances, 'At eight hundred a night it's a killer for me. But what the hell, its only money and we're worth it.'

'Amen, sistah!' So we begin to tackle the bills. Toby is inner circle, so he knows that things aren't as rosy as I paint them. But it's my job to worry, and to keep everyone else motivated, onward we plow.

'Are we going to make the bills this month?' Toby quietly asks, concerned for the bottom line.

'Yes, by the skin of our teeth.' Isn't that an odd saying? What the hell is that supposed to mean anyway?

'What's your plan to generate more business? I know you have an idea, you always do, and you always come through.' Toby is my personal cheerleader, another good reason keep him around.

'Fingers and toes crossed for Puerto Rico,' meanwhile thinking to myself, better add eyes, ears, boobs, and anything else we can cross. This constant search for new income streams is becoming exhausting.

As we are wrapping up, Penny knocks on the door.

'Can you help me a sec? I have a woman on the phone who says her credit is bad because her cousin's sister-in-law's boyfriend is in jail for robbery, but her pastor says he will co-sign on a note for her.'

Welcome to my world of high finance, we house the masses, whatever it takes. 'Get the pastor on the phone and let's see if he understands what he is getting into.' This should be a doozy.

And so my day goes. I feel in our small way in our small corner of the world, we are helping those who would otherwise be renters. We are helping families realize the American Dream of home ownership; a slice of the Americana pie. The remainder of the day goes without significant incident. Toby and Penny end the day on a positive note – drinks after work, should make for lively gossip tomorrow. Mable is headed to have martinis with her family in the compound where she is safe and only drives a golf cart.

Sandy pops her head in my office to see if I need anything else before she leaves. She is a very kind soul, odd, but kind. She also has sweaty hands, leaves soggy paper towels all over the office, and I think combs her too long hair with a shoe. But good help is hard to find so if those are her worst traits, she's a keeper.

'Thanks Sandy, I'm good; enjoy your evening,' which I know will consist of smoking a joint and eating cereal from a large mixing bowl. To each their own, we live in a judgment free zone.

Quiet falls over the office, no retorts, no jabs, just me and my shadow. I look around the office, I am Yertle the Turtle, the master of all I survey, but is it enough? Is this the life I am destined for? Selling mobile homes? Is there something bigger waiting for me? I know one thing for sure, if I can't bring in more business, I have no choice but to change my path. But is the grass really greener? Ouch, alone time is not good, my brain hurts. I seem to go down this rabbit hole, thinking the next big thing is waiting and not staying focused on the here and now.

My cares and woes neatly packed, singing low, I head out the door. Warm, balmy sea breezes greet me, so naturally the top goes down on my Mitsubishi Spyder. I bought this car right off the showroom floor. Stopped at a red light, a Spyder pulled up next to me, one look and I headed right to the dealership. The sales person saw me sitting in the car and asked me if I wanted to test drive the car, I answered no, just put up the top to make sure my hair fits. It did. Popping in my favorite Cher CD, I crank to full blast, the perfect recipe to clear the head and not obsess on what tomorrow will bring, or won't bring.

As always, my driveway of worn Chicago pavers is a welcoming site. Engine off, I take a moment to admire my casita, a 1930's Mizner inspired cottage in Delray Beach, just a block from the Intracoastal. Lush greenery surrounds me, curving coconut palms, giant mango trees, jasmine, birds of paradise, ahhh, my paradise. Not too big, not too small, just right for me at least. As I walk in, another big sigh escapes me, home sweet home. Decorated in beach cottage shabby chic, the overstuffed furniture has a bold, orange floral print that says, '*Come In, take your shoes off, do you want a cocktail?*'

Don't mind if I do, a Belvedere martini, complete with hand stuffed blue cheese olives should hit the spot. Feeling the need for a light nosh, I scrounge around the fridge and find a nice slice of brie, cut a crisp apple, and head for the patio to soak in the twilight. Sigh number three.

Don't get me wrong, I love what I do, and most of the people in my life. But we all need space and alone time.

My comfy chaise lounge whispers for me to sit. I fondly admire my martini, gently pull the olive out of the glass, let the excess vodka slowly drip into my mouth. The brain kicks in. Crap, just when I was getting relaxed, looks like it's going to be a night of introspection. I begin to look at my journey, I should be satisfied, nice car, nice house, my own business, family, friends...

Then why do I not feel satisfied, why do I feel restless? Shouldn't I focus on taking my business to the next level instead of looking at other paths to take?

Do you ever look back and connect the dots that brought you to where you are? When I got out of college,

I worked for a big company developing new security software. My family and friends were so very impressed, I even had stock options, *whoo hoo!* That lasted about three weeks before boredom started setting in, I felt like a working Stepford wife. So I went out to lunch one day, had a few beers, got a haircut, and never went back. My illustrious career path had begun.

Sales are really more my thing, it's in my DNA, my mother can sell snow to an Eskimo. At one point she owned a bridal store, her favorite line to the bride-to-be while trying on gowns was *hold your flowers low, show off your waistline while you still have one*. Nice.

Shattering the silence, a loud, *Helloooooo* comes from the other side of the coconut palms on the side of my house. Yay! Saved by my neighbor, Jillian.

*'Hellllooooooo*, we'd love to have Santa come stay with us!' I replied with our standard greeting, my favorite line from miracle on 34th street, where Mr. Shellhammer plies his wife with martinis so she will let good old Kris Kringle spend the night.

'Yum,' Jillian's eyes are transfixed on my martini, a bit of drool starting to slide from the corner of her mouth..

'Plenty inside as usual, help yourself'

'And you know I will.'

Jillian is my blond bombshell neighbor. Not sure if she is a natural blond, not a question I am going to ask. She has a smile that disarms, a laugh that is infectious, a heart of gold, and tits for days.

When I moved in, we bonded instantly; her ex like mine, is also an attorney. Hers however, is hell bent on making her life miserable. Our relationship was solidified when I told her my favorite attorney joke:

*A woman goes into her gynecologist, and says she needs the doctor to settle an argument she is having with her husband. 'My husband says I cannot get pregnant having anal sex.'*

18

'Of course you can,' says the doctor. 'Where do you think all the attorneys come from?'

Bah dum dum…

Jillian is blessed with the kind of body women and men would die for, happily for the later, she loves to share it. My sex life would almost be non-existent if I could not share hers; the stories of her sexual escapades that is, not actually share sex.

'So,' she remarks with a raised eyebrow, 'Thinking too much again, weren't you.'

'Let's talk about you, tell me about your latest dalliances.'

'Oh My God! Remember that chef guy we saw at the crepe place? We hooked up, we hooked down, we hooked all around.'

'Then?' Unsure why I bothered, I know the answer.

'I said thanks, now you can go, we are done,' she coolly answers.

'Don't you ever want more?' I question, feeling a bit melancholy. It's been quite a while for me in the intimacy department, in fact, I probably should check for cobwebs.

'No cuddle time for me. Get in, get out, get gone.'

'No sense mincing words or actions,' I conclude.

'So what's up with you? Do you plan on seeing anyone anytime soon?' Jillian of course already knows the answer.

'Okay, I am going to give you the answer and that will be the end of the conversation. No.'

Jillian bites her lip, dying to push me into the dating game, but she has known me long enough to know it ain't happenin'. 'Then tell me why you are so restless?'

'My career path has been taken over by my gypsy blood, or the, *is that all there is syndrome*,' unfortunately the only answer I have to offer. 'Don't you ever feel that something else is calling your name?'

'Someone else for me, I am a gypsy slut.'

'Well aren't we the pair,' and as I say it, she looks at me and in unison we say, 'a pair of what is the real question!' Ba dum bum.

'What's going on with your work?' I ask. Jillian is an endodontist, oh yeah, root canals. She only needs to work part time, and is always booked solid, probably because of the valium she uses to relax her patients.

'I always think of Bette Midler when I work, but I'm on the wrong end of the punch line,' and she starts to sing, *'Cause you thrill me when you drill me, Dr. Longjohn, I have a cavity I need filling.'*

'Let's have another martini.' I get up, take her glass and head to the bar inside. 'Have you eaten yet? You know the rule, if you drink, you gotta eat.'

Looking in the fridge, I scope out my odds and ends, check out the pantry, and decide I can whip up a fresh pasta primavera. Easy peasy.

'Jillian, while you make the martinis, I'll do dinner.'

She grabs the glasses and expertly shakes our martinis while keeping me company in the kitchen. My house has the perfect open floor plan; the kitchen, living and dining room all flow together in one big room. I love to cook although it doesn't happen often so I have the proverbial cook's kitchen with all the goodies. The feel is that of a Tuscan kitchen with granite counter tops in neutral tones and weathered wood shelving instead of closed cabinets.

Pasta ready, we decide to take the feast back outside on the lanai. Dusk is settling in, so I turn on the pool lights for additional ambiance. We eat in silence, watching the light sparkle and bend in the pool.

'This is boring,' Jillian states, after slurping her last fettuccine noodle. 'Let's walk over to the Ice Bar, see what's shaking.'

'Sounds good except it's a school night for me, but don't let me stop you.'

'Would you mind?' Like she even has to ask.

'Not as long as you give me details of your debauchery.' I give her a quick hug and send her on her way. Its only eight, too early for bed, even for me. I need a life, like perhaps even personal one. Maybe even a new romance? Nah...I'll just call Toby and see what he is up to.

'Yo, Lanalu!' I can barely hear him, I assume he is imbibing at one of his local haunts.

'Where are you?'

'At The Tool Box, its two for one night, drinks, not boys,' he screams. 'Come meet me!'

'No can do, I have already had two martinis, plus it's all the way into Lauderdale.'

'Stop being boring, live a little, take a cab.'

'Tempting, but it is a school night.'

'Oh come on, I have my lucky socks on, it'll be fun.' His lucky socks say *Fuck my Sox off*, not much luck needed there. Knowing Toby, he has his feet up on the bar so no one can miss the message.

'You enjoy, I'll see you in the morning in the Lauderdale office.'

My life is in no way boring, not with the crew I hang with. And I can party with the best of them, oh yeah, I've closed bars down. I've even had one night stands, well, once I had a one night stand. I look at the clock, eight-thirty... think I'll head to bed.

# Chapter 4

I am not particularly looking forward to meeting John, Sol Milichek's lackey, to finalize the Puerto Rico trip. Sol I like, he is a manufactured home community owner that I do a considerable amount of business with and we have a great rapport. When I hatched the idea of pitching manufactured housing to Puerto Rico, I knew I would need a partner with deeper pockets, hence, Sol. But Sol delegates, makes calls while relaxing by the pool at his hacienda in Arizona, hence, John. Allegedly, John, who is a young whippersnapper community manager, has a government contact in Puerto Rico that has promised to get us the ear of the Governor.

John is waiting for me in his office, sitting behind the big boy desk, in the big boy chair, with his feet up. Immediately, I want to smack his feet down, but instead I extend my hand. Showing off his professionalism, he comes in for a fist bump.

'John, nice to see you, are we set with the conference call with Sol?'

'Yea, sure, let's do this thing.' Now can I smack him?

'Lana, pleasure to speak with you again,' Sol is of course polite, his business etiquette oozes through the speaker phone, 'I am excited about this opportunity we have before us.' Now that's the way to do it.

'Likewise Sol, I am all set on my end, we have the presentation printed with impressive facts and figures, I'll just go over the final travel plans with John, anything else you want to add?'

'Just call me if you need me as back up, you have my banker's statement that we can handle the initial purchase and shipping. Now go get that contract, I have complete faith in you and John!' He would make a great cheerleader.

'Thanks Sol, fingers crossed.'

John hangs up the phone, looks at me, 'Yea, I got this.'

'Who else is coming with you John?' I ask.

'My wife and her friend and my buddy.' Great, bringing in the heavy hitters.

'Alrighty then, let's just go over our presentation points.'

'No need, I got it all up here,' he taps his head where his brains are supposedly housed, I'm sure I heard an echo. He inspires confidence.

'Okay then, don't forget all the home specifications, see you in Puerto Rico.' I scram out of there before I either pull my hair out, or his. I need this deal to work, I can't believe I am saddled with this ass. No matter, I'm used to doing the heavy lifting.

I feel like my day is shot but its only early afternoon, I might as well swing by the West Palm office and see what's happening. On the way, my cell rings and it's Toby.

'Sooooo, how was the meeting?' he inquires.

'Ugh, what a putz,' I tell him. 'I don't get what Sol sees in him, he must be a great ass kisser. No matter, we'll carry the ball, and try not to let him speak.'

'I wanted to remind you that Uncle Larry lands tomorrow and he will be expecting to see you first thing.'

'Any idea what is on his agenda?'

'I am sure just the usual; what have we sold, what do we have in inventory, and what do we have coming up, blah blah. Are you going to ask him about financing new model homes?'

'Yes, that's on my agenda, and I think that would be great for business, yet another idea to stay in the black. So be on your best behavior and you may have to take one for the team, that would ensure the financing.'

'Hah! Won't be me sistah,' he exclaims, 'but fortunately we have plenty of loose employees that I am sure will be happy to volunteer.' Truer words were never said.

'Okay, see you in the morning,' and I hang up.

Something seems amiss in the office, too quiet as I walk in. 'Penny? Mable?' Not evoking much of a response from either.

'It was their idea' Sandy looks nervous, her eyes wandering over to the water cooler. I squint to take a harder look because I can't possibly be seeing what I think I am seeing. Something is floating in the bottle, and there seems to be orange around the spigot.

'Are those olives in the water bottle?' My brain in denial, 'And Mable, that looks like your color lip stick on the spigot!' This is new.

'Well, the martinis stay nice and cold that way, it's been a rough day so far,' explains Mable. As long as there is a good reason.

Alright then. 'Sandy, put a fresh bottle of water in the cooler, Penny and Mable, go next door and eat something and drink lots of coffee.' Sheesh.

'And we have a kinda nasty letter from an unhappy homeowner,' Sandy reluctantly tells me.

I just look at her 'and…?'

'They feel they were myzzled.'

'Okay, wait… what?' I am confused, 'Can I see the letter please?'

I look over the letter 'Sandy, could that be 'misled'?'

'I guess, but I like myzzled better.'

'I'll put a call into the Urban Dictionary, I am sure they will add 'myzzled.' With that I head for my office and close the door. Is this day over yet? Oh wait, it's not. Still one more piece of the puzzle to insure I have my best shot at the Puerto Rico opportunity, advice from the dreaded ex.

He's a walking, talking oxymoron, yummy and annoying. Unfortunately, I need his help tonight and after one more martini, I'll probably sleep with him. Recumbent on his sleek, butter soft, russet brown sofa, I pretend I am glued to his every word as he spews his words of wisdom. All I am really hearing is *blah, blah, blah*.

'Lana?!? Are you listening to me?' Patrick says a little too loudly for my taste.

Without answering him, I get up; slowly move around his subtle but unmistakably masculine living room, with its sleek, transitional furniture of muted tones. Perfectly placed are the exquisite pieces he has collected in his world travels plus a few awards touting his excellence in lawyering. Missing in my opinion is an award for anal retentiveness. Deliberately, I make him nervous, slowly heading toward his precious Chinese vase. Just for the hell of it, I move it ever so slightly, mentally making a bet with myself on how long it will take before he will move it back to its proper location.

'Yes, I'm listening,' I finally respond, trying to avoid looking at his perfectly tousled, sandy blonde hair, tan sculpted calves, azure blue eyes. Shaking myself back to reality, I know I should really be paying attention as Patrick is a damn good attorney and annoyingly right ninety-nine percent of the time.

'As I was saying,' he starts again. 'How I see it, you are in the black, but barely. I know you are hoping that this trip to Puerto Rico will fix your financial woes, and it is a solid plan…' and here it comes, 'but what I don't understand is why you just don't focus on what you have right in front of you? You're always going off on a new or different direction, hoping for the pot of gold when there is no rainbow. Why don't you hire a solid sales force instead of that rag tag group?'

Now it's getting personal, my staff is like family, crazy, quirky family. 'They can sell snow to the proverbial Eskimo! I know they're characters, but they are my characters.' I want to stab him with my toothpick, but alas, there is still an olive on it. Instead for spite I move from collectible to collectible, slightly moving each one. To no one's surprise, he is right behind me, moving them back to their designated spot.

'Characters? That's how you describe them? Mike has a wooden leg, not that there is anything wrong with that, but hello, there have been advancements in prosthetics. And your Palm Beach people are drunks. The only downside is if you fire them, I can't imagine anyone else hiring them.'

Angry, I cut him off. 'They are like family to me, replacing them is not an option!'

'Well now it all makes sense, your family is certainly a cast of characters.' Are you getting a sense of why we aren't together anymore?

'Do you really want to go down this road?' I fire back. 'I came here tonight because I thought you would help me, so let's stay in the judgment free zone and just help me fine tune my game plan.'

'Okay, okay,' he says backing down, shifting his Chinese vase back to its perfect position. 'I know you are struggling, and if you can land this contract, it will be a definitely be a boon to your bottom line. But Lana, it's me, you don't have to put on a brave front. By the way, you look lovely tonight.' Smooth talker, eh?

Rolling my eyes, I take another gulp of my martini, and we begin to review my plans; cost analysis, profit margins, yada yada. His advice of course is spot on, and I should really be paying more attention, maybe even taking notes. And I probably should not be sucking down a second martini as my thoughts seem to be wandering with every sip.

Oh boy, I realize I am staring at his plump, very kissable lips and not hearing his endless words of wisdom.

Hmm, my glass is empty. Oh so subtle, I wave it directly in front of his face. Dutifully, he gets up to shake us another round. Apparently his focus has shifted as well as Cher begins to drift through the built in speakers, singing *If I could Turn Back Time*. Damn, he knows me so well. What the hell, they say Tequila makes your clothes fall off, well, martinis don't do a bad job either. I am down to the bare facts by the time Patrick returns, and great minds must think alike as he is also in the buff.

Okay, so I did not exactly solve all of my financial issues, and I most likely regret this tomorrow, but I will certainly be smiling tonight.

◆ ◆ ◆

# Chapter 5

All herald the arrival of Uncle Larry! At some point in time, we all have to kiss a little ass, today it's my turn.

'I see his car pulling into the lot,' Junes squeals with nauseating delight. Rounding the corner out of my office, June is pushing up her girls and checking her lipstick, oh brother.

Cool, Larry has a mysterious shopping bag in hand, maybe he comes bearing gifts.

'Larry, good to see you as always, how was your flight?' Greeting him at the door, I am cordial as always. 'And nice car!.' Toby is snickering in the background.

'Lana, good to see you as well, flight was good and the car is do-able. I have a little something for all of you.'

Larry sets the bag on a chair and produces five identical, festively wrapped gifts. The crew is on the edge of their seats, eyes open wide, like its Christmas morning.

'How thoughtful of you Larry,' I unwrap the gift to find that it's Trailer Trash Barbie, complete with a cigarette in her hand and bruises on her face. Her hot pink shorts are up her wazoo and a red flowered tube top completes the ensemble. This should elevate the trailer stereo type. I don't even allow my people to use the 'T' word.

Toby crosses his legs he is laughing so hard. 'Larry, I love it!' he shouts. Oy.

'Larry, I shall treasure this always,' Mike says, mentally calculating the fortune will make a fortune on Ebay someday. 'I am sure it will be a collector's item, I will never take it out of the box.' He looks over at Diane who already had hers out of the box and is playing with it. 'Kinda looks like you Diane.'

She responds with a classic hand gesture.

'I have more for the crew in West Palm,' Larry assures us, 'I thought they might be here to greet me.'

'They are on probation for turning the water cooler into a martini shaker,' explains Toby. Larry looks at him, unsure what to say to that one.

'Okay then, Larry, come on into my office and let's get started,' I reward Toby with my stink eye, 'Toby, if you are able, won't you join us?'

'So,' Larry asks, 'how is our venture going?'

'Very well, five of our six rehab houses have closed, we have three more underway and two more in the pipeline,' Toby proudly reports.

Larry looks pleased as I hand him his sizable check and the contracts. As he is putting them into his brief case, I spy his boarding pass for his flight here, it's dated for yesterday. That could only mean one thing, he stayed at June's last night. Shit, this is going to be awkward, I hate confrontation, but I need to address this and nip it in the bud. June sleeping with our investor is just bad business, plus I think I just threw up a little. Toby must have seen it as well, he appears to be gagging.

'Toby, can you excuse us please and ask June to come in?' Time to deal with Larry and June's indiscretions.

'Of course.' He mouths the word 'nasty' on his way out.

Larry's head drops when he sees the look on my face, the jig is up. Actually, this might be to my benefit, maybe I can use this as leverage to persuade him to finance my model homes. Hmm, the wheels turn.

June just takes one look, and lowers her gaze.

'Sit down June,' I command. 'I thought I made this clear to both of you, no commingling, period.'

Larry attempts to defend their actions. 'We just sat and talked, June can't even have regular sex because of her...'

'Stop!' More throw up, too many visuals going through my head, please make them stop. 'No intimacy in any form is allowed. If it happens again, June, I will fire you, do I make myself clear?'

'Yes Lana,' they reply in unison.

'June, go back to your desk and send Toby in please.' She opens the door as Toby almost falls in, his cell phone held out and presumably on speaker phone, sharing the juicy goings on I assume. My guess is the West Palm office, why should they miss all the fun.

Look, both June and Larry are nice enough, although quirky. But when you go to rent an X rated movie, those are not the two you want to see in HD.

'What do you say we head out and look at the homes we are rehabbing? I could use some fresh air,' I suggest. Toby and Larry quickly agree.

The silence is deafening as we make the drive to the first community. Toby has laid out a tour of all the ongoing projects. This will be a long day if the tension doesn't break.

'Lana,' Larry starts, 'we are just friends, I hate to see June lose her job over nothing.'

I look at Toby in the rear view mirror, his lips saying *friends with benefits*.

'Larry, you've been in business long enough to understand that its simply not good business, and I can't allow it. Let's just leave it at that.'

'But she has some real health issues,' he pleads. Why would he even know that? 'She can't have vaginal sex.' Lalalala, I so *do not* want to hear about this.

'Larry, its business, so let's focus on what we have in hand.' I shoot Toby a look before he can open his mouth. But I have to stifle a giggle, great minds think alike.

30

We pull into the first community, and head for the first home. Proud of the job we have done, this home used to be truly trash. Now the home is freshly painted inside and out, new carpet and tile, new appliances, ready for a new family to move into. Larry slowly scans the home, taking in all the details. He is obviously pleased. 'This looks great, what did we spend and what are we selling it for?' he asks.

This is Toby's wheelhouse, so I give the floor to him. 'This was actually a freebie from the community, we spent just under eight thousand on rehab, and we'll sell it for twenty. And it is still a bit underpriced so it should move quickly.'

'Excellent, let's have a look at the rest.' Happy Larry means more investment money, so Happy Lana. We tour the rest of the homes, including the ones we have yet to start on. It's a productive day.

'Lana, I am delighted with the work you've accomplished, I am sure my partner will feel the same, what do you say we have a drink to celebrate.'

'Fine, we'll drop Toby back at the office and get your car. Where shall we go?'

'I haven't checked into my hotel yet, why don't we just have a drink at the bar there?' Really? I guess I'm next on the hit list.

At least Larry is not a cheapskate, he is staying right on the beach at the Hilton. I wait at the lobby bar for him to check in and order two Grey Goose gimlets. Subtle suggestion should be my tack to pitch Larry on funding new model homes, but that will take too much time. More time for him to make a move, I am thinking right to the point.

Lost in thought, I don't notice Larry sliding onto the bar stool next to me, until I feel his hand on my leg. I remove it and start my pitch, 'Larry, I have another idea to make us money. How about fronting the money for new model homes? I have a deal with the communities and they will not charge any lot rent until they are sold. I have negotiated the best pricing available from the factory. We know what the average consumer wants, it's a slam dunk. Even June agrees.' I had to throw that in.

'Send me the breakdown, but I think it sounds like a winner. What will you need for initial capital?'

'Probably $100K, that will get us two houses move in ready.'

'And what do you think our return will be?'

'You'll make 35% on your money in 120 days or less.'

'I'll drink to that,' he says, and we clink glasses. I do a mental high five.

'So,' he drawls, 'June is off limits, but how about you?'

And it was going so well. I politely decline, business and all that. He says he understands, I just want to go home and take a shower.

'So when is your flight, Larry?'

'This is a quick trip, I am out first thing in the morning. Sorry I didn't get to see the West Palm crew, but next time, and please make sure they get their Barbie dolls.'

A bit more chit chat and I head off wishing him a safe trip and promising to get him the details on the model homes. The night is clear, the stars have aligned, time for some Cher. Top goes down, volume goes up, Cher belts out, *'All I really want to do, is baby be friends with you'*. She always knows what to say, I love her.

◆◆◆

# Chapter 6

The rest of the week goes without serious incident. Friday night comes and I politely decline offers from both Tedi and Toby to go out, instead, I fall asleep in front of the TV before ten. I'm a party animal.

The sun warmly shines through my bedroom bay window, waking me up gently, thankful for the slow roll. It's early, only seven, that gives me plenty of time to have a leisurely cup of coffee on the patio before I start my day.

Traditionally, Saturday mornings I call my family members and we catch up on each others lives. I received an email early this week from my older sister, Rikki, who lives in Fayetteville, North Carolina. She unfortunately had to euthanize her fifteen year old German Shepherd. We only had to chance to speak briefly, so she is first on my list. 'Hey Sis, so how are you doing?'

'I'm okay, Bubbles was like my child, in fact, there were many times I liked her better than my children.' Rikki has four boys, ages nineteen down to eight, and Sadie, five. She is better known to the family as Fertile Myrtle. I would need a constant supply of Xanax if I had five kids.

'How did the kids take it?'

'Pretty well; it was hardest on Sadie, but she'll be fine.'

'Did you bury Bubbles in the back yard?'

'No, we cremated her and put her in the *dead things in a jar* room. We'll put mom there when her time comes.'

'Huh, good to know,' I'm unsure if that's the correct response, but it's the best I can come up with.

We chat about the upcoming family reunion, the first ever, and most likely the last. Most of our cousins, except Tedi's family, are quite a bit older than us, and I doubt much fun, but who knows they could surprise us. Rikki is on board with coming up a day early for quality sister-cousin time.

'Is mom bringing her latest boyfriend?' I ask.

'I think he is married so the answer is probably no,' she says.

I do a mental head shake. 'Well, good for mom, she gets more action than me.'

'A lot of people fit in that category. So, how's business?' Rikki goes for the quick zing then smartly changes the subject.

'It's going great, we head to Puerto Rico next week.'

'Are you sure it's okay? Patrick called me.'

'Seriously!' My hair is on fire. 'Why is he calling you? I never should have asked for his advice.' Damn him, sticking his nose too far into my business.

'Don't be mad at him, he just cares.'

'Oh bullshit, he's just using you to get to me; he always has to complicate things.'

'Well, whenever you want a stable job, Peter is ready to hire you.'

I catch Jillian out of the corner of my eye, dressed in her serious work out clothes. She can tell by my expression the turn the conversation has taken.

'Yeah, thanks, I'll keep that in mind, but I am fine. I will call you when I get back from my trip, kiss the kids for me.' With that I hang up. Peter is Rikki's husband, he is a pie maker and has a fairly successful business called The Pie Hole. Unfortunately he is an a-hole, at least according to Rikki, plus I don't look good in aprons. I know she means well, but she never has faith in me. Okay, so I have bounced around a bit, okay, a lot. But I cannot see myself covered in flour the rest of my life.

'More family support?' Jillian has heard many conversations between my family and me. With all my career changes, they are always worried about my financial welfare.

'I don't want to talk about it. I still have to call my mom, grab a cup of coffee or whatever, I will try to make it quick,' I say.

I dial my mom's number, holding the phone away from my ear, knowing what's coming. 'Don't cry for me Argentinaaaa… hiya Leebee, I can't talk long, I am headed for a protest march.' My mom lives just outside of Washington, DC making for a multitude of possible protests.

'Hey Mom, what are you protesting now?'

'I'm not really sure, I will find out when I get there. I am wearing all white, like a blank canvas so I am ready for anything. What's going on with you? Patrick called and said your business is failing. Rikki says you are going to make pies with Peter. And did you know your sister plans on putting my remains in a room with her dead dogs?'

'First, my business is fine, stop talking to Patrick, we are not together, he is using you to get to me. Second, no, I have no plans on being a pie maker. Third, no comment, its Rikki, all those kids have warped her thought process.'

'I think it was warped well before her kids. Do you remember that time she interviewed a dog? 'This is Sam, Sam is a dog,' yikes.'

'In her defense, she was inebriated.' Not much of a defense, but it works.

'Whatev. Are we all sharing a room at the reunion? I really want my own, but you'll have to pay for it. Your Aunt Rita offered to pay for me, but I don't want her to think I can't pay my own way. Can you put my flight on your credit card, too? I would ask your sister but she has so many mouths to feed, I know I explained birth control to her. Don't get me wrong, I love all four of my grandkids, no wait, five? And your brother Max, well… so can you?'

I am exhausted just listening. 'Mom, I will take care of it, you can have your own room, Rikki and I will share one. She is not bringing the kids or Peter, I think she needs the break.'

'No shit,' Mom was short and sweet on that one.

'I can't find the creamer,' yells Jillian from the kitchen.

'Is that your neighbor?' asks Mom, 'She is quite the looker, but I think she's maybe a ho.'

'Okay Mom, go do your whatever protest, and I will call you during the week, love you.' I hang up before she can gather steam for round two.

'I am glad I can amuse you,' I say. Jillian just smiles, taking it all in.

'Your family is very entertaining. Okay, let's go work off some frustrations,' she suggests. We head off to the local gym. Delray is a quaint town, very walkable, and of course the day is full of sunshine. We pass the Crepe Store, both of us drooling for different reasons.

Once in the gym, we head our separate ways. I have a standing appointment with a personal trainer, Martina Twist. And yes, I have aptly nick named her Martini with a twist. She always kicks my ass and today is no exception. Session done, I try to catch my breath as I catch Jillian's eye. We are both glistening with perspiration, actually downright sweat soaked. Sweat is good, it cleanses the brain at least temporarily.

It's only ten am, but the heat is already evident as it bends the air coming off the street. But I love, love it, and feel energized from our workout. Our gait is slow as we gaze into the windows of the eclectic boutiques and knick-knack shops.

'Sally! How are you? You look great! How are the twins?' A strange woman has approached and is practically shouting at me, next she comes in for the hug. Once again,

I am recognized for someone who I am not, maybe one day it will come in handy, but not today.

'Whoaa there sister, you've mistaken me for someone else!' I exclaim, rapidly backing up out of her reach.

Jillian rolls her eyes 'This never gets old, oh wait, yes it does, come on.' She grabs my arm and hustles me away.

'Bye Sally, tell Bitsy hi!' yells the crazy lady while she is waving to the point of being off balance, figuratively and literally.

'So, are we stopping for a crepe?' I ask Jillian, hopefully.

'Well, if you insist. But all that work you did will be negated with that one crepe. I, on the other hand, I can actually burn calories with what I have in mind for that crepe maker, and I know what I want mine stuffed with.'

'Ew, I am losing my appetite. And I thought you said it was a one and done?'

'I may have to rethink my policy,' she says, eyeing the crepe maker as we walk through the door.

'I'll have the banana strawberry Nutella,' I order, wiping the drool sliding down the side of my mouth.

'I'll just have my usual,' Jillian says as she licks her lips. Antonio the crepe guy mouths, *give me five minutes,* as he starts my order.

Walking home alone, I can't help but admire Jillian, she seems so free. Maybe I should just get rid of the business, sometimes I feel like the weight of the world is on my shoulders. Maybe I should have a business with no employees, and then I could do what I want without worry about how it will affect their lives.

Wham! Without warning I am flat on my ass, what the hell happened? I look up into Patrick's eyes, is this some kind of freaky dream?

'What happened?' I ask groggily, unable to fully focus.

'Maybe you should watch where you are going instead of daydreaming, you smacked right into that sign. Good thing I was sitting here at Starbucks to save you,' Patrick is smugly proud of himself.

Mental eye roll, 'Oh yes, my knight in friggin armor, don't just stand there, help me up.'

'Easy,' he instructs, 'you are going to have a nasty bump. Sit down; let me get you some water.' He reads my *are you serious* glare, and quickly changes his tune, 'I'll get you an iced mocha.'

Ouch, this lemon on my forehead is a nice bonus accessory to my sweaty clothes, how attractive I must look. Patrick finally returns with my mocha, I ask,'So what are you doing in my neck of the woods?'

'You know I love Starbucks, great people watching.' By people, he means babes, ones you can bounce a quarter off their stomach. I'm in good shape, but nothing is bouncing off this stomach.

'Actually,' I say, ramping up to vocally slap him, 'I am glad I ran into you. I need you to stop calling my family. Like the song says, we are never, ever getting back together. And what did you tell them about my business? Sometimes I just want to shoot you.'

'I am just concerned.'

'Telling my mother and sister fixes that how exactly?'

He casts eyes downward, 'How about dinner tonight?'

'What? That's your response? Let me think about it, No! Besides, I already have plans.'

'With your harlot neighbor?' he sneers.

I give him the evil eye, get up and head home. Jillian is not a harlot, even if she is at the moment getting her crepe stuffed in an alley. And really, who says harlot anymore?

Exhausted by my day already, I am thinking maybe just a twenty minute power nap, so I plop on the couch...

'Must be a hell of a dream the way you're smiling.'

I open my eyes, its Tedi. Whew, I must have really zonked out. 'It was, Cher was singing at my birthday party. What time is it?'

'Time for you to get your ass up and get into the shower, Stacey's here, remember?'

I look around and sure enough, there is Stacey, Tedi's sister, in from DC. 'Shit, I am so sorry!' I jump up and give Stacey a big hug. 'So happy you could visit, give me just ten minutes, make yourselves a drink.'

In a flash, I soap up and down, and I am out of the shower. Putting on my usual Saturday night outfit of capris, sleeveless silk top, and sandals, I give myself a nod of approval in the mirror. Gotta love South Florida, this is dressed up.

The girls are outside sitting poolside enjoying a yummy Moscow Mule in the traditional copper mugs, with one waiting for me. 'So girls, where are we headed tonight? Mmmm, tasty,' as I take a sip.

'Let's go to Dada,' Stacey suggests. 'Tapas under the tree.'

'Works for me,' Tedi agrees as she chugs her drink.

'Since we are walking, let me get a to-go cup for mine' as I pour mine into a plastic cup, I'm definitely not ready to follow suit and chug. And off we go.

Dada is an old Victorian style beach house, converted into a delightful restaurant. As you walk in through the opening in the weathered white picket fence, an enormous hundred year old Fichus tree greets you, covering the front lawn area like a huge umbrella. Benches surround the massive base of the tree and are married with tables for quaint outside seating. The wrap around porch has couches and coffee tables perfect for drinks and a leisurely nosh. The porch is our easy choice. Tedi looks up in the sky, and taking her cue, orders three Sunset Martinis. The breeze is gentle and warm; a sigh escapes all of us.

When the server brings our martinis, Tedi adds, 'And we'll share warm brie with honey and fruit, plus an order of pumpkin ravioli.' Done and done, life is good.

'So Patrick says the business is in trouble,' Stacey states, then screams 'Owww'. I assume Tedi has kicked her under the table.

'Arrgh!' is all I can manage.

Tedi sets the record straight and warns, 'Okay, let's make this clear, the business is fine, we don't like Patrick and there will be no more talk of business tonight.'

Stacey watches me down my martini, hails the server. 'Then let's have another round.'

I take a cleansing breath. 'So Stacey, how are things with you? Getting closer to the altar?'

'Close enough, but not that close,' she says. I follow where her eyes have wandered, into the inside bar where a man is wearing a hula skirt. This is a Zagat-rated fine dining restaurant, so he apparently opted not have the upgraded accessory of a coconut bra, just the standard Tommy Bahama shirt. My fears are realized when I look back at Stacey; too late, she is already making a beeline inside. What the hell, Tedi and I move closer to listen.

Stacey gently taps Hula man on the shoulder, not hesitating to ask the question that has been on millions of minds. 'Whatcha got under there?'

Without blinking an eye, the man responds, 'Just the lipstick of the last woman that asked.'

Huh, wonder what shade, I'm thinking red. We all go back to our spot, quiet for a few minutes, pondering the man in the hula skirt. We look over his way again, he raises his glass to us, at least he did not raise his skirt.

'So where do we head next?' Stacey is ready to roll.

'Let's just walk down the avenue, and see what inspires us,' Tedi suggests.

The avenue is busy, as always. Most of the restaurants have outside seating, taking advantage of the tropical weather. Delray is very dog friendly, all shapes and sizes accompanying their owners, some in special puppy carriages. Overall, it's a festive, happy place to be.

Thumping music is coming from the Copa, we keep going. A Frank Sinatra tune is coming from Joel's. I look at my cousins; I can see that is not happening. Soft jazz is coming from The Moon Rose, we all nod in agreement, no craziness for us tonight.

'What will you have ladies?' asks our bartender.

'Let's do a vodka gimlet, straight up in a martini glass, and make it Grey Goose,' I order, I know my cousins.

'That'll work,' Tedi and Stacey agree in unison.

'Oh crap,' hisses Tedi. 'Patrick is over in the corner with what looks like a rent-a-babe.'

'He is like a freakin' stalker!' I feel like my head is going to explode. 'Maybe she is nice and he will fall in love and leave me the freak alone.' I am not jealous in the least, and I'm sure her boobs are not real.

'Me thinks thou doth protest too much,' notes Stacey.

'Blah blah blah,' is my response as I do another sideways glance at Patrick. He catches me looking, and heads our way.

'Lana, I want to say that I am really sorry about talking to your family, and wish you nothing but success in Puerto Rico,' He sounds sincere, with those damn baby blues, perfectly coiffed hair, dimples and cleft chin.

'Whatev, do it again and I will cut your balls off.'

'Duly noted. How about Starbucks when you get back so you can tell me all about your trip?'

He gives me a soft kiss on the cheek.

'Sure,' who am I to say no to Starbucks? 'Ladies, what say we take this back to my house where we can get comfortable.' We throw back our martinis, slip off our barstools, and head out. I give it my best sashay, knowing he is watching. Hah!

Back at my house we don on our swimsuits and head to the hot tub, oh yeah, I have all the comforts. 'Let's do a shot of Lemoncello!' I am suddenly feeling in party mood.

'Oh boy,' Tedi says knowingly, 'let's not, you remember how you felt the next day last time we did shots?'

'Right, so how about just Belvedere and sour. Thanks Tedi, for reminding me, hate feeling like shit.'

'Anytime.'

We slide into the hot tub, relax, watch the palms swaying above us, the stars beyond. It's comfortable, just family, no stress, no expectations, nice.

Comparing Tedi and Stacey, I wonder to myself if Tedi is the milk man's baby. Stacey has my uncle's fine features, big smile, curly light brown hair, fair skin. Tedi in contrast has an olive complexion, dark brown almost black hair, and eyes as dark as the abyss.

'What are the plans for a cousin day at the reunion?' Stacey inquires. 'Is Rikki coming sans family?'

'Yes, and we'll figure something out for sure,' I answer. 'Rikki is primed since she is going to be free as a bird.' We exchange glances as we know that spells trouble.

The rest of the night is spent laughing about old stories and making fun of our families. Last I remember, I am stretched out on the chaise lounge, Cher is singing *Strong Enough*, how does she always know? It boggles my mind.

◆ ◆ ◆

# Chapter 7

The day of the Puerto Rico trip is finally here, and I'm off to pick up my traveling partner, Toby. He lives in a quaint neighborhood of Fort Lauderdale called Shady Rivers; the trees are massive, unruly, hanging like a canopy over the narrow streets, I just love it. One day he dragged me from the office to get my opinion on the house he now lives in. It was truly a no-brainer; classic old Florida home with the pool in the front surrounded by a wooden six foot privacy fence. The bathrooms inside tipped the scale for me, done in old style small pink and green tiles. The only thing missing I told him, were the plastic pink flamingos in the yard, which of course I presented to Toby as a house warming gift.

We have an eight am flight to catch, but I know Toby, that's why I am pulling into his drive at five-thirty. He lives just five minutes from the airport, but I anticipate a bit of a coaxing will still be needed to get him on the plane.

'Knock, Knock,' I just walk in, not worried about seeing anything that might shock me.

'Good Morning!' Toby is in his boxers, dancing with his dog Billy, a big black lab. Billy is, of course, on his hind legs with his paws on Toby's shoulders, they make a cute couple.

'You're up early, got anything to eat?'

'I never went to bed, I knew I wouldn't sleep so I went to the Philling Station (his local boy bar), closed it down, and danced the rest of the night away with Billy. He keeps stepping on my feet though,' complains Toby. 'Look in the frig, I am sure you'll find something in there.'

Great, Toby tipsy from the night before, this should be an interesting flight, hopefully he'll sleep. Yikes, there's only Toby's standard fare of jar food in the frig. Toby's theory is that it's easy to see the contents, and how much is left, no mysteries. I decide to pass.

'How about a Bloody Mary to kick off the trip?' he asks 'Use my infamous homemade mix; it'll wake you right up.'

'What the hell, I'll take a short one, but in the meantime, please put on some clothes and let's get going.'

Bloody Mary and I go out by the pool while Toby finishes getting ready. The sun is starting to rise, another balmy day in store, and the winds are thankfully calm which I hope translates into an uneventful flight to Puerto Rico. Looking around, I admire the fabulous job Toby has done decorating his pool area; potted tropical foliage surrounds the perimeter in colorful ceramic pots, even a few pineapple plants. Many a weekend afternoon has been spent here resulting in many wise sleep overs.

Mentally preparing myself for the meetings to come, I ramp up my confidence by reviewing my facts. I have been told that people can sense my confidence by my walk, and I really need to strut my stuff to win this opportunity. It also helps that my height, or so I am told, makes me a bit intimidating. Focus is the key, focus is the key, focus is the key, my pre-game mantra.

'I'm ready for my close up Mr. DeMill,' out swoops Toby, uncharacteristically business like in khaki pants and navy blue Izod shirt. But wait, the shoes warrant a comment.

'Where did you get the Pilgrim shoes? I ask, 'the buckle on the shoe matches your belt buckle.'

'Ha... ha... ha,' he says as he looks down at his shoes, 'huh, you're right, what a bonus!'

'Let's go if you want to get your Bloody Mary at the airport.'

Toby kisses Billy good bye, and out we go...focus...focus.

Amazingly, we zip through check in and security with plenty of time to head to the bar adjoining our gate, which to no one's surprise, is only selling coffee. No problem, Toby knows the bartender, and, magically, our V8 is spiked.

'I met him at the Philling Station last night, I was on a mission' Toby explains. I only employ goal oriented people.

He glances over at me staring out the window 'Stop obsessing, you will do great and all will be right with our world. Can I call Penny, wake her up and make her jealous that I am going and not her. I always feel better when I can throw things in her face.'

My eye roll answers his question. But he is right, no sense over thinking this, they either get it or they don't, I just have to give it my best shot. As far as all being right with our world, I am again questioning just what I want my world to be.

Boarding call for our flight comes over the loud speaker, 'Down the hatch, that's us,' says Toby. We clink glasses for good luck, and knock back the rest of our drinks. Toby is really not a good influence on me.

Barely in our seats, Toby already has a death grip on the arm rests, panic written all over his face. He is far from a touchy feely person, but I take his hand any way. As soon as we level off and he hits the call button, clearly not understanding that we need to wait our turn for the drink cart. But somehow, in another feat of Toby magic, our flight attendant shows up with two Bloody Marys.

'Seriously?' His depth of influence never ceases to amaze me.

Toby just grins, 'It was a fruitful night at the bar,' emphasis on the fruit.'

The silver lining of Toby's previous night's escapades is that he sleeps most of the flight, and thankfully I do as well. We both awake to the captain's voice announcing our landing in ten minutes. Toby reaches for the call button, quickly I grab his arm, halting another round of alcohol.

Smart airport navigation on my part also keeps Toby clear of the airport bars and gets us directly to the baggage claim. Thirty minutes later a taxi drops us at the Ritz Carlton lobby entrance.

'Grab the bags,' I instruct, 'I'll get us checked in.'

'Ooo, I love it when you are in control,' he croons.

Quick eye roll and I head for the check in desk. Smiling, I know I am in control and he does love it.

The eight hundred dollars gets us a room with a spectacular view of the azure sea, and yay, the tiki bar. I am starting to question whether my mother's propensity for drinking is rubbing off on me, but then again, there are certainly more forces at work in my life than DNA.

'I need to call John, see if he's landed and make arrangements to meet him tonight. It's imperative we are on the same page for our meeting with his government contact tomorrow.' Crap, just getting only his voice mail, whatev, I just leave a message. 'Okay, let's go exploring,' code for lets hit the tiki bar.

The bamboo stools are more comfortable than they look, we lean back, and watch the brilliant blue waves crest and break in to a bubbly white froth, coconut palms swaying in the wind to the background samba music, both of us thinking that life at this moment does not suck. Breaking the serenity, my phone rings, its John, he missed his first flight but will be in this evening, asking me to make reservations for dinner. What a putz, yep, will do. I hate relying on anyone else, but that's the way the world sometime turns.

'John and his crew are going to meet us for dinner,' I tell Toby, 'so let's relax and enjoy until then'. Toby just nods, his eyes roaming the pool area, enjoying the tanned native eye candy.

'Carlita! *Como estas?* I have not seen you in so long!' I spin around to see an attractive, older balding gentleman with a wide smile, and pencil thin black mustache, coming in for a hug. Seriously? In Puerto Rico? I look over at Toby, who has fallen off his stool due to excessive laughter.

'I believe you are mistaken,' I politely explain to the gentleman, 'I am not Carlita.'

'Yes you are,' he states adamantly. Wow.

'No, I think I know my own name, I just have a familiar face.'

'No, you are Carlita!' he actually stomps his foot. Unless I have amnesia, I am pretty sure I am not Carlita. Plus, the only Spanish I know is *Donde esta el bano*.

What the hell, I'll play, 'Okay, I am Carlita, you got me.'

'No, you are not Carlita! She would never speak so rudely with me!' With a flip of his head and a harrumph, he turns on his heel and walks away. I tried to tell him.

Toby turns to me, 'Another drink?' Does he really need to ask?

Reason winning the moment, we look at the bottom of the glass of our second drink and wisely Toby and I head back to our room. My brain is screaming for a power nap. Crossing the lobby Toby suddenly halts and says, 'Isn't that John?

'Where?' Weird, I just listened to my voicemail that said he would not be in until tonight.

'Right there, standing with the woman, the one in the tube top,' Toby points to a secluded corner of the lobby.

'Huh, who knew tube tops are back in style,' I remark.

'Wow,' Toby exclaims. 'She wears more make up than a drag queen, her face will melt in this heat.' John glances around furtively, spots us and with a look of badly concealed guilt, gives me the upward head bob. What a sneak. Not wanting to appear rude, we walk over to greet him, but really wishing we could be rude.

'John, thought you were coming in tonight. And this must be your wife?'

'Yea, made the flight after all. This is my wife, her name is Precious.' And I am sure she is.

'You remember my General Manager. Toby this is John and his wife Precious.' I so want to roll my eyes at the absurdity of it all, but instead I play nice.

'Yea,' mutters John. Brilliant, we should really bowl over the governor's people with John's people skills and oratory acumen. Toby puts his hand out to shake with John, who promptly ignores it. Interesting, we may have a homophobe. Toby, ever the statesman, grabs him instead and gives him a big hug and a wet kiss. Poor Precious, she needs to pick her jaw up off the floor.

'So we'll see you at dinner at seven-thirty in the Mamba room,' I say, and with that we take our leave, smiling ear to ear.

A quick twenty minute nap, and refreshing shower later, we are ready for Happy Hour. Toby and I are both dressed in appropriate tropical linen; Toby's shirt is a classic Gauyabera in a soft pastel print; of course I have on white linen capris and loose flowing white linen top with delicate lime green embroidered flowers.

'We look so pretty,' remarks Toby, 'too bad we have to waste it on that ass John.'

'I believe we get the introduction to the governor connection tonight, let's hit the bar and soak up some local color first.'

The lobby bar is crowded, but luckily we are able to secure two seats. Glancing around, I spot John tucked away in the corner of the bar with another gentleman, but this time he does not see me. Looks like they are deep in a conversation that I am thinking involves skullduggery. Instantly my hackles are up. 'I don't trust John,' I tell Toby.

'He's a slime ball, we need to make sure we get every one's names and contact info. John is the type that would cut everyone out of a deal.'

'Agreed.'

The bartender with little effort has coaxes us into a colorful rum concoction garnished with papaya chunks and orange slices. We spy on John over the rims of our glasses, undetected. Another man joins John, who now finally spots us. Momentarily, John looks like the kid with his hand caught in the cookie jar, but recovers quickly and waves. We wave back, and he heads over to the bar by himself, slithering like the snake he is.

'Yo,' he articulates. 'So you ready to do dinner?'

Serious mental eye roll. 'So who are your friends?' I ask, curious to know.

'Oh, the government dudes that are having dinner with us, we just wanted to get some preliminary stuff out of the way.'

Toby kicks me, then turns to John and says, 'Great, look forward to your introduction, let's move to the dining room.'

The restaurant is absolutely fabulous, the décor stunning. The wall of windows facing the ocean are wide open, framed by sheer white panels undulating with the gentle sea breeze. The tables are bamboo, the seats wicker with overstuffed cushions in bold floral prints. The host seats us, placing napkins on our laps with flourish and a snap of his wrist. I like this place.

John's contacts join us at the table. Not waiting for John, I introduce myself and Toby, 'Such a pleasure to meet you gentlemen, my name is Lana Turner, and this is my associate, Toby Gile.'

'The pleasure is ours. My name is Robert Rodriguez and this is my associate, Carlos Adams.' His English is perfect, with a captivating accent and charming lopsided smile.

Our server appears with perfect timing, 'May I take your drink order,' he asks, almost like a song, maybe because a drink right now is music to my ears? Okay, bad pun, happy I did not say that out loud.

Locking in on me, the server wonderfully ignores John's attempt to order, hah! 'I will have a Belvedere gimlet, straight up, martini glass. My companion will have the same.' Toby simply giggles.

As we await our drinks, we make small talk about the island, places we should see if we had the time, and the general charm of the island. Drinks in hand, we get down to business.

'John tells me, Lana, that your group has the answers to our housing problem. We have been given $165 million dollars by the federal government to replace the lost housing. John has given us the preliminary budget details on your plan, on the surface, it seems like a winner,' Robert states.

Wait... what? I have to recover quickly, that information was not to be shared until we presented together. John strikes again. I notice from the corner of my eye, a look between John and Carlos. I see how this is being played. Toby kicks me again, he gets it, too.

'If you like what you see in the preliminary, wait until you see the full report,' I say. A slight choking sound comes from John, aw, too bad. Toby and I were wise not to share everything with him. I turn to John, 'Is your lovely wife joining us? Or shall we go ahead an order?'

'Yea, order.' He is so eloquent.

'Robert, anything you recommend?' I ask.

'Camarones al Ajillo con tostones, very flavorful shrimp with fried plantains,' he suggests with a warm smile.

'Done,' I look at the server, 'and he'll have the same,' pointing to Toby who just smiles. We definitely enjoy seeing the confused looks on people's faces when I do all the ordering and talking. Toby kicks me again, ouch, I am going to need shin guards.

The meal is absolutely delicious and thanks to Robert, the conversation is humorous and stimulating. At one point I think Toby had a little drool happening as he watched Robert, so it was my turn to kick him. Turnabout is fair play. John and Carlos don't have much to add, they are conspicuously quiet, two peas in a deceitful pod. Toby as usual, interjects his humor at just the right moment.

The table cleared, our server inquires if we would like dessert or an after dinner drink. Politely we decline, keeping in mind the big meeting tomorrow. I know it's hard to believe, but we really did decline. The server discretely leaves the check on the corner of the table, Robert immediately snaps it up. John conveniently is looking the other way.

Not wanting to insult the man, I simply say, 'Thank you Robert, how very gracious of you, and now if you will excuse us, tomorrow is an important day. Toby?'

Toby jumps up and pulls my chair out, barely keeping a straight face. I have him trained well. We head straight up to the room, waiting until we are alone to discuss the dinner.

'What a sneaky bastard!' Toby blurts out as soon as our door closes.

'We anticipated this,' I'm trying to stay calm. 'He only has the basic info. Remember, we held back the most important info, our foundation system specially designed for hurricanes. There is nothing like it and I'm good friends with the patent holder. So don't stress, we are golden. Let's get a good night sleep, and be ready for battle tomorrow.'

'Oh Lana, you're so smart,' says Toby the wise acre.

'And you are a smart ass. Break open the mini bar and lets have a night cap, who cares if its fifteen bucks for one ounce of booze!'

We toast our anticipated success in the morning, and put on Nick at Night and the sleep timer on thirty minutes. The Mary Tyler Moore show is perfect accompaniment to a miniature bottle of rum, chin-chin.

# Chapter 8

'I know I said I wanted to get an early start Toby, but can we at least wait for the sun to come up?' My eyes are still slits, but I can make out Toby standing by my bed with a petite cup of coffee that smells intoxicating.

'Cuban espresso,' he says, waving it in front of my nose. 'Slug this down and get in the shower sister, we have worlds to conquer.'

Oy, where does he get his energy? But I comply, down the espresso and head for the shower. I have a few tricks up my sleeve so getting an early start works in my favor.

Today I have to don the power suit, black slacks and jacket with a sleeveless power purple blouse with a hint of cleavage, sensible black flats. I could do the heel thing, but I am already tall enough, I need to exude power but not intimidate. The hair is still crazy, but I think that just says very subtly, *watch out world, I can kick your ass if I want to and I am crazy enough to do it.*

Outside the lobby entrance, the cabs are lined up and waiting. We have no intention of waiting for John, et al. Wanting the advantage of being the first to the meeting, we quickly instruct the cabbie where to take us, and we're off. Before we enter the building, we give each other a final appearance check; no black things in the teeth, hair in place, good to go.

The elevator door opens to the third floor, Robert is already there, but no John or Carlos, perfect. 'Buenos Dias Robert,' I begin, greeting him with a warm smile. When in Rome...

'Buenos Dias Lana y Toby, pleasure to see you again this fine morning. Please come into the conference room and make yourselves comfortable while we wait for the others.'

Strategic placement is in order; accordingly we seat ourselves facing the door near the head of the table. This is the perfect opportunity to exchange direct contact information with Robert. As soon as we finish, an older, silver haired gentleman enters the room, Robert stands to introduce him, 'This is Cordero Rivera, he works directly for the Lieutenant Governor as his affordable housing adviser.'

Charm oozes from my lips. 'I am Lana Turner, and this is my associate Toby Gile, we are honored to be invited to meet with you and discuss your housing recovery.'

'Ah, Lana Turner, like the movie star! The Sweater Girl,' he exclaims. Like I haven't heard that one before from any man over sixty, thanks again mom, but I will use it to my advantage.

'Yes, but she was blond,' I reply, so sweetly his teeth must hurt.

At that moment, John and Carlos enter; John is obviously pissed, we did not wait for him to begin the meeting, like I give a flying fig. 'And here are our other associates, John Granger and I believe you know Carlos'.

Robert takes the lead, 'Let us begin, please, everyone be seated.'

John starts his presentation, not even glancing my way. In my head I am having Rikki interview him, 'This is John, John is an ass.' He is explaining how we can use manufactured housing to replace homes at half the cost and in half the time. Cordero looks like he has heard this all before, he keeps glancing at Robert.

Time for me to jump in and work my magic, 'If I may interject,' I start. John shoots me daggers, I just ignore him. 'I know one of your concerns is to also to create jobs. We have a training plan that will address that. We also have a patented foundation system so that will not only address your hurricane concerns, but earthquakes as well. Let me go over the details of both.'

John looks as if his head is going to explode; he knows nothing of the training or foundations. I now have Cordero's full attention. 'Please,' he says, 'this is intriguing and may be exactly what we need.'

In my element, I go through the details we have worked so hard at assembling. Toby gives copies of the presentation to Robert, Carlos, and Cordero so they can follow along; they are eating out of the palm of our hands. John looks like he could spit nails.

'Do you have any questions?' I conclude.

'This was very thorough Lana. Our next step is to give this presentation to our committee, we will be contacting you as soon as we have had additional time to review. But I can tell you, I am impressed,' remarks Cordero, nodding his head.

Game, set, match. All John can do is sit and take it all in, he can't add anything of real value. 'Yeah, great,' is his feeble attempt at input.

After shaking hands and saying our goodbyes, we head to the elevator. By the time John comes out, I am already on the phone with Sol, bringing him up to speed. 'It went well, Sol, I will send you the info on the training program and the foundation as promised. We'll talk again next week.'

John is frothing at the mouth, 'What the hell was that?' he demands, 'Why didn't I know about the training or foundations?'

'Same reason I did not know about your side deal with Carlos,' I fire back.

'We are only making $20,000 a piece...' He stops suddenly, realizing he has let the cat out of the bag. 'I mean, we're all making $20,000 a piece for bringing the deal, including you and what's his name,' pointing at Toby.

'See you in Florida.' The elevator door slides shut as we smile to see smoke coming out of John's ears. I turn to Toby and proclaim, 'And that's how it's done.'

A cab is waiting outside and whisks us directly to the airport, this trip has been short, exhausting and with luck, productive. Sprinting through the airport, we just make our flight, no time to stop for a rum concoction. However, fate is on our side as our flight attendant is the same one from the flight over. No sooner we are up in the air then he brings us rum runners that are definitely not on the menu.

'Well done Lana,' Toby raises his plastic glass to meet mine, 'Here's hoping the rest of the committee has the same vision as Cordero. Chin-chin, bottoms up, down the hatch.' With that he drains his cup.

The flight is blissfully uneventful; we retrieve my car and head directly to Toby's. 'Stay for a drink?' he asks.

'I am going to head home, tomorrow is a work day, I'll be in the West Palm office. Let's talk first thing in the morning.' As he heads into his house, I put the top down, and of course turn on Cher for the drive. Vintage Cher I think will work. It's like she is in the passenger seat. She begins, *Half Breed, that's all I ever heard*, why yes Cher, I'd love to sing along. The driver in the car next to me is staring; I just wave, sing louder, and hit the gas.

The drive up gives me time to contemplate the trip. If it works, it means the business would be back on solid ground. Again I wonder if that is really what I want. I turn Cher up louder to drown out my thoughts.

My little home is a site for sore eyes, at heart I am a simple home body. Jillian is watering the plants on her front porch, I give her a wave but I notice she does not have her happy face on.

'Give me a minute,' I understand that look, she has had another run in with her ex. Quickly, I dash into the house, change quickly into shorts and a tank top.

Joining her, I make myself comfortable on her steps, 'So what now?'

'Join me in a cocktail?' pleading with her eyes. She dashes into the house and returns with two vodka sodas, twist of lime in festive Tervis tumblers. She knows me.

'John is an ass!' she starts. John is also the name of her ex, seems to be a John theme. 'Now he is taking me to court to get back the potted banana tree. I am going to take the bananas to court with me and stick them right up his …'

'Whoa!' I exclaim. 'It's just a banana tree Jillian. If you go to court it's going to cost you a ridiculous amount, just let him have it.'

'I think he is still stinging over the curtains he won back in court three months ago.' She gave him back the curtains but not before sewing shrimp in the hem. It took John more than six weeks to finally find the source of the stench. 'Your trip was fruitful?'

'Time will tell,' I take another sip of my drink, it tasted yummy but I think I am too tired to finish it. 'I'll give you the details this weekend, I am pooped, rain check on a refill?'

She nods, I give her a hug and head back home. Too tired to even unpack, I flop down on my pillow top bed, wondering what adventures tomorrow will bring.

# Chapter 9

'I am calling for Salvatore Tortalini; he requests your presence today for lunch at Denny's in Lake Worth at high noon,' booms the gravely male voice.

'Excuse me?' I am confused once again, a now familiar state. 'May I ask what this is in reference to and who is Salvatore Tortalini?' Its only seven-thirty in the morning, I haven't even left for the office yet, sheesh.

'Mr. Tortalini would like to discuss business with you, a proposition that will benefit both parties.'

I look around my living room to see if I am getting punked. 'Is he not capable of calling himself? Can you give me a clue as to what type of business?'

'Mr. Tortalini understands you are in the mobile home business and he is also, but it is best left for him to discuss with you. May I tell him you will be there?'

My curiosity gets the best of me. 'Yes, I will be there,' and hope I will not be fitted for cement shoes. As the caller hangs up I find myself scratching my head, I need to call Toby and see what he knows about this Mr. Tortalini.

Toby picks up on the first ring, but all I hear is *Do you believe in life after love*. Toby is blaring Cher in his car, one more reason to like him. He can't hear me so I sing along until the song is over.

'What's up Lanalu?' He is in his usual chipper mood.

'Have you ever heard of a Salvatore Tortalini? Supposed to be in the mobile home business?'

'As a matter of fact, I was talking to one of the park managers last week and his name came up. He is fairly new, he finances mobile homes for a somewhat unreasonable interest rate. Kinda of like Uncle Larry, but for the real *get me dones.*' Translation: for those who have the worst credit, but have significant cash.

'I just got a call from one of his minions, requesting my presence at lunch today,' I explain.

'Huh, well, word is he ex-mob.'

'Seriously? What was your first clue Sherlock, and no one is ever ex-mob, you're in it for life. Well, I guess I'll go and see what it's about, if I don't come back, you get all of my Cher CDs and wigs.'

The rest of my morning is typical, talking with sales people and suppliers, but my eyes are constantly watching the clock. Time seems to crawl by; I decide might as well see if Penny or Mable know anything about my new Mafioso friend.

'Hey gals,' I start; they stare blankly up at me, 'either of you ever heard of Salvatore Tortalini?'

'Is he the one with the cooking show on PBS?' guesses Mable.

'No Mable, he is on that kid's show on Disney, dances with the asparagus I think,' says Penny.

Sandy looks at me, 'Sounds like a mob boss to me.'

I just look at the three of them, and walk back into my office to watch the clock some more. Do I need to be nervous? *Tick tock, tick tock,* finally at eleven forty-five, I am out of here.

Good start, no burly men in black with guns hidden badly in the Denny's parking lot, no dark sedans. Walking into the restaurant, I catch the eye of an seemingly tall, older gentleman wearing a short sleeve button down plaid shirt with navy blue Dockers, not very mob like.

He rises to greet me, 'Lana, nice to meet you, I know so much about you.'

Wait... what? 'Mr Tortalini, the pleasure is mine I think, and I know next to nothing about you.'

'I took the liberty of ordering you an ice tea, since that is what you normally have at lunch, except of course the occasional Belvedere martini.'

At this point I am thinking martini. 'Thank you, shall we get down to business, after all that's why we are here.'

'Shoot from the hip, exactly what I heard about your style. Let me explain the reason for the meeting. I finance the, shall we say, the hard to finance. I understand that you have an excellent rapport with the communities around here, and you are a person of honor in business.'

Oh brother, did I step into The Godfather? 'I appreciate your compliments, what is it that you propose, Mr. Tortalini?'

He takes a long sip of his tea, his eyes never leaving mine. 'I propose that I use my funds to buy homes to repair and you find the buyers for me to finance into these homes. You have the boots on the ground to find the right homes, and the marketing to find the buyers, I have the cash, perfect partnership. And, please call me Sal.'

I take a long sip of my tea, my eyes never leaving his, tit for tat. 'Sal, that's an interesting proposition, but now it's my turn as I know nothing about you.'

'I have money, Lana, what more do you need to know.'

'Point taken, Sal. I propose we take a test run to see if we are indeed compatible. I have a home in mind right now; I can send you the details and analysis. Also, if we are going to work together, we need to meet at Starbucks from now on and I take an Iced Mocha Latte, which I am sure, you already know.' A girl has to have her standards.

With that I stand up, say my goodbyes, and head out the door. The meeting was a little creepy, but my brain is smoking with possibilities. With both Uncle Larry and Sal, the business can definitely boom. I head back to the office, do a joint text to Toby and Tedi to meet me this afternoon in the West Palm office.

When I get into the office, both Penny and Mable are out of the office showing homes and won't be back until tomorrow. Perfect. Sandy is busy trying to solve Rubik's Cube. Obviously slow, I send her home for the day, she does not even question why.

Somewhere in this pile on my desk I need find the info on the home I have in mind in The Crossings, an older fifteen hundred square feet home and a total mess. But we can get it for a song, and make a small bundle. I hear the front door open, its Tedi and Toby who have come up from Lauderdale together.

'So spill your guts, you rat!' says Toby. 'Did he make you an offer you can't refuse?'

I can see this is going to be cliché heaven. 'Tedi, anything to add?'

'Not yet, give me time, so how are we going to play this? Do you think it's a conflict with Larry?'

'I don't think it is, but it doesn't matter anyway.' I explain, 'There is no exclusivity with Larry. Let's start with the house in the Crossings; Toby, do you have the repair numbers?'

Our concerted effort produces a sweet package; pictures of the home, complete cost analysis, and what we can sell the home when it's finished. We figure a twenty thousand profit when all is said and done. The question is, how much is our take, what will the split be?

'Okay, let me call Sal and get the ball rolling.' He answers, I ask him for another meet. 'Sal, I have everything together for our first project, let's meet tomorrow morning and get started.'

'Excellent Lana, I will meet you at Starbucks, eight am.' Nice, he's a fast learner.

'The game is on,' I nod at Tedi and Toby; we are all pleased with the new venture.

'Don't forget,' warns Tedi, 'Take the cannoli, leave the gun.'

'Bada bing, bada boom,' chimes in Toby. *Oh brother.*

The next morning, I am on time at Starbucks, but Sal has beaten me here, and as requested, an iced mocha is waiting for me. 'I have a small gift for you and your wife, a goodwill gesture of our pending success,' I say, handing him a rectangular box, festively wrapped. I am a good schmoozer.

Sal cautiously unwraps his gift, a smile creeps across his face, its *The Soprano's Cookbook.* 'My wife loves this show; this is a thoughtful gift, thank you. Now let's see the information on our first venture.'

Not sure if it's good to be a wise ass with a wise guy, but I think the book was a nice touch. I hand him the file on the rehab, and as he reviews, I enjoy my iced mocha. His poker face does not betray any thoughts. Closing the file, he says, 'Lana, I smell a successful partnership, set up the buy on the property.'

With that we toast each other and our venture. Immediately upon leaving, I call Tedi, who of course is sitting next to Toby in the Lauderdale office. 'Just put me on speaker. The meeting went well, all is a go, so I need you both to put the wheels in motion and lock down that house. Let's get the entire repair scheduled so we can flip this fast.'

'We're on it!' Tedi exclaims enthusiastically.

'Don't forget you have to talk to the new hire today,' Toby reminds me.

'I'm only ten minutes out, see you then,' and I hang up, once again my mind racing faster than my car. Yet one more opportunity to increase cash flow, maybe I'm meant to stay in this crazy business.

The office is a buzzing beehive of activity when I walk through the door. Mike has a customer at his desk writing an offer, Diane is on the phone making an appointment to show homes, June is drawing pictures of Larry's... wait, what?

'June, don't you have something productive to do?' I inquire one eyebrow up.

Tedi and Toby have apparently been waiting for my arrival, anxious to see my expression regarding June's artwork. The two of them are nearly double over in laughter, falling over each other into my office, makes me happy I can be so amusing. Who's this? I spot a new guy, seated, waiting patiently; its the prospective sales person.

'Hi, you must be Charles, give me a moment and we'll have a chat.' I shake his hand. His blond curly hair is kinda crazy, his glasses are black rimmed and thick, his smile is a bit crooked, but overall he seems like the pleasant sort.

In my office, I glare at Toby and Tedi, 'Okay, not sure why it's so funny that our admin person is drawing a penis.' But I can't keep a straight face; okay, it is kinda funny, never a dull moment around here.

'Give me the scoop on Charles; his resume?' I ask.

'He doesn't really have one; he comes recommended by one of our community managers. She just asked that we speak with him, no commitment,' explains Tedi.

'Send him in, and stick close by,' I instruct Toby.

Charles makes himself comfortable across from me staring at me with his crooked smile. I notice he has on two different sneakers, this should be interesting. 'Charles, tell me a little about yourself, I don't have a resume on you.'

'I have years of sales experience, but just not lately. And if I work for you, can you pay me in cash?'

'Well, Charles,' I explain, 'I can't pay you in cash, the government frowns on that. So how long ago were you in sales, and what did you sell?'

'I sold marijuana, I had to stop when my brother, who was my supplier, was arrested and they came looking for me. That was about five years ago, I have been on the lam ever since.'

Am I just a whack job magnet? 'Charles, that's not really the kind of sales experience we are looking for...'

He interrupts me. 'I get it, I also have some chiropractic experience, I could adjust your back for you, just lay down on the floor.'

Not complying, I ask, 'So you went to school to be a chiropractor and ended up selling pot?'

'No, my first stint in the joint I learned a few moves from a chiropractor that was in for Medicare fraud.'

And they say that there is no reform in the prison system. 'Charles, I want to wish you luck, Toby will show you out.'

'Can we please get back to reality?' I plead with Toby and Tedi once Charles is escorted out, 'Let's talk about our deal with Sal.'

Toby starts, 'I had the plumber, A/C and construction guys all go over today to give us bids, we should have them in the morning. But overall, we are not expecting any surprises on the pricing. I'm thinking we should be able to rehab the house for about $8500.'

Tedi goes next. 'I spoke with the manager over at The Crossings, she will let us have it for the back lot rent, less than $1000.'

Now Toby, 'Diane has a customer that can pay cash for the home, fair value is $31,000. We'll just need to 'help' getting her approved at the community.'

'I see, just put that in the budget. Let's get this done fast since we have a cash buyer, tell her she can pick her carpet color and get her under contract.'

'Hey!' exclaims Tedi, 'you never did go over the details of your Puerto Rico trip with me. I say we go have lunch at Los Amigos and you can bring me up to speed.'

'Sounds like a plan, Toby are you in?'

Toby makes a pouty face 'No, you girls go. I want to look at that house in The Crossings again, make sure we didn't miss anything.'

'We'll miss you,' says Tedi. She drags me out the door.

'Your car or mine?' I ask.

'I am not in the mood to listen to Cher and since your car only gets the Cher Channel, we'll take my stang.'

We roll out of the parking lot, top down, Billy Joel on the radio. Billy is Tedi's Cher. The drive is short, the parking lot not too full which means the primo seats will be available. Los Amigos is an old style Mexican restaurant with lots of character and colors, the food is excellent, the beer icy cold and the limes juicy.

A table by the large open window near the bar beckons us, gotta love Florida, always able to dine and drink al fresco. The server of course knows us and brings two Coronas.

'Wait!' shouts Tedi, 'don't put the lime in yet. Let me show a trick I learned at Comfortable Shoes last week, you cover the top, turn it upside down, and the lime gets infused all the way through the beer.' With that she jams her lime wedge into the bottle, puts her thumb over the open top, and turns the bottle upside down. Did I mention that Tedi is of small stature? I look at her, then look at the beer pouring on to the ground.

'Okay, I got this.' Rikki always tells me I have baseball mitts for hands. I push my lime in, cover the top with my thumb, quickly invert the bottle, then flip back right side up. Oh shit, the beer is now fizzing and spraying all over the guy at the bar. Guess I didn't quite cover the top, and maybe, just maybe, I turned it upside down a bit fast. Tedi and I look at each other and turn nonchalantly look out the window as the guy turns around, not happy about his spattered soaked shirt.

'So tell me about the trip,' Tedi says casually.

I open my eyes, relieved to see the guy at the bar has turned back around. 'I think it went okay,' I say, 'And let's not try that trick again.'

'Give me the details on the meeting; what was Puerto Rico like, did Toby behave?'

I start at the beginning with picking Toby up and finding him in his boxers dancing with his dog. Tedi listens with rapt attention, smiling and laughing. 'So sorry I missed the trip,' she concludes, 'Never a dull moment with our crew.'

'Hey, since its Friday, let's play hooky!' I suggest. I don't have to twist Tedi's arm, it's good to be the boss.

'Let's move up to the bar,' Tedi suggests. Grabbing our beers, we pick out a couple of stools so we can have a view of the lake across the street. 'I have to go to the bathroom, don't talk to anyone while I am gone, and don't let anyone sit next to you.'

'Whatev,' I reply. I can take care of myself, thank you very much. No sooner than Tedi disappears around the corner do I hear a voice from the once empty stool behind me, 'I like to make cakes.'

Do I dare turn around? Of course I do, I can't help myself, and oh boy, I'm not sure if it's a man or a woman, kinda like Pat on Saturday Night Live. 'Good for you,' I say trying to avoid looking at her or him, and now I have opened the flood gates.

'I use an easy bake oven, the cakes are small but it's just for me. Light bulbs are powerful.'

Tedi rounds the corner almost at a run. 'What did I tell you? Don't talk to strangers!' She has the strange right.

The bartender is watching from a distance, having been with me in this scenario before. With a simple head nod, she has my new friend escorted from his or her seat to a new one.

'How about some nachos on the house?' she asks.

'And two more Coronas, please,' I request. I look over at Tedi, 'What? I was just minding my own business'.

Tedi just shakes her head. 'Never ceases to amaze me.'

# Chapter 10

My typical Saturday routine once in a while takes a back seat to the biz, and I field sales calls for one of the sales people, who alternate weekend phone duty. I don't really mind, keeps me in practice. Today I am taking the West Palm phones for Penny; she called me saying something about an ex in town and a urinary tract infection. I cut her short and just agreed. With the phones forwarded to my cell, I can work from home, just need to be ready to go if I get a decent call.

'Home Store,' I answer on the first ring.

'Hi, can I make an appointment today to see the house in Magic Meadows you have advertised?' A happy male voice asks.

'Of course, what is a good time for you?'

'How about noon today? I can pay cash,' he replies.

*Cha ching* goes my brain, 'Noon is good, how about if I meet you at the community entrance. My name is Lana, I'll be driving a blue Mitsubishi Spyder.'

'Cool, my name is Lance; see you then.'

Sometimes it's that easy, mostly not. Noon gives me a couple of hours to maybe clean my house, hah, not. Think I'll call the family and catch up. First on my list is Evita.

'Hey Mom, what's new?'

'Not a damn thing, how was your trip? Did you land the deal? Are the men there as sexy as they say? Did you bring back any rum? How was the Ritz?'

Long ago, I learned to let her get all her questions out. 'The trip was quick and productive. We did get in front of the alleged powers that be who seemed enthused, but we'll have to wait and see. No time for hot guys. No, I did not bring back any rum. The Ritz was beautiful, right on the beach and coffee was six dollars a cup.'

'Holy shit, did they lift the cup to the mouth for you?'

'You would think. No protests today?'

'I am putting on my pigeon suit right now,' she replied.

Wait... what? Do I dare ask? 'And what is the protest?'

'The city is banning feeding pigeons in the parks because they poop on all the statues which are expensive to clean. But there are pigeon food sellers that have been in the parks for years and they will be put out of business.'

I love that she is so passionate about the little guys. 'Well, that sounds like a great cause.'

'I just have to remember to take my umbrella, last time I was at the park, the damn things were dive bombing me.'

Oh, the visual I have. 'Well good luck with all that, I'll call you during the week, love you.' With that I hang up.

Onto Rikki. 'Hey sis, what's happening? How are the kids?'

'I almost broke my favorite pair of heels because of Jonah. I saw the little bastard, and I use the term lovingly, at Wonder Wiener when he was supposed to be in class.'

'And... ' I prompted. Jonah is her 'free spirited' fifteen year-old.

'I had to chase him down! You know how fast he is, and my heels were slowing me down. I think I may have twisted an ankle, but once I kicked off my heels, I was able to tackle him and take him back to school.'

'Guess those cross fit classes are paying off,' I noted.

'Then, I bought a shirt at the Wonder Wiener, 'I love wieners' with a picture of a giant hot dog with arms and legs, and made him wear it to class. I figure that was consequence enough. Punishment should fit the crime.'

'Dostoevsky's got nothing on you. Anything new on

the reunion? It's coming up in two weeks.' I make a mental note to schedule a therapy appointment.

'All I know is song sheets have been mimeographed, oh yeah, I said mimeographed. And we are all supposed to look at the Cluck U Chicken Shack menu and send our favorites to order for the picnic.'

I can hear my arteries clogging. 'Are you coming in early for the cousin day?'

An ear piercing scream interrupts us. 'Crap, gotta run,' Rikki shouts. 'Sadie is beating on Jonah again.' Click and she is gone. Rikki's husband was out of the country when Sadie was born, I was the surrogate birth coach. The second I laid eyes on Sadie I said aloud, *this girl is not going to take shit off anyone*, and she has lived up to those words.

Always great to catch up with the family, whew. I look at the clock, still have an hour to kill before I go to meet Lance. The house needs cleaning, could probably at least get the kitchen clean, again, nah, drive-thru Starbucks is more appealing. Anything is more appealing.

A couple of minutes early, I realize I forgot to ask Lance what he is driving, poop. So I sit and wait, glaring like a goof at everyone that is driving in. Fifteen minutes go by, nothing, my max wait time is thirty minutes. Twenty five, still a no show. I don't get pissed, this is all part of sales, I'll give him ten more minutes.

As I slurp the last of my Frappuccino, I see someone riding a bike my way, waving. No, can't be… but it's Lance.

'Sorry I'm late but I was working on my car. I forgot I needed it to come here,' he explains.

Warning bells are going off in my head. I look down at his tires, which actually are not there, he is riding on the rims. 'Bet that wasn't the smoothest ride, how far did you have to come?'

'Just two miles,' he says with a toothy grin. His clothes look like he has been working on a car, and possibly using his head as I spot grease marks above his eyebrows.

'Let's put your bike in my trunk,' I suggest, 'It'll speed things up.'

We quickly load his bike into my trunk and proceed to the house he wants to see. Unlocking the door, I start my pitch. 'The home needs a bit of work, but the good news is you can pick your carpet color. We will also paint the entire home and put in all new appliances.'

'I'll take it!'

Wait... what? Can't be that easy, 'So Lance, you have the $19,000 cash for the home? Is it available now?'

'Yes, I just have to sign the papers I have from my lawyer that says I won't sue.'

'And when are you supposed to sign the papers?'

'I have them at my house, they are ready for me to sign, I'll give you a copy.' The words are bubbling out of his mouth, literally, he is making bubbles.

'Okay, so how about if we leave your bike in my car and I run you home, and you can give me a copy of the papers. Then we can write the contract.'

'Oh yes!' More bubbles.

His directions are not the best, he confuses left and right, but we make it to his house without incident. The entire trip I keep glancing his way, hoping his bubbles don't drop onto my car seat.

'I am so excited to have my own place, can I get it painted any color I want?' he asks. 'I am so tired of white'.

Knowing better, I ask anyway, 'Where were you living before?'

'The sanitarium,' he says matter of fact, 'you know, the nut house, got out two days ago, everything was white, white, white, even the throw pillows.'

'Hmm, and usually throw pillows can liven up any décor,' I remark.

'Here we are! I'll be back in a jiff.' I look at his car, which he is indeed working on, up on blocks, with no engine.

'I'll be right here, hurry back,' I try to make a bubble but am not successful. As soon as he is in the house, I jump out, throw his bike in the yard, and floor it out of the neighborhood. Cher, save me please! I turn on the CD player, and out comes 'Big crowd at the crazy house.' Cher and I are always in sync.

I'm thinking I deserve another Starbucks after that adventure, and I promised to meet Patrick to give him the scoop on the Puerto Rico trip. He is not answering his cell, so I leave him a voicemail, 'Yo, Starbucks, you're buying,' short and to the point. It is, of course, another glorious day, so I decide to leave my car at home and walk. As I am leaving, I see Jillian also heading out.

'Hey there, where are you going?' I ask. 'I'm on my way to Starbucks to meet Patrick, join me?'

Jillian looks at me like I have two heads, she has no use for Patrick. 'Gee, thanks, and I am tempted, but I think I'll pass on the Starbucks however, I'll walk with you.'

We walk and talk, I share with her my adventure with the bubbly bicycle man. 'You have all the fun,' she notes, then, 'Looks like your boyfriend is stepping out on you.'

Following her eyes, I see Patrick sitting with a perfect bottle blond, although I am doubting her parts are real. I'll bet even her baby blues are contacts.

'Well, fancy meeting you here, I just left you a voicemail,' I say with a snide attitude. Patrick is, as always, annoyingly composed. 'Introduce me to your friend.'

'Lana, this is Bambi, she is a client of mine,' he explains. Yeah… right. Is that seriously her name? Looks like he is the client. I start to open my mouth, Patrick's look shuts me down.

72

'Bambi was just leaving.' Then he turns to her, 'Please don't stress, we'll win this case on Monday.'

'I'm Lana,' I put my hand out to shake hers. She just nods nervously, with a look that says *she looks like she might be a bit crazy, so I think I'll just get the hell out here.* Whatev.

I lock eyes with Patrick, 'Can't wait to hear this lawsuit.'

Jillian looks at me, amusement in her eyes, 'I'm out, let's catch up in an hour or so at Scallops, have a late lunch. She glares at Patrick, 'As always,' turns and sashays away. Love her.

Patrick starts, 'So tell me all about your trip.'

'Oh no, spill mister.'

'It's simple, do you remember a couple of months ago, when some joker put detergent in the fountain in downtown West Palm?'

'Go on.'

'Well,' he continues, 'Bambi slipped on the suds and injured her shin.'

'The way she left, she did not look injured to me.'

'She has a scar, and being a dancer, it affects her income,' he explains meekly.

'Are you kidding? Can you say frivolous? And, since when did you become a slip and fall attorney? Plus, that is so not her real name.'

'Let's just say I'm doing it for an old friend.'

'You don't have any friends!'

'Well what about you?' he fires back. 'When did you start doing business with mobsters, Lana. Not a wise choice.'

We engage in a stare down. 'Truce?' I ask. He nods in agreement. 'Good, now go get me an iced mocha, and be quick about it. Then I'll tell you about my trip.'

Once I finish my account of the trip, Patrick says, 'That John character seems like he can possibly cause problems, maybe even legal ones, watch him carefully.'

Agreeing with him, I reply, 'I have a spy on the inside,' meaning Robert. 'I want this deal, but not at any cost.'

'I have a couple of nice rib eyes marinating at home, join me for dinner?' Does he think I am that naive?

'Bambi a vegetarian?' I slurp up the last of my mocha, and sashay off. Oh yea, I can sashay with the best of them.

Jillian is waiting at the bar, a large plate of chilled, seasoned shrimp straddling the line between her stool and the empty one next to her. I plop down on the stool, and dig right in. The shrimp are huge and cooked just right, yummo. A squirt of fresh lemon, a quick dunk in the cocktail sauce and I am in heaven.

Jillian raises an eyebrow and asks, 'Are you imbibing?'

'I just met a woman named Bambi, having Starbucks with my ex.'

Jillian waves down the bartender, 'Nuff said, two Belvedere martinis barkeep. So what is the so called lawsuit?'

'She slipped on fountain suds and scarred her shin.'

'And the sad thing is that Patrick will probably make a couple hundred thousand and get laid.' True dat.

Our drinks are placed before us, we clink and take a welcoming sip. The martinis here are tumbler sized or 'one and done' size as we call them. Jillian looks like she has something on her mind, so I start the conversation. 'What's burning your brain?'

'Crepe man.'

'Good or bad?'

'Why haven't you ever taken me to Comfortable Shoes? I've always wondered what it would be like to bat for the other team.'

I'm going with bad due to the subject change. 'Worlds would collide, possibly altering the future.'

'Oh come on, just once, please,' she pleads. 'This lunch is on me.'

'Okay!' Yes I am that easy, 'But I have to set it up so the gang will all be there. If we are going to alter the future, we're going to do it right.'

We finish our shrimp and gianormous martinis, welcoming the walk home to clear our heads. Just as we step out into the dusk, we hear 'Boobalas, it's been ages, you both look marvelous!'

Here we go again. I am face to face with a rather large woman, lovely black bouffant hairdo with a skunk strip right down the middle. Before I have a chance to even speak, she has both Jillian and me in a death lock. Jillian looks like a raccoon in a trap ready to chew her arm off to escape. Try as I might to push away, my arms sink into the... the... the ampleness of whoever this is.

'I can't breathe!' I scream.

She finally releases us, both of us, who are now sporting fire hydrant red lipstick tattoos on our cheeks. 'My God, Babs and Tiffany, I never thought I would see you again,' she shrieks.

Staying out of arms reach, I loudly explain, 'We are not Babs and Tiffany, please keep your distance.'

Jillian, looking shell shocked, turns to me, 'Unbelievable, you are contagious!' She grabs my arm, and next thing I know we are at an all-out sprint. Turning a corner, we look at each other, trying to catch our breath.

'I think my ribs are cracked.' I feel a sharp pain in my side. We walk the rest of the way home in stunned silence.

'That was a real buzz killer, do you have martini fixins?' Did she really just ask that? Is the Pope Catholic?

'Meet you poolside,' I say, heading to my bar.

'I was going out tonight,' Jillian says, definitely traumatized, 'but I think a nice quiet night home is in order. How about if we rent a movie? And no, I am not watching Burlesque.'

Feeling guilty, I bypass Cher on my CD player, put on jazz, then finish making the martinis. Jillian's color seems to be returning as I sit in the chaise next to her. 'Wow, that was one for the record books,' she remarks.

I just nod, take a sip, put my head back, closing my eyes. 'Do you think if I had a different hair style it would make a difference? Maybe a fake mole?'

Jillian looks over, just shakes her head. It was just a thought.

'Wanna talk about crepe man?' I ask.

'He's just getting too clingy, why can't we just have fun and sex.'

'Sounds reasonable, you would think that would work for him. Has he told you he wants to be exclusive or wants you to wear his letter jacket?'

'Ha Ha. He just wants too much of my time. And I don't really want to talk about it. Did you drink my martini?' she inquires, a look of consternation on her face.

'Uh, no, you did,' I am thinking that hug from hell squeezed out some brain cells. 'Maybe we should call it a night, I think you need some rest.'

'What? Maybe you are right, I'll take a martini to go if you don't mind, I don't know what happened to mine.'

I make another martini, and leave it in the shaker for her. With a pat on the head, I send her off to her house, telling her to text me she has made it okay.

◆◆◆

# Chapter 11

Phones are ringing off the hook as I walk into the West Palm office. Poor Sandy looks like she is ready to pull her hair out so I grab one of the ringing lines.

'Home Store,' I answer with a smile in my voice – that's another of Mom's nuggets.

'I saw your ad in the paper and I want to buy a mobile home, the pretty one,' a male voice states.

'Well sir, I think they are all pretty; my name is Lana, let's see how we can help you.'

'I'm Gilbert, how do I buy it?'

'Well Gilbert, are you paying cash? Are you going to finance?'

'I have money to put down!' He is very excited, I wonder if he is making bubbles?

'That's a start Gilbert, how much do you have to put down?'

I can hear him counting, change jingling, 'I had $20, but I needed cigarettes, I still have nine dollars and thirty one cents!,' he says proudly.

And so starts Monday, 'Gilbert, thanks for calling, keep saving your money, let's talk in a month and see where you are,' click. Sandy looks at me 'Needs to save more money,' I tell her, and head to my office.

As soon as I get settled, I hear Tedi make her entrance, saying her good mornings on the way my office. 'I come bearing good news!' she announces. 'Diane's buyer on our mafia house is ready, willing and able to close as soon as the house is move-in-able. Is that a word?'

'No, and nice. I just got off the phone with a guy that had nine dollars and thirty one cents to put down on a house.'

Tedi just looks at me and rolls her eyes, 'You should jump on that one. So let's call Toby and get the status of the repairs.'

'I needed to call him anyway.' I am already dialing. 'We are supposed to do a shrink and drink this afternoon, I have to get a tune up for the family reunion.'

'Lanalu!' Toby answers, I love how cheery he always is, 'what's shakin?'

'Tedi is here with me and I understand Diane's buyer has the cash burning a hole in her pocket. What is our time frame to complete repairs?'

'I just need to have Gus do the final clean up and it's ready to move in. Am I good or what?' Gus is our charity case, Mr. Fixit, he'll do anything for a buck kinda guy.

'Did I tell you I saw Gus the other day, he was pulled over picking up a piece of sod that must have fallen off a landscaping truck. I just kept driving.' I tell him.

'He is sodding his yard, one found patch of grass at a time,' explains Toby.

One more character to add to our cast. 'I'll have Diane get the buyer into the office, let's close this then we can move to the next project with Sal. Don't forget its shrink and drink day, meet at the Infusion Bar about three?'

'With bells on,' Toby says, and disconnects.

'Do you think this shrink session will really do you any good?' Tedi questions.'You know Babs in not a real shrink, I don't care what Toby says.'

'She has a degree… in something, and Toby says she has helped a couple of people he knows.' According to Toby, Babs practices what they call NLP, she is supposed to help me shift my thinking. I'll just be happy if the elevators stop going sideways.

Tedi just looks at me, 'Probably get more therapy with the peach infused martinis afterwards.'

'Not true,' defending myself, 'I am sure I will leave there thinking my mom is just quirky not whacky.'

'Uh huh, let's go with that. Moving on, I am heading down to the Fort Lauderdale office and getting the contract ready for Diane's buyer. Are you going to call Sal and give him the good news? We really slammed this deal through, only one week, he should be ecstatic.'

'I am sure he will jump for joy, have you met him? Keeps a poker face,' I reply. 'I'll see you in the morning, let's shoot for ten o'clock.'

Tedi just nods and waves as she heads out the door. I dial Sal, 'Mr. Tortellini, we are closing on our project tomorrow morning. Are you available to meet in the afternoon?'

'Two o'clock, Starbucks,' click.

Hmm, I think my phone dropped the call, what the heck, I call him back. 'Did we get disconnected?' I ask.

'No,' click. Alrighty then.

No sooner than I hear the click, my cell rings again. It's an Arizona area code, must be Sol.

'How are you Sol?' I answer.

'Quite well Lana,' he responds, 'Thanks for asking. John concurred that your meeting in Puerto Rico went well, have you heard anything further?'

No repercussions from me blindsiding John in the meeting, that's a relief. 'Nothing yet Sol, you know government wheels grind slowly. I assume that John has not heard anything from his contact?' You know what happens when you assume.... ass... me...

'Not that he has told me,' Sol replies.

'I will call Robert Rodriguez next week and follow up, see what his thoughts are.' Sol seems to have his eyes open as far as John goes, meaning the possibility John may go behind his back for a side deal.

I read between the lines. Good to know.

'Thanks Lana, I wanted to give you the heads up that I may be selling my Florida communities. I'll be in town soon, let's do lunch, I should know by then.'

'Wow, what brings on the sale?'

'I'm no spring chicken, Lana, I want to focus closer to home. There may be an opportunity for you.'

'Sounds like a plan Sol. I'll look forward to lunch and I'll connect with Robert before I see you.' Hmm, maybe a new opportunity? Geez, what a roller coaster I am on, its exhausting.

'Knock Knock!' Penny waltzes in, not waiting for my invite. 'Just wanted to see if you want to do lunch with me?' Uh oh, she wants something.

'Sure, I have a few things to finish on my desk, in about a half hour?'

'Cool, been a while since we hung out,' with that she turns and walks out. I met Penny when she was working at flooring store, she measured my house for new travertine tile. We bonded instantly. I could see she had the sales gene, within a week she was working for me. Of course, I was not aware at the time of how colorful her background is, just a bonus.

Thirty minutes later we are in her Escalade headed for the The Atlantis, a local pub that serves surprisingly fresh food. After we order, we make small talk until our lunch arrives. I opt for grilled shrimp salad, she ordered burger and cheese fries, just ice tea for both of us.

'Okay, spill it,' I say. 'I know you have something on your mind.'

'Now Lana, what makes you think that? But since you ask, I am wondering why all the good stuff is happening in the Lauderdale office? That bitch Diane just told me your new goombah investor bought a house down in The

Crossings and she has it sold already? Plus, when Uncle Larry was in town we didn't get to see him, and he is going to finance new homes.'

The usual interoffice, sales person rivalry; jealousy of course exists between the two offices. And we also, of course, take it to a new level. Once Penny had a dream that Diane stole her sale, she came in the next morning and demanded I fire Diane… truth.

In her standard whiny voice, Penny says, 'You know I have a high overhead, Lana, I need to make sales.'

Penny has a high overhead because she spends a lot. Who has a soda machine in their house? She has every gadget imaginable, not sure what she is trying to compensate for and I don't want to know.

'This is just the first go round with the new investor, we'll do the next project in Palm Beach, I promise.'

'And what about Uncle Larry and the new houses?' I cringe as her voice goes into full, over the top, whine mode.

I reassure her, 'Penny, we are doing new houses for both offices. In fact, you should get with Toby and figure out the best location for the first new house.'

'Do I have to? I don't think Toby really likes me.'

Geez, now I have to put on my couples counseling hat. 'You know that's not true, Toby is just, well, Toby. He acts like he doesn't like anyone, but you know he has a heart of gold.'

'Oh yeah, he's a real giver.' She starts to whine again, but I am saved by the cheese fries. Penny has a healthy appetite. I never have to worry about the temptation of eating the crap she orders, it's never around long enough.

Lunch is finished in wonderful silence. The check arrives, Penny just looks at me, 'You're paying, right?' I thought she asked me to lunch, I'm confused.

'Sure.' There's no use arguing the point.

We wrap up and head back to the office, Penny seems placated for now that she will get her fair share. I do my best to keep all the sales people happy and making money, who says you can't buy loyalty. Plus, not sure who else could deal with their craziness except the me who seems to be the mayor of Crazy Town, which is just another weight on my shoulders, and keeps me plugging away at keeping the biz going.

Puppy dog eyes from Mable greet me as I walk back into the office, guess she feels left out. It's like having kids. 'Hey Mable, how about lunch next week? Just you and me?'

She smiles, orange lipstick stuck to her teeth, 'Well, if you really want to, sure.' Oh brother.

I turn to Sandy, 'Any messages?' Sandy, thankfully, is not the jealous type, she is happy in her own little world.

'Nope, but next time you take someone to lunch, maybe you could bring me back a waffle.'

'Well, if we go to IHOP, I'll certainly do that,' I say.

'Cool.'

My watch tells me it's time to get on the road to my first session with Babs. I am confused, Babs will diffuse, then I'll infuse, perfect.

Dr. Babs' office complex is a typical Florida one story building with outside individual office entries. Not high end, but pleasant looking enough. Not sure what I was expecting, maybe a big brick asylum like building with bars on the windows and lots of people in white coats.

Okay, here it is, suite 132. Anxiety raises my heart rate, I open the door anyway. No one in a white coat is waiting for me, a good sign. Actually no one in the waiting area at all, but I hear voices behind a closed door. I look around and find a nice comfy overstuffed chair. The atmosphere is relaxing, lots of sunlight, plants strategically scattered around, welcoming furniture. Maybe this won't be so bad.

The door opens abruptly and I jump up, startled, great, nice first impression, Lana.

A pleasant looking woman smiles warmly at me, 'You must be Lana, please, come in. I am Barbara Windsor, but call me Babs.'

Into her lair I go, okay, her office. Again, very pleasant, overstuffed chairs, plants, lots of light, and soothing colors. She blends in with her decor in a gypsy like long flowing skirt, salt and pepper hair up in a bun that has partially fallen framing her face.

Settling in, I am not sure what to do next. 'Sooooo,' I say. Wow, I'm on a roll. 'How does this work, Dr. Babs?'

'First, I am not a doctor, I am a therapist specializing in NLP or Neuro Lingusitic Programming. If I can help you shift your thinking on one small thing, your whole world can shift. I can tell you are a therapy virgin, I promise to be gentle.' Her voice is reassuring and kind. 'Tell me what brings you here.'

'Elevators,' I respond. I see her raise an eyebrow, 'and my family reunion.'

'Fear of riding in elevators?' she asks.

'Not real ones, only the ones in my dreams. They never just go up and down. They go sideways, they blast through the roof, they are more like roller coasters.'

'Okay... okay... sounds like you may think your life is out of control.'

I could buy Tedi a martini and get the same insight.

'But I am sure you have heard this before,' she continues. 'The real question is when do these dreams occur? Before a major event, after a major drama, randomly?'. Babs reads the look of confusion on my face. 'Let's start with the events around the latest dream.'

'Well, I would guess the trigger would be the family reunion that's coming up in a week,' I answer.

'Do you get along with your family? Is there anyone in your family in particular that causes you anxiety?'

Therapist Babs is patient as I take a moment to collect my oh so many thoughts on my family. Then it happened, my inner thoughts come out like upchuck, 'I love my family but they are crazy. My mother thinks she is Evita, and goes to every protest march no matter what the cause. The last one was for pigeon poop. My sister is married to Peter the pie maker and thinks I should make a living in crusts, and she has a room just for dead things in a jar. My brother Max, well… My cousin, Tedi, is my business partner; she's good, stable, but not so successful in the dating world, but who is? Oh, and she's a lesbian, not that there is anything wrong with that. My Aunt Sylvia, married to my mother's brother, she's just a bitch that thinks she's June Cleaver on steroids, that's Tedi's mother and Tedi will agree. Most of my other family, cousins and so on, are all older and I don't really know them. I do know that they are a couple of decades behind the times and from what little I know, judgmental, and I like to think I live in a judgment free zone.

Then there's the people who work for me. Diane is loose to put it mildly, but of course, no judgment. She used to date Mike who also works for me and has a wooden leg, but is a great dancer. June is one of my admin people who is sleeping with my investor who wants to sleep with everyone, but June can't have vaginal sex. My other investor is Mafia, and I don't want to go to the mattresses if a deal fails. Sandy, my other admin person, she just gets stoned and eats cereal. Penny and Mable turned the water cooler into a giant martini dispenser. And then there's Toby, he is my savior because he also loves Cher. Did I mention my ex? I still sleep with him once in a while, because the sex, well, its mind blowing. I'm also tired of everyone thinking they know me. A few days ago I was walking with Jillian my neighbor, who sewed shrimp into the seams of her ex-husband's curtains, and a woman grabbed the both us thinking we were old friends. She was rather large and I thought we would never make it out of her folds. I think Jillian is now suffering with PTSD.' I take a breath and decide to stop there as Babs looks like she has been tasered.

'Maybe we should take one person at a time,' she suggests. 'Let's start with your mother, Evita? I assume that is not her real name?'

'It's Isabel, she is your 'Harper Valley PTA' mom,' I reply.

'Then again, maybe we should just focus on getting you through the family reunion, sound like a plan?'

'That works, I am just afraid that once I get to that crazytown, there will be no way out.'

We talk for the next thirty-five minutes, Babs giving me tools to keep all the drama and madness in perspective. How to let each person own their craziness, and how my perception of the reunion should be just to enjoy and then leave it all behind. She puts it in such a way that it made sense, it will be an adventure. Yeah, let's go with that.

'Well Lana, our time is up. I can't wait to hear the reunion stories. You are coming back, aren't you?' What's she trying to say?

'I must say, I am looking forward to the reunion now, I'll call you when I get back to set another appointment.' Meanwhile I'm thinking she may well move with no forwarding address.

I bounce out to my car, definitely feeling lighter than I went in. The Infusion Bar is just a Cher song away, I let Cher choose this time, out of the speakers comes *And the Beat Goes On,* excellent choice. The parking gods are with me as I find a space right in front.

Toby is easy to spot since he is waving and screaming.

'Lanalu!' he shouts. It's loud in here, but not that loud. Stationed directly in front of the peach infused vodka, I am thinking he started without me. 'Soooo, how did it goooo? Are you shrunk? Are you diffused?'

'Actually, I am. Not sure that Dr. Babs will ever be the same though, once I started, the crazy spewed right out.'

'Uh oh, how cra cra?'

'I think I recited the whole cast of characters, even stoner Sandy. Is this my drink?' I ask, taking a sip anyway, yum. Anxious to change the subject, 'So what's going on with Eduardo?' Eduardo is Toby's latest fling.

'He came over the other day unannounced, you know he's a health nut, right? I was sitting in my Jacuzzi with Billy the dog, having a 7&7, sharing my jar of food. I don't think I will hear from him again any time soon. His loss.'

With that we clinked glasses and take another swig. 'You've never had trouble getting dates, and I have a feeling you will have one before you leave here tonight. Toby, are you listening to me?' I can see he is fixated on a well-tanned young man across the bar, Toby is the proverbial Canadian Mountie.

'Sorry Lanalu, what did you say?'

'Never mind.'

Toby looks thoughtfully at me, 'We need to find you a man, or a woman, just plain old get you laid. And not Patrick!' He looks around, taking on the task of shopping for me. 'And we have a winner! The red head over there seems to be staring at you.'

Uh oh, it's Sherri from Comfortable Shoes. 'Quick, hide me!' Too late, Sherri is making a bee line for us.

'Lana, so nice to see you in the daylight,' Sherri is licking her lips.

I gulp. 'Sherri, this is my friend Toby.'

'Ohhh, Sherri, *The* Sherri, so nice to finally meet you,' he moves his leg so I just miss giving him a swift kick.

'Lana, I am here with someone, but if you want to join me, I will get rid of them, just say the word.'

'That's nice of you, I guess, but Toby actually works for me and we have some business to discuss.' I see Toby out of the corner of my eye, mesmerized by the exchange.

'Okay then, hopefully next time,' Sherri says, and sashays off, sashaying as only she can.

'Even I'm tempted to let her put her shoes under my bed,' remarks Toby. We look at each other and burst out laughing. 'Seriously though, what are you waiting for?'

'She scares me.' I leave it at that, changing subjects. 'So I am actually excited I think for the family reunion.'

'You leave Friday?' Toby asks.

'Yep, Tedi and I fly out early in the morning. Rikki and Stacey are meeting us at the hotel a day early so we can have a cousin's day. That also scares me.'

Toby observes, 'With good reason. And Evita, June Cleaver, and the rest come in on Saturday? How will you know anyone? Most of them you have only seen a couple of times years ago, and some you have never seen.'

'I am going to look for tall people with big hands and big feet.'

'Hmm, I use the same criteria,' Toby says, knocking back the rest of his peach infusion.

I finish my infusion as well, wanting another, but alas, I must drive. 'I am outta here my friend, I do not live in stumbling distance like you do. I'll be in the Lauderdale office tomorrow, see you there?'

'Absolutement, I think that's a word.' Good enough for me.

◆ ◆ ◆

## Chapter 12

My office door cracks open, I peer up from my mountain of paperwork to see June's face peeking through, 'Diane's buyer is here.'

'Put her in the conference room, and please send Toby in to see me,' I reply. My heart beats just a bit faster than usual, the adrenaline rush of closing a deal kicking in. It never gets old, makes me wonder if I could ever find anything else that can give me the same rush.

Toby lightly knocks, comes in a sits across from me. 'How did the walk through go?' I ask, 'Any issues I am going to have to deal with?'

'There is an old water bill for $26 that we need to take care of, but other than that, we are good to go.'

'Then let's do this thing!' The excitement makes me a little louder than I would like.

Diane and the buyer are seated at the conference table when I enter. The conference room is nothing fancy, just a well-worn light oak table, six comfortable cushioned chairs around it. I have the contract in one hand, and with my other I reach out to shake the buyer's hand.

'How are you today Gladys? Ready to be a homeowner?' I say, smiling pleasantly.

'Well, Lana, I hope this is not going to be a problem,' she starts, uh oh. She reaches down by her side, lifts a large, stuffed satchel, 'but I only have cash.' And with that she dumps $31,000 in fives, tens and twenties into a money mountain on the table top.

'Not in the least,' I am trying to keep my eyes from bugging out of my head. Holy Crap! Toby reads my thoughts, and like a stealth ninja, he quietly gets up and closes the blinds to both the outside and the sales floor.

'I was hoping you would say that, I just have never trusted banks. My daddy used to own a business, and use the night drop at the bank. One time he was leaning over while putting in the drop and his toupee fell off and got deposited. You know that bank never would give him his toupee back? Ever since then I keep my money safe under my compost pile. Can't trust them damn banks,' Gladys explains.

'Well, I certainly wouldn't think of looking there,' I respond. Everyone around the table eagerly nods in agreement. 'Toby, why don't you start counting while I go over the contract with Gladys.'

Toby, opens his arms and scoops the money toward him, making a gigantic pile. As he starts counting, I am reminded of George's cousin Eustace, counting the money at the end of *Its a Wonderful Life*.

Turning my attention back to Gladys, 'Okay, so you are buying a 2001 Fleetwood 24 x50, final sales price of $31,000. All appliances are brand new and under warranty from their manufacturer.'

Gladys interrupts, 'Just show me where to sign, Lana, Diane already went over the particulars. I got my grand boys sitting in front of my new house right now ready to unload my belongings.'

'Alrighty then,' I turn the documents toward her and start pointing out all of the highlighted signature lines. Doncha just love when a deal comes together this easily. If only they all… 'Thank you Gladys, Diane will give you your keys and you can be on your way. May you make many happy memories in your new home.'

'I just wanted to get away from my bossy daughter, but I thank you all,' and with that Gladys follows Diane out to get the keys.

'Well, another satisfied buyer,' I say. I look over at Toby, he gives me the nod.

'It's all here, now what?' he asks.

'Now I go meet with Sal, and look forward to our next deal with him. Do you have anything lined up?'

'Yep, up in Happy Acres, and Penny is chomping at the bit, thinks she already has a buyer.' This brings a visual of Penny with a bit in her mouth, totally plausible.

'Do I get paid in cash?' Diane asks as she pops her head in the door.

'No, but you do get a *Well Done* from the boss,' from her look I think she would prefer the cash, oh well. 'Seriously, excellent job, let's go do another.' She nods, and backs out the door.

'I have a Starbucks shopping bag in my office, grab that to stash the cash and I will be on my way to meet Sal,' I instruct Toby. I hope it all fits.

My eyes dart to every corner as I pull into the parking lot, anticipating a mugger jumping out and snatching my bag of cash. Sal is already here, I can see him in the window, sipping his iced coffee, relaxed, waiting patiently.

'Hello Sal,' I pick up my iced mocha he has so kindly ordered for me. 'I have a pleasant surprise for you, we were paid in cash.' I discretely open the bag so he can get a gander inside.

Do I detect a slight smile? 'Perhaps we should conclude this in the privacy of my car, Lana.' I am sure I hear the clicking of a camera as we head to his car, and I am equally sure that my picture has been added his most likely voluminous FBI file.

In his car, he thumbs through the bundles that Toby has put together. 'Excellent Lana, and as per our agreement, here is your half of the profit. I believe this is going to be a lucrative partnership. To that end, my wife and I would like to invite you to dinner at Tuesdays in Delray. I assume you are familiar with this restaurant?'

Am I! I have been dying to try Tuesdays, but would be lucky to afford one drink at Happy Hour. 'I would love to join you and l am looking forward to meeting your wife.'

'Seven thirty then, and bring your cousin, Tedi. And one more thing, Lana, next time you buy the coffee.'

'With pleasure Sal,' knowing his old school mentality will never allow me to pay, works for me. With that I exit his car, a big smile on my face.

◆ ◆ ◆

# Chapter 13

The day of our flight to Boston and the family reunion is finally here. Tedi and I park my car in long term, and wait with our bags for the shuttle.

'Do you think we left early enough; I hate to take off my shoes; it seems really windy; did you remember your ticket; did you print your boarding pass; what time do we land again; how does something so heavy fly, I just don't understand; what if I don't recognize any of the family; my mom is going to hate my outfit; is it too early to get a drink?' Tedi does not travel well.

'It's only eight, Tedi,' I say, trying to calm her.

'You drank with Toby at five am.'

'Yes, but he likes Cher.'

'Whatev. Why are we doing this again?' she asks.

'Because our mothers told us to,' I reply. 'Plus, we get a cousins day today, and you know that will be a hoot.'

'Whatev.'

We climb aboard the shuttle, tossing our bags onto the racks, and find a seat. The ride to the terminal is thankfully short. My hand keeps pressure on Tedi's knee so she doesn't bounce the whole bus up and down like a low rider.

The check-in line is tolerable, we zip through and head to the security check. Off go our shoes and we put everything into the dog bowls, then wait to pass through the x-ray thingy. Poor Tedi is frozen in place so I give her a gentle shove, wait my turn and follow behind. No beeps, yay. Tedi spies the bar on our way to the gate.

'It's too early, Tedi, they don't serve booze till eleven,'

'Then how did Toby get Bloody Marys at six am?'

'Connections.'

'Whatev.'

'We only have fifteen minutes before we board, I am sure you can get a drink on the plane,' I tell her, 'Let's just sit until they call us.'

We settle into a couple of seats to people watch as the hoards move to and fro. A handsome, very well built man, catches my attention and makes me smile as I watch him try to corral two energetic kids. They give him kisses and head off to another gate. Suddenly he turns my way, a big smile crosses his face and he begins to make his way toward us. Tedi gives me the eye, another one who thinks they recognize me, and I am thinking I may just answer to whatever name he calls me.

'Lana? You look great!' he exclaims.

After recovering from the fact that this person actually knows me, I realize I have no idea who he is. 'Hi...' I wait for a bell to go off, nothin.

'It's me, Paul.'

Still nothin.

'High school chemistry class? We made the green goop that ate right through our lab table?'

Whoa! Last time I saw Paul he was a hundred pounds heavier with scraggly hair and bad skin. 'Paul! Wow, you look great!' I exclaim. Finally, ding ding ding.

'It helps when you don't live on junk food. What about you! Those braces did a great job, and your hair looks better brown than purple.'

I can hear Tedi suppressing a giggle. 'You remember my cousin Tedi?'

'Yes, of course, you were a year behind us.'

'So, you're married? Were those your kids?' I ask, hoping the answer is no.

'We are legally separated, and yes, they are my kids,' he answers. Yeah, okay, how many times have we heard that one. 'My ex, well almost ex, is taking them to her parents for a vacation.'

*Passengers for Flight 613 to Boston, we will begin boarding in five minutes?* Saved by the loud speaker.

'Well, that's our flight, it was nice seeing you again,' I say to Paul, anxious to make my escape.

'That's my flight, too! I am headed to Marblehead, I have a research gig on whale mating habits.'

Crap. 'Enjoy,' I grab Tedi and get in line.

'What's the matter with you?' Tedi yanks her arm away. 'He said he was separated, legally. Let loose a little.'

'Whatev!' I keep moving down the runway. Tedi stops short and I smack right into her with a grunt. 'Now what?'

'Don't look,' she hisses. 'Look at the flight attendant.'

Wait... what? She said not to look. I follow her eyes. 'Whoa, is that Karen? Didn't you date her in high school? Freaky, it's like a high school reunion.'

'Welcome to Flight 613, Welcome to Flight 613, Welcome to... hello Tedi.' Karen doesn't miss a beat, 'Welcome to Flight 613.'

Tedi and I just nod and continue doing the airplane aisle shuffle, banging our bags into people that are already seated, until we locate our row. Paul passes us on the way to his seat, glancing at us sideways with an uneasy smile. This should be an interesting flight. The plane doors close and Karen stands two rows up from us in the aisle, explaining how to use the oxygen mask when the plane loses pressure or we are about to crash. Both Tedi and I look up, wishing the masks would drop now.

Finally up in the air, the beverage cart makes its way toward us. 'Can I get you something to drink?' Karen asks in her lilting flight attendant voice. Tedi plasters herself to the back of her chair as Karen leans across her to put a bev napkin on my tray. Yikes.

I look at Tedi, who seems to have lost her voice. 'How about two Bloody Marys? Nice to see you, Karen,' I say, elbowing Tedi in the side.

'Yes,' Tedi apparently doesn't want to waste words.

Karen leaves us with a can of Bloody Mary mix, four mini bottles of vodka, and sweat on Tedi's upper lip. Looking at Tedi, I can't help the huge smile on my face. I give her back her advice, 'Let loose a little.'

She looks at me and we both crack up. 'She was the one that got away,' Tedi sighs, reminiscing . 'I wondered what happened to her after her family moved. I've always regretted not staying in touch.'

'Oh please,' I remark, 'Your class ring didn't even get cold before it was on that cheerleader's hand.'

'Didn't you spend the junior year Home Coming making out with Paul for an hour under the bleachers?'

'He was a nice guy, I saw him for who he was, not the science nerd everyone thought he was. And our braces got caught,' I explain.

We leave it at that and drink our Bloody Marys, both of us deep in thought about our unsuccessful experiments in high school relationships. My full bladder snaps me from my deep thoughts. Tedi has fallen asleep, meaning I need to gently, well, as gently as a plane will allow, climb over her to get to the restroom at the rear of the plane. It also means I need to pass Paul; damn he looks good, and as I recall he was a great kisser even with braces. Good, no line, so I can go right in and accomplish my mission. A quick look in the mirror before I return to my seat, hmm, maybe I should loosen up. Whatev.

Opening the door, I am shocked to find myself face to face with Paul. Looking up into his eyes my temperature jumps thirty degrees. Well, no time like the present, I have always wanted to join the mile high club. Without a word, I grab Paul, pull him into the restroom, lock the door, and plant one on him.

Gasping for air, I ask, 'Legally separated, right?' That nod is good enough for me. As we embark on our own mission, I am amazed at what can be accomplished in such a small space in such a short amount of time, whew! Adjusting my outfit, a quick check in the mirror reveals my hair looks like squirrels have made a nest, yikes. Paul on the other hand looks perfectly coiffed, damn. We simply nod to each other, take a deep breath and open the door.

Holy shit! Tedi is coming out of the restroom across from us and Karen right behind, her once perfectly coiffed chignon bun looking like squirrels also have used it as a nest. Picking our jaws up off the floor, Tedi and I regain our composure and casually head back to our seats. Paul slides back into his seat, Karen heads to the galley to make a fresh pot of coffee.

Resettled, I face Tedi, 'Where'd you get the wings?' I ask, pointing to the gold and blue wings pinned to her shirt.

'I earned them. Your pants are unzipped.'

'Secret handshake?' I ask. Tedi nods, we spit into the palms of our hands and do the if-you-ever-speak-of-this-again-I-will-kill-you-cousin-secret-keeping handshake. Then we both close our eyes and wait for the flight to be over.

'Welcome to Boston folks, the temperature is a pleasant seventy degrees,' the captain announces. Tedi and I gather our belongings, do our best again not to hit anyone as we take down our carry-ons, and painfully wait our turn to deplane.

'Hope you enjoyed your flight today, thanks for flying with us. Hope you enjoyed your flight today, thanks for flying with us. Hope your enjoyed your flight today, thanks for flying with us.' Karen just smiles as we pass.

I look at Tedi, 'I would say we enjoyed it, wouldn't you?'

As we exit into the terminal Tedi looks over her shoulder, Paul is right on our heels, she pulls me into the ladies room. 'He probably thinks he'll see us at baggage claim, but we don't need any more baggage, get it?'

With a roll of my eyes and my luggage, we head out and down the escalator, do not pass go, and hail a cab. Whew, well that was a flight I won't soon forget, no one can accuse me of not knowing how to loosen up.

'Where to ladies?' asks the cabbie.

'Revere Inn,' I reply, then turning to Tedi, 'What time is Stacey getting in? Rikki should already be here.'

'I think Stacey is in, too. I'll text her when we get out of the tunnel. They may have already connected and may well be at the hotel bar, after all, it's already noon.'

The sun is blinding as we emerge from the Ted Williams Tunnel. The sites of Boston come into view, including the Boston World Trade Center. Roads are mostly one way, very confusing, makes me glad we didn't rent a car. The good news is, Boston is known as America's Walking City, guess we'll find out soon enough when we head out for our Cousin's Adventure.

'That'll be thirty dollars,' demands the cabbie with his hand out. Guess they don't help with luggage anymore.

Exiting the cab, we look at hesitantly at each other, 'Are you ready for Cousin's Day?' I ask.

Tedi takes a large gulp of air, 'God help us all.'


'Whooo Hooo!' Comes from inside the lobby bar.

Tedi and I sideways glance at each other, knowing this most likely signals that Rikki and Stacey must already be in the lobby bar. Crossing the comfortable, but way too colonial for my taste, hotel lobby, we peek into the bar. Rikki and Stacey are high fiving each other, empty shot glasses are in front of them, oh boy. Taking deep breaths, we brace ourselves for what's to come.

'Whooo Hooooo!' Rikki screams and comes flying towards us for a hug at full speed, almost knocking us down. Stacey, being a bit more subdued, simply orders four more shots, then screams. It's all about priorities.

For being high noon, the bar is fairly empty. Anyone that was here, I am fairly certain made a mad dash for the exit. It's a typical lobby bar, dark woods, lots of brass, fake greenery, and leather high back bar stools. The bartender is hoping for a big tip, or she would have left with the other patrons.

'So what are we drinking?' I ask, looking dubiously into my glass. I can tell this will be a one and done, smells nasty.

'Boston Burn Out,' Rikki tells us, 'Bottoms up!'

We pick them up, and slam them down. Holy Crapola! I think my eyebrows were singed off! Whew! I look over at Tedi who has tears coming out of her eyes.

'Wow, alrighty then,' I say. 'Tedi and I need to check in, then let's head this Boston Cousins' Day out to the city. And Rikki, no more Burn Outs, we'd like to last at least until 5 tonight, I have been looking forward to Legal Seafood for months.'

'Whatev,' she replies, using the apparent word of the day. Heading off another round of shots, I grab her by the arm and drag her with us to the elevators. Stacey and Rikki have already checked in, so we really just need to drop our bags in their rooms. Should be interesting sharing a room with Rikki, it's been a while. We did share growing up, I survived, but I am scarred for life. Maybe a topic for Dr. Babs?

I stop dead in my tracks as Stacey reaches for the up button. 'Do you not see that?!' I scream, frozen in my tracks.

'Uh oh,' whispers Tedi.

'What… What?,' asks poor Stacey. 'Ohhhh.'

We all stare at the *UP* button, which in fact is not pointing up, but sideways. My nightmares are coming true. I am freaking out!

'What does this mean?' I cry, 'I am so not getting in that elevator!'

Rikki takes control , 'Here, give me your bag, I'll take it up to our room and be back down in a flash. It's just a silly button, look, I've made it point upwards. Go have a seat in the lobby.' She grabs my bag and Tedi's, then enters the elevator. As the doors close and she disappears, I wonder if I will ever see her again.

Rikki is a great big sister, always ready to kick someone's ass for me. At six foot tall, she matches my height, but since she is my big sister, she insists she is taller. She is always fiercely loyal to her family. Once, in elementary school, a couple of girls who were crosswalk patrols kept giving me a hard time. I just had to tell Rikki once. Next day, Rikki and her posse had a friendly chat with the girls, problem solved. Any time after that when I approached the crosswalk, they were all smiles, and safely ushered me across the street.

'Come on,' Stacey guides me to the exit, 'let's get some air and figure out our game plan.'

'The quest is simple,' states Tedi matter of factly. 'We have to find a bar that has Harpoon beer on tap and Boston Clam chowder. The little octagonal oyster crackers are bonus points. If the bar does not have the combo, we have a shot and move on to the next bar.'

'Should be easy to accomplish,' says Stacey, quietly mumbling a little prayer.

I am still trying to get the visual of the sideways *UP* button out of my head. My imagination is running wild, visualizing poor Rikki plummeting to the basement, only to circle the garage, and shoot out the roof. Thankfully, my fears are laid to rest when I spot Rikki headed our way, love my sister.

'Let's get this show on the road!' she announces, then grabs Tedi by the arm and marches out onto the streets of Boston. Stacey and I just look at at each, link arms, and follow suit. Women on a mission, look out Boston.

We only get half a block before we hit a locals pub, dark and smoky, no tourist traps for us. 'So can I clarify the rules?' I ask. 'It's the trifecta, Harpoon, Boston Chowder and oyster crackers, or we do a shot and leave? Don't you think we should eat something?'

'No,' barks Tedi, 'Barkeep!' I think we're going to make oodles of friends along the way.

Stacey steps up, 'Here's the deal my friend, we want Harpoon on tap, bowls of Boston Chowder, and cute little oyster crackers. If you cannot accommodate us, we shall leave this establishment post haste... after we do a shot.'

The bartender looks like he needs a translator. 'Let me dumb this down for you,' Rikki says, she has real people skills. 'Let's start with step one, do... you... have... Harpoon... on... tap?' And this is only bar number one.

'No... we... don't,' replies the bartender. That brings smiles to our faces, it's always fun when someone plays along.

'Alrighty then,' it's my turn to chime in, 'shots it is, set us up with Patron Espresso my good man.' Might as well be able to stay awake, this quest could take a while.

The bartender lines up the shots, we bring it in a circle, clink shot glasses, 'Nostrovia,' we knock them back, salute the bartender and head out to continue our mission, kinda like Don Quixote.

The bartender salutes back, 'And may you fair ladies be successful in your quest!'

'So where to now? I think we head towards the wharf, they must have Harpoon Beer there,' suggests Stacey.

'Sounds like a plan, which way?' Rikki asks.

'I think we just head down State Street, I am sure we'll find it,' this from Tedi who can get lost one block from the office.

Heading down the street toward the wharf, I gaze around at the city full of history, observing the hipster college students. We are lucky given Boston's reputation for not so nice weather, to have a brilliant sunny day, sparkling blue skies with smattering of white puffy clouds. I am sure the sunny weather followed Tedi and me from Florida.

'Ding Ding Ding!' Rikki has signaled the next stop on our trifecta search. Once our eyes adjust to the lack of light, we appear to be in an old man's bar, signaled by lots of hair in ears. Rikki nods, and looks at us 'Okay, I got this one,' and with a wink starts her magic. She has a way of flirting with older men that as good as guarantees us free drinks.

Quietly, we stand near the bar and observing Rikki at work, all smiles. Not two minutes later she is motioning us over, and I see shots being poured. I am assuming no trifecta.

'Benny, this is my sister Lana, and my cousins Tedi and Stacey. Girls, this is Benny, he is a true Bostonian.'

Benny smiles at us with his summer teeth, you know, some are here and some are there. By the look on his face he appears to be thinking he hit the trifecta or fourfecta, whatever.

'Well ladies, Rikki herah tells me you four are on some kinda reunion, pleased ta meetcha,' he says, reaching for Stacey to bring her closer. Lucky girl. 'Let's do this shot together, on me. What's this called Rikki?'

'Slippery Nipples,' she announces.

Benny laughs a little too loudly, a little spittle falling from the gap in his upper gum where his has lost one of many teeth. We all take a step back and look at Rikki to get us out of this.

'Benny, you are one of a kind,' Rikki slaps him on the back. 'Thanks so much for the drinks, but we have a mission to complete. Enjoy the rest of your day.' And with that we make a speedy retreat.

'But... But... But,' we hear Benny stutter as the door closes behind us.

'No more stops until we get to the wharf or we will never make it,' Tedi wisely observes. Then she sees something shiny. 'Ohhhh, look!'

As we pass the Children's Science Museum, Tedi becomes mesmerized by an exhibit outside that uses sonar to tell you how tall you are. Rikki, Stacey and I just look at each other as Tedi runs over and stands underneath. The machine makes a few bings and bongs, then in its machine voice states, 'You are five foot three and one half inches'.

'I knew it,' exclaims Tedi. 'I knew I was over five foot three, I may have to buy some new pants!'

The three of us exchange glances again, silently agreeing to let Tedi have her moment in the sun. We start walking toward the pier again, Tedi grinning like the Cheshire Cat.

The Wharf Bar is exactly what you would expect from a Boston waterfront bar. Very nautical, ropes hanging, wooden helm wheels, pictures of sail boats; cliche in other words. Even smells salt watery.

Finding seats at the bar, we are hopeful that our mission will end here. 'What can I get you ladies?' the bartender asks as she distributes bev naps. She is a very attractive blond, dressed suggestively but not showy. In other words, no boobs hanging out of a tube top or cheeks hanging out of her shorty shorts, but her physical attributes are still noticeable.

To no one's surprise, Tedi takes the lead. 'We are hoping you will be the one to help us complete our mission,' she smiles with her best flirty smile. Oh brother.

'Your mission is my mission, my name is Brandy. Tell me how I can help you.'

Huh, this is interesting. Stacey just rolls her eyes. 'Our mission is a simple one, Harpoon on draft, Boston Clam Chowder, and oyster crackers, yay or nay'.

'Yay,' says Brandy, smiling at Tedi.

'Yay,' responds Tedi.

'Yay,' Rikki, Stacey and I respond.

Brandy leaves to get our beer and chowder, Tedi can only stare after her. Stacey gives Tedi a slap on the head, warning, 'Don't compromise the mission!'

'Here you go ladies,' Brandy lines up our beer and chowder, 'anything else I can get you, just give me a holler,' and with a big smile, she sashays over to wait on her other customers. Brandy is a fine girl, what a good wife she would be.

'I don't even like beer,' Rikki makes a face, 'who thought of this mission? And I am not really a fan of chowder. Can we just do a shot instead?'

'No,' I answered. 'Eat the damn chowder, drink the damn beer, then we'll talk about a shot.'

'Whatev!'

Mission complete, I see Brandy heading over with five shots. I glare at Tedi, knowing damn well she somehow orchestrated this. 'Ladies, this one is on me,' she holds up her glass, 'to a job well done.'

Whatever is in this glass looks like pee. 'Thanks Brandy, but what exactly are we drinking?' I ask.

'Mountain Dew me,' she replies, meeting Tedi's eyes. Rikki, Tedi and I look at each other, feeling like three extra wheels. What the heck?

'Down the hatch,' orders Rikki, 'we need to head out, time for some Legal Seafood.' Tedi not so discretely scribbles her phone number on the credit card receipt, surprised she just didn't write it on the back of Brandy's hand.

Food is a good idea since our afternoon has consisted of mainly alcohol. We pass the Children's museum again, poor Tedi cannot resist. The rest of us keep walking, but stop when we don't hear a *whoo hoo* from Tedi. Glancing around, we spot Tedi following us with her head down.

'What happened,' I ask, 'did the measuring thingy stop working?'

'I think it's broken, now it says I am only five foot two and an half,' replies Tedi sullenly.

Suppressing a laugh, Stacey consoles Tedi, 'It's the beer, it weighs you down.'

Tedi frowns, 'Stupid beer, whose idea was the Harpoon anyway?'

'Yours,' the rest of us say in unison.

'And speaking of beer, I really got to go.' I need to walk with my legs crossed. 'Like now.'

We are surrounded by large, dingy white, utilitarian looking buildings with bars on the windows that seem to be signaling we are walking through some kind of industrial area. No lounges, no convenience stores, no retail of any kind. Our bladders are not happy, we continue our painful walk.

'I think we got something!' shouts Tedi excitedly.

There steps up to what seems to be some kind of sketchy pub. Not that we care, things are getting urgent. Up a steep set of narrow concrete stairs, we walk into a smoke filled, pool hall. Without taking much notice of the clientele, we all just smile and head straight to the little girls room, aware of multiple sets of eyes following us. There is only one stall, so we wait with our legs crossed until we all get a turn. Four big sighs later, we head out to the pool hall, wondering if we can get away with not imbibing.

'Well Tedi, you sure are hitting the jackpot today,' remarks Rikki. As we look around, we realize there are only women in this bar. Big women, scary women.

I glance over at Tedi. 'Keep your eyes down, move slowly towards the door,' she instructs. We look at Rikki, she seems to be slipping into her *workin' it* mode. 'Even you Rikki.'

'I am sure these are very nice women,' Rikki says. 'You know what they say anyway, 'Butch on the streets, fem in the sheets.'

Definitely no more alcohol for Rikki, Stacey takes one arm and I take the other, hustling her out the door. Luckily, we are closer than we think, we arrive at Legal Seafood in just five minutes. The restaurant is typical of the chain, comfortable four top tables, aquariums inside the walls. The hostess eyes us up and down, undoubtedly smells the copious amount of alcohol, and decides to seat us anyway.

'Can I get you started with an adult beverage,' our server asks.

'No!' I yell. 'Oops, sorry, we'll all just have water.'

Plastic bibs adorned with red lobsters are quickly around our necks as we all request yummy lobster, and each of ordering different sides that we can share. Conversation is limited to pass the potatoes au gratin, everyone busy with full mouths. Last but not least, we order a slice of Boston Cream pie and four forks.

The downside to our excellent food – it has somewhat killed our buzz. Tomorrow will be a long day so we do the smart thing and wisely decide to head directly back to the hotel. Stepping outside into the sunset, Rikki whines, 'Let's get a cab, I don't think I can walk another step.'

Stacey, steps off the curb and whistles for a cab like a sailor. One roars up to the curb immediately; in we pile, Tedi riding shot gun. 'Where to?' asks the cabbie.

'Revere Inn,' Tedi replies.

'Are you sure?' questions the cabbie with raised eyebrows.

Tedi turns around to us, her look conveying, WTF, 'Uh, yes, I'm sure.'

'I only ask, Miss, because it's right across the street.'

One by one we slide back out of the cab, Tedi throws a five dollar bill at the cabbie, and we trudge across the street. In the back of my mind I hear Cher singing *Taxi Taxi, give me ride, I'm gonna to take you to the other side.* Without a word, we head into the lobby and get into a waiting elevator.

'Well, that was fun,' states Stacey, her voice not conveying any enthusiasm. Nodding in agreement, we head into our rooms to get a good night sleep, even though it's only seven o'clock. Tomorrow is going to be a doozy of a day.

# Chapter 14

'I need breakfast, or maybe I should just swallow a sponge,' groans Rikki.

Without lifting my head off the pillow or even opening my eyes, I ask, 'What time is Evita due in?'

'I think ten; call Tedi and see if they want to join us for breakfast. I hope it's a buffet.'

Not wanting to sit up, I search the end table with my hand until I find my phone, and speed dial Tedi. 'No,' she says answering the phone.

'Yes, come with us to breakfast,' I tell her. 'Be ready in fifteen minutes, we'll meet you at your door.'

Rikki and I drag ourselves out of bed, brush the moss off our teeth, and throw on comfy clothes. Heading out the door, we do an outfit check, a nod of approval and we're ready. Stacey and Tedi exit their room at the same time, I hope we don't look as rough as they do.

'Jet Lag,' states Stacey. Not sure how that works since we are all on the same time zone. The hotel restaurant is not too crowded; the hostess is able to seat us right away. The decor is what you would expect in Boston in a hotel named the 'Revere Inn,' lots of red, white and blue, vintage flags, rusty antique tchotchkes.

Without being asked, our server brings us a big pot of coffee. Savoring the first few sips, we start to feel human again. 'What time do the festivities begin and what's first on the agenda?' I ask.

'*Don't cry for me Argentiiinnnnaaaaaa!*' None of have to look up to know that Evita has arrived; the knowing nod is exchanged, let the Crazy Town reunion begin. Turning towards the door, there is Evita in all her glory, long flowing, loud peasant skirt, gypsy blouse and cowboy hat. Queen of the fashion statements.

'Hey Gals,' says Evita. 'You four look like shit, how about a hair of the dog?'

We all get up and take turns giving Evita a hug. 'So how was your flight Mom?' I ask, pulling up an extra chair to the table.

'Same old same old, you're up, you're down. So, Tedi, Stacey, what time does your Mom fly in on the broom stick express? Boy, my brother sure is whipped. You both look great by the way. What's going on with that boyfriend of yours Stacey, still afraid of marriage? Not that that's a bad thing. And Tedi, how's Lesbo Land? Gettin any lately?,' she takes a breath to re-energize, 'Lana, surprised Patrick didn't follow you, hell you two are doing the Patti LaBelle thing, getting a divorce without ever being married. Rikki, my sweet, how is that brood of yours, how many, four? Five? That little one sure is a pip, Sadie is going to rule the world. Are you sure she is Peter's daughter?'

Not bothering to acknowledge any of her questions, I ask, 'Mom, do I want something to eat? Or you can just go check into your room, it adjoins mine and Rikki's.'

'Really? I don't think I want to be that close to you two, what if I want to entertain?'

Oh my god. 'Fine, see if they can change it,' I reply, eager not to have additional material for Dr. Babs.

'And who picked this place?' she starts again. 'I love Rita, but she has horrible taste. This place looks like George Washington, Ben Franklin, and Betsy Ross had a three way, produced a baby and it threw up all over this hotel.' Evita suddenly shivers, looking like she has seen a ghost. 'It just got twenty degrees colder in here, John and Sylvia must be in the building.' Meaning Tedi's parents. 'I think I'll just go check-in.'

Sure enough, Uncle John and Aunt Sylvia are standing at the entrance of the restaurant. I love my Uncle John, he is so laid back, dressed casually in plaid cargo shorts and an orange polo shirt. Aunt Sylvia, well, I love her too, of course, but not so laid back. Typical of her style, she is wearing a pale blue pleated skirt that ends just below her knees, with a simple floral blouse, round collared. I didn't think they even made rounded collar shirts any more. Only things she is missing are the pearls and clip on earrings, oh wait, no she's not.

We all get up again, ready to greet them with hugs and kisses, Evita is already in motion. Without missing a step, she goes in for the hug with her brother John, 'Johnny! Looking well, can't wait to catch up and hear about everything going on in your life. June, I mean Sylvia, love the outfit. See you all at the kick off lunch!' Backwards wave, and she's out.

'Hey Mom, hey Dad,' says Tedi with affection. She moves from the table to give big bear hugs. Her parents live in Maryland, and of course it's my fault their little girl is a lesbian and has moved away from home. Nothing different, it was always my fault growing up, whatever it was. Other than that I have a great relationship with them. Stacey lives in Washington DC, giving her the opportunity and the obligation to see her parents more often.

'Hi sweepea,' Uncle John says to Stacey, embracing her. She gives him the one armed hug, Stacey is not a fan of hugging.

'Sylvia, good to see you, even though we saw each other last Sunday,' Stacey says as she greets her. Hmm, perhaps their relationship is a bit strained?

Rikki and I both hug our aunt and uncle. 'We were about to have breakfast, would you like to join us?' I offer.

'Breakfast? Its ten o'clock!' Sylvia is taken aback.

'Mom, why don't you and daddy check-in, get settled, and we'll see you at the luncheon,' suggests Tedi.

'Well, if that's the way you want it Theodora,' huffs Sylvia. I can actually hear Tedi cringe.

'Gotta love parents,' Rikki notes, and whistles for our server. 'I'll have the right side of the menu.'

Bellies full, we head back to our rooms to get ready to face the rest of the day. In a timely manner, the Turner Family Reunion Official List of Fun Festivities, has been delivered by sliding it under our door.

'Oh yeah, Rita is here, she just waiting to make her big entrance.' Evita is standing in the doorway that connects our rooms.

'Mom, I thought you were going to change rooms?' I ask.

'No such luck Leebee, all rooms in this red, white and blue hell are taken if you can believe that. If my thong is hanging on this doorknob, I suggest you wear ear plugs so you can sleep.'

'Ew, there goes my breakfast,' Rikki whispers to me. 'Looking at this list of activities Mom, not sure where you will find the time.'

'It's me you're talking to Rikki, I'm a man magnet.'

Someone please help me.

'I think I'll call and check on the kids,' says Rikki, making her way to the corner of the room.

Evita returns to her room, and I plop on the bed, hoping for a little calm before the storm. 'Hang on honey, okay, I'll put her on,' I hear Rikki saying as she makes her way to me.

I hear my niece Sadie's sweet voice coming through the phone, 'Hi Aunt Lana, I am sorry that I am not in Boston with you, but Mommy says it's not a kid friendly reunion. I just wanted to invite you to my first concert.'

'Oh,' I reply. 'When is it?'

'Soon as I am famous. I am only going to sing three songs, no more, even if they give me a standing ovation. I am sure it will be sold out, but I will reserve a ticket for you, no discounts.' Crazy in training.

'That's very kind of you pumpkin, I'll look forward to it,' I hand the phone back to Rikki as she rolls her eyes. I close mine again, resting up for the remainder of the day.

By eleven forty-five, the three of us are ready to head to the luncheon. Tedi, Stacey and parents are going to meet us there. Evita has somewhat toned down her outfit, no cowboy hat. Off we go into the fray.

In the elevator, I turn to Evita and ask, 'How will I recognize our cousins? I haven't seen them in years.'

'Just look for the people that look like you, hands as big as baseball mitts with big feet to match.' Huh, Toby will be happy to know that I was spot on.

Aunt Rita is easy to spot in the restaurant since she is standing, perfectly coiffed, under a big banner announcing the Turner Family Reunion. Rita is very cosmopolitan, she was always hob knobbing with the elite of DC when her husband was alive. Uncle Perry was a favorite doctor of Washington's upper crust. He also played the trombone, and sang *That Little Pink Nighty of Mine* after a few gin and tonics. Are you sensing a pattern to this family tree?

Since his passing, Aunt Rita has become the self-proclaimed glue of the family. Spotting us, she smiles and waves, rushing to greet us. Me first, yay, she has always been my favorite aunt. 'Hello sweetheart!' she exclaims, hugging me tightly. She moves down the line, hugs and kisses all around.

Last but not least is Evita. They take each other's hands, size each other up, and finally go in for the embrace. Evita and Rita were the Tedi and Lana of their generation, without the lesbianism. Always in trouble,

111

always together. Until that is, Rita met Uncle Perry, and life became about being the perfect hostess slash wife. Evita was sad to lose her running partner, but doesn't hold it against her, it's evident they still have a very special bond.

'So let's get this shin dig started,' exclaims Evita. 'Where is the rest of the crew?'

As if on cue, a gaggle of cousins enter the restaurant. A bit apprehensive, I am not really sure how to start a conversation even though they are family. Everyone takes a seat at the four tables reserved for our gang, and we begin to mingle. It becomes almost like speed dating, moving from table to table, getting to know the basics.

'So, Rosie, I'm Lana, Evita's, I mean, Isabel's daughter. I live in Florida and have a manufactured home business with Tedi.' Rosie is a bit intimidating, at five foot eleven; she has the perfect proportions, perfect teeth, perfect natural blond hair. Try as I might, I cannot find a flaw, tip to tail.

Rosie takes my hand, smiles sweetly, 'I understand your business is not doing well, so sorry to hear that. But on the bright side, I hear you may be getting married!'

This is going to be a long reunion. 'My business is fine, and no I am not getting married,' I reply. 'Tell me about you.'

'Well, I was crowned Miss Pork Roll at the state fair two years ago. While I was at the fair I met Mr. Corn Hole, the corn hole champ of the county, and now just three months later we are married and expecting our first child.' I smile, bingo, as perfect as she appears, the crazy cannot be denied.

My next cousin sits down, looking up I am happy to see its Tedi. 'How's it going with you?' I ask.

'Well, cousin Martha says its okay to be a lesbian, just don't tell anyone. If someone asks why I am not married at my age, tell them I was but my husband died in the war.'

'Sage advice from a Crazytown elder. I just met Miss Pork Roll,' I say. We both roll our eyes and move on.

The *get acquainted* session continues, meeting and greeting, lots of smiling and laughing. Rita has a satisfied look on her face that makes me happy, she has put so much effort into making the reunion special. Looking around for Evita, I spot her sitting with her cousin, Melvin, giggling away. Against my better judgment, I decide to see what they are talking about.

'Hey Melvin, how are you? You look great,' I exclaim. Although Melvin is my cousin, he is close to Evita's age. Don't ask. 'I just came over to see what you two are giggling about.' As soon as it comes out of my mouth, I regret asking.

'We were remembering how we used to play Doctor,' Evita explained. 'This one time…' My mind screams, *Run*! I obey and high tail it out of earshot before Evita has a chance to finish her sentence.

Thankfully, Aunt Rita is clinking a knife on her glass, signaling it's time to move onto the next activity. 'Okay everyone, time to get on the bus, our first stop is the waterfront site where they had the Boston Tea Party.'

'Let's go have our own tea party,' Rikki whispers in my ear. I see Tedi and Stacey right behind her, their heads bobbing in agreement.

'Come on, get on the bus,' I order. 'Let's at least make it to the waterfront, Aunt Rita will be mad at us if we don't stay with the group.'

As if on cue, Rita looks our way, giving us the eye, the *you better not ditch this reunion* eye. All aboard! Each of us are mentally plotting a dalliance that can go unnoticed.

The bus is one of those open air jobs like they have in London. The *kids* all scramble to sit on the top level, enjoying the sunshine. Rita narrates the trip, instructing the bus driver not to slow down enough for any of us to tuck and roll. Rikki keeps kicking me, flicking her head to the side indicating we should the make the jump anyway, road burns be damned. Stacey is asleep with her head on Tedi's shoulder.

Round the city we go, through Beacon Hill, past Boston Commons and Faneuil Hall, past all the old churches. It would probably be interesting if I had any fascination with history. Finally the bus rolls to a stop back in front of the hotel. Tedi shrugs her shoulder to wake Stacey, whose head promptly slides off with a jerk, leaving Tedi with a nice drool spot on her shirt.

'Okay everyone,' Rita announces. 'You all have a bit of free time to rest and get ready for dinner. See you in the restaurant at seven, and don't forget to wear red, white or blue.'

'I'm going to vomit red, white and blue,' Evita says as she walks beside me into the lobby. 'Where is Rikki? She must have been the streak I saw headed into the hotel bar. What are you gals going to do now?'

'I am thinking nap,' I reply, as I am being steered towards the bar, Tedi on one arm and Stacey on the other.

'Sometimes you are so boring Lana, I wonder what Patrick sees in you,' states Evita. 'I am headed into the bar to see if anyone interesting is there, please pretend like you don't know me.' I'll try real hard...

Shots are waiting for us at the bar along with Rikki. 'What are these?' asks Stacey.

'Brain Hemorrhages, I thought they were appropriate.'

They look nasty to me. 'Fine, but one and done, I seriously need a nap.' I feel like I need toothpicks to keep my eyes open.

Salud, we down the shots, then head out of the bar to the elevators. Evita is singing to a group of three men, the lyrics have to do with her lipstick matching her eyes. Taking her advice, I keep walking and pretend not to know her. Rikki starts to go over but thinks better of it. Silently, we wait for the elevator, fried from yesterday's and today's events. As elevator doors open, and we hear an ear piercing scream. Rudely jolted out of our tired trance, we are face to face with a woman dressed like Betsy Ross.

'Jerrianne! As I live and breathe! They told me you moved to Fiji!' Of course she is coming straight at me.

Tedi drags me into the elevator, feverishly pushing all the buttons. 'Shhh, we are US Marshalls, Jerrianne is in witness protection and you may have just blown her cover,' she hisses.

'I knew when you dated Vinnie, he was trouble,' Betsy Ross exclaims. Then she gives the sign of locking her lips and throwing away the key as the elevator doors closed. Nice one, Tedi.

Without a backwards glance, we go to our rooms, and crash. Just twenty minutes, that's all I need. Not even ten minutes into our nap, we hear giggling from Evita's room, ewww. Rikki and I simultaneously put pillows over our heads. Whose idea was adjoining rooms anyway. Thankfully, I fall into a blissful sleep.

# Chapter 15

'Hey! Hey!' Rikki shouts as she is shaking me. 'What the heck were your dreaming about? You were talking about wigs.'

Roused from my slumber, I simply reply, 'Cher was asking my opinion for her next number before she went on stage.'

'Why do I ask. Maybe this should be a topic for Dr. Babs, your obsession with Cher. Come on, we need to get ready, we have to meet Stacey and Tedi at the bar before dinner.'

I do not reply, I stay in the Cher moment to keep me sane. Finding attire for the dinner shindig is not as challenging as I thought it would be, Rikki has on a red clingy dress, I have on white capris and a navy blue pin stripped sleeveless blouse. Outfit check, teeth check, all good… out the door we go.

Tedi and Stacey are already at the bar waiting, thankfully no nasty shots are waiting. 'Martinis?' suggests Tedi.

Nodding in agreement, Tedi orders Chopin martinis all around with blue cheese olives. Girl after my own heart. We all sip our martinis, enjoying the quiet before the red, white and blue chaos. There is a rumor of a surprise during the dinner event; I don't even want to venture a guess.

As the clock strikes seven, we take the last sip of our drinks, and head into the dining room. I note the movie screen and stage set up behind the tables, please don't let that be for us. There are place cards for each family member, Tedi and I look at each other, crap, we will be separated for sure.

Finding my table, I am happy to see that I am sharing it with Melvin and Aunt Rita. On the down side, Aunt Sylvia is also at my table, I mentally remind myself she really is a nice person, somewhere deep down. Thankfully Rita is between us and they immediately engage in Washington upper crust gossip.

'Rumor is your business with Tedi is struggling a bit,' starts Melvin, 'but I don't believe in rumors.' He smiles and takes my hand. 'Also a nasty rumor you are getting married. I know that one is not true, I've met Patrick.'

'Oh Melvin, no wonder you are my favorite,' I respond, squeezing his hand.

'So tell me what's really going on.'

'Well, truth be told, business could be better. I have taken on projects with a couple of socially questionable people, but nothing I can't handle. Trying to think outside the box, I bid on a project in Puerto Rico. Patrick is, well, a friend, and an adviser.'

'Listen Lana,' Melvin looks me dead in the eye, 'Owning a business is hard work, something you are not a stranger to. Just weigh your pros and cons, it has to make you money, and make you happy. There is no shame in deciding when the time comes to take another direction. I know you worry about your employees, but they are grownups, they'll all be fine. As far as your love life, well, you have time Lana, take it.'

A big sigh escapes me, he is spot on as usual. I know I have some thinking to do when I get back home. Aunt Rita silently takes my hand, gives me a wink. Then says, 'You'll be fine, I have oodles of faith in you.' Family isn't so bad after all.

The servers bring Boston favorites to our tables, Fish and Chips with a side of Boston baked beans. Tedi is in my line of sight and I can see she is as skeptical as I am about the meal, but it's surprisingly good. More kudos to Aunt Rita.

The meal winds down, the lights are dimmed and the movie screen comes alive. Uh oh, time to be very afraid, pictures of family members are appearing. I look over towards Tedi; she has her face buried in her hands. Evita is at the table next to me trying to look innocent. This means that the pictures that parents think are cute, but will mortify their kids are soon coming to the big screen. I contemplate crawling under the table, giving Evita the evil eye.

This has turned out really not so bad, everyone is smiling and giggling as one picture after another goes by, cowboy outfits, frilly dresses, pouty faces... family. My moment in the sun comes with a picture of me in the bath at three years old, a large purple floating sponge flower strategically placed. Next is one with Rikki and I in matching Hawaiian Moo Moo dresses. Tedi and Stacey appear on screen in ballerina outfits, then Tedi and I covered in mud. No one is spared a slightly embarrassing picture including one of Evita and Rita on a cruise ship in scandalous outfits, two piece swim suits in a lovely floral print.

The finale is recent pics of all of us since we have been here, *We Are Family* is playing in the background. That's Evita's cue, she jumps on the stage, microphone in hand, encouraging everyone to sing along. Aunt Rita wastes no time in joining her, waving for me to come up on stage. Oh what the hell, I grab Tedi, Stacey and Rikki on the way.

*'We are family... I've got all my family with me... We are family... Get up everybody and sing!'* One by one, everyone stands up and joins in, even Aunt Sylvia. Pointer Sisters got nothing on us. 'And... link arms... do the stroll...'

We spend the rest of the evening just chatting, enjoying our time together. Promises are made to stay in better touch, phone numbers and emails are exchanged, Facebook invites are sent. A good time was had by all.

Most of us are flying out tomorrow, so we call it a night by eleven, even bypassing a nightcap. Rikki and I settle into our room, both thankful there is no thong hanging on the door knob. We hear a tap coming from the door to Evita's room, she gingerly opens the door.

'Love you girls,' is all she says, and looks at us with a warm smile, then closes the door.

'Love you back,' Rikki and I say in unison, and with that we slip into peaceful slumber.

'Good Morning! Good Morning!' sings my alarm as it goes off at seven am. Tedi and I have a flight at ten thirty. Opening my eyes, I see Rikki watching me from her bed. 'What?' I ask.

'Just miss you that's all,' her eyes are a bit misty.

'Are you tearing up?'

'Hell no, it's the dirty air ducts in the damn hotel,' she exclaims.

'Ya, okay, miss you too. I'll come up soon, I want to see the kids anyway, I know you don't like Florida, but you need to come down with Stacey so we can have a tropical cousins vaca. I am sure Tedi will come up with a great mission for all of us.'

'Knock Knock!' Evita sweeps in wearing a bright blue flowered jumpsuit, and a very large floppy hat. She sure knows how to make a statement. 'What time are your flights, girls? I was flying back with Rita, but instead I have opted to drive back with Melvin to Baltimore, boredom does not suit me. What about Tedi and Stacey? Can Sylvia fit Stacey and John both on her broom? Damn it was fun seeing everyone.'

'Tedi and I fly out at ten-thirty, Rikki is out about eleven,' I reply.

Evita is not one for emotional scenes, 'Okay girls,' she gives us both a quick hug, then turns her back and walks away. 'This butt jiggle is just my way of waving good bye.' And with that she shakes her tail, does a backward wave, kicks up her left foot, and is out the door.

Rikki and I exchange smiles. 'Gotta love her,' I remark. 'Are we all taking a cab together to the airport?'

'Yes, Stacey and Tedi are meeting us in the lobby at eight-thirty. Stacey opted not to drive back with her parents. I sensed a bit of chill in the air between her and Sylvia.'

'What else is new,' I go about the task of packing. An hour later Rikki and I are showered, packed, and headed to the lobby to meet Rikki and Stacey.

Seems everyone is leaving at the same time, the whole gang is in the lobby, hugging and promising it will not be so long before we all get together again. Aunt Rita, is locked in a hug with Evita. Seeing me over Rita's shoulder, Evita gives us a wink, then heads out the door arm in arm with Melvin. Just before the door closed, Melvin turns around, gives me the thumbs up and a big smile. I nod and wave back, not easy to find a voice of reason in this family, his is much appreciated.

Tedi and Stacey are saying their goodbyes to Uncle John and Aunt Sylvia, so I take the moment to say my goodbyes to Aunt Rita.

'The reunion was wonderful, you did a fantastic job,' I tell her as I put my arms around her and kiss her soft cheek.

'Thank you, sweetheart. You know, you don't have to wait for a big reunion to come and see me. I am sure your mother would like a visit as well. And if you need anything at all, you just call me.'

'I know that, Aunt Rita, but I am fine, really. And I will come up, Tedi wants to see her parents as well, so we'll plan the trip. Love you lots, can't wait for your follow up family newsletter. By the way,' I ask. 'What was with the chicken menu and song list?'

With a sly smile, Rita replies, 'Just wanted to mess with everyone.'

And so we make our way around the room, hugging and kissing all the relatives, ending up next to Stacey and Tedi. With a nod, the four of us look at each other, give the final wave and get into shuttle to the airport. The ride is unusually silent, each of us thinking about the last couple of days, the meaning of family. I, for one, am thinking it was not as bad as I thought it was going to be, it was actually kinda fun.

'Well girls, one for road before we head to our separate gates?' suggests who else but Rikki.

'What the hell, a Bloody Mary will help me sleep on the plane,' I agree. Tedi and I exchange glances, both thinking its very doubtful we will have a repeat of the crazy flight up.

Situating ourselves at a high top facing the busy tarmac, we order four Belvedere Bloody Marys, on the spicy side and take a moment to watch the planes taxiing.

'So, Stacey, what was with the cold shoulder you were giving your mom the whole reunion,' I ask. Tedi swift kicks me under the table, damn, she needs to stop doing that.

Stacey stares at the planes again, pondering the question. 'She just needs to lighten up, I don't see the big deal with Justin and I moving in together.'

Rikki's mouth drops open, then she screams, 'We just spent three days together and you are just telling us!'

'Good for you girl!' I say, and we all clink drinks in congratulations and take a long draw. 'Tedi, we better get to our gate, we'll be boarding soon.'

With a final slurp, we do a group hug, promising to have another cousins' vaca in Florida within the next two months. The voice on the loud speaker announces they are beginning the boarding process for the first class passengers just as we get to the gate.

Then, 'Passengers Tedi Turner and Lana Turner, please report to the podium,' comes over the loud speaker. All I can think is *uh oh, we probably got bumped off our flight.*

'We're Lana and Tedi Turner.'

'You have been elevated to first class, you may board now,' the airline worker tells us.

'What?' But before the question can be answered, Tedi grabs my arm and propels me down the gangway.

Her answer is simple, 'You know what they say about gift horses.'

Without further question, we quickly settle into our big, cushy, wonderful seats. I have come up with a working theory, I turn to share it with Tedi, 'I think Karen had something to do with this.'

As if on cue, our very attractive female flight attendant is handing Tedi a note, 'Karen is right, you are very cute,' and with a wink, she is gone.

'Well, that answers that,' I retort. 'What's the note say?'

'Thanks for being a member of the Mile High Club.'

We both giggle, and get comfortable for the flight home, hoping it's uneventful. Soon both of us are quasi-sleeping, opening our eyes only when the captain announces our descent into the Fort Lauderdale area. Looking out the window, I can see the tropical blue ocean beneath, boats of all shapes and sizes speeding along the coastline, leaving a trail of white wake. Ah, home sweet home.

As soon as we are parked at the gate, we are up retrieving our carry-on luggage, waiting our turn to disembark. Passing the flight deck opening, we notice the co-captain is a woman, and she is staring directly at Tedi. Really? How does she get so much action?

'Thanks for flying with us,' The Captain is sporting a big smile. 'I hope someone has explained how our Frequent Flyer Program works.' Oh brother!

Not letting Tedi even pause, I pull her along, 'Seriously? Do I even want to know?'


Timing is good for a change, the shuttle to the parking garage is at the curb as we exit the airport. The humidity hits us like a wet towel, ugh, but the sun is shining brilliantly, and the palm trees are swaying. With a content sigh, we both put on our sunglasses and board the shuttle to my car.

Traffic is light going up I-95, for that I am thankful. Tedi seems to have something on her mind, 'Okay, spill,' I tell her.

'You know I am a big girl,' she starts, 'and I can take care of myself.' Tedi moved to Florida after three years of being a casino dealer in Atlantic City. Try as she might, she is not one to tow the corporate line. She showed up on my door step late one night, mumbling something about a hole in the casino director's office and viola, I had a new partner in my business.

'I know that,' I reply.

'You have to think of you for once Lana, I know our business is not exactly in the black. But, all of your employees are grownups as well.'

'I know, I know. But they have become family to me, I feel responsible. And we still have Puerto Rico or Uncle Larry or Sal. We have irons in the fire, let's see where they go.' My head knows she is right, but my heart is not so sure.

'Everything will play out as it's supposed to, just don't ignore the signs,' Tedi sagely says, just as we are pulling into my driveway. She throws her luggage into her trunk, gives me a hug. 'See you tomorrow at the office, love you.'

'Love you back,' I respond. My home as always is a welcoming oasis. Not bothering to unpack, I put on my workout clothes and head for the gym, feeling the need to sweat out all the alcohol I have recently put into my system. Just walking to the gym will makes me feel better. Half way there I get a call from Jillian.

'Hey Kiddo, you back?' she asks.

'Just got back, headed to the gym, feeling the need to perspire. What's with you?'

'I'm at the dog bar with Sookie, why don't you join us when you are done?' Sookie is Jillian's old college roommate and always entertaining.

'I don't think I can do any more alcohol, but I will meet you for an iced tea. See you in about an hour,' I reply.

And sweat I did, whew, I feel a hundred percent better after my work out, the fog has lifted. The dog bar is actually McGinns Irish Pub with a fenced outside patio to keep the pups in and safe. Jillian and Sookie are seated at a table on the patio, tall frosty half empty beers in front of them.

Spotting Sookie and Jillian is easy, Sookie always has her parrot, Johnny Depp, on her shoulder, plus she has flaming red hair. To complete her ensemble, Sookie has a ninety-five pound boxer named Tiny that gets his own bowl of beer. And I thought I left Crazytown in Boston.

'Hey girl!' Jillian greets me with a warm smile. 'How was the reunion? How was Evita?'

'Evita was Evita in all of her glory. And I have to say, to my pleasant surprise, the reunion was a success.' I turn to Sookie, 'So how are you? And what is that rock on your finger?'

'It's a shut up ring. I agreed to wear it so Duke would shut up about getting married. It ain't ever happening,' Sookie is very independent. Duke is her long time live in, who desperately wants to make an honest woman out of her. Sookie has other ideas. 'I hear *you* might be getting married.'

We all look at each other and laugh. Sookie is well aware of my tumultuous relationship with Patrick. 'Yeah, Jillian and I will have a double wedding when she gets back with her ex.'

'Sounds like fun, I'll be there with bells on,' Sookie remarks. 'I am going to leave the two of you to catch up, its paws and claws day, taking Johnny and Tiny to get their nails trimmed, enjoy!' And with that she is off.

'Okay, now give me the real scoop,' says Jillian.

I proceeded to tell her about cousins' day, Tedi thinking she was over five foot three,' meeting all of the family, and left the best for last. 'I ran into an old flame on the flight there, we had sex in the bathroom, coincidentally Tedi had sex simultaneously in the bathroom across from me with the flight attendant,' I waved to the server, 'can I get an ice tea please?'

After Jillian picks her jaw up off the floor, she says, 'You what? I am so proud of you!'

'It was so quick I am not even sure it really happened. What's going on with you?'

'Oh, nice segue way, fine, we'll talk about me. I broke it off with crepe man, just too clingy. I wanted sex, he wanted love.'

'But you really seemed to like him, and you seemed simpatico.' I am bummed for my friend, her ex really did a number on her.

'I know, but I just don't want all the crap that goes with so-called love. So here is a juicy tidbit, Richard Cabeza is dating a lunatic.'

125

Richard Cabeza is her ex's code name, code for dickhead. 'Do tell, and where did he meet this lovely lady,' I inquire.

'Word on the street is she is his manscaper. The nutball is accusing me of stalking her at the grocery store.' We both get a good laugh out of that one, Jillian probably can't remember the last time she was in a grocery store. She only shops at two places, the liquor store and the produce stand. We hang out a bit more, chatting about Patrick, her ex, Evita, and in general solving all the world's problems.

'Soooo, come on, give, what else is on your mind,' Jillian asks me.

Geeze, I hate that she knows me so well. 'I had a brief but *makes me ponder life* conversation with cousin Melvin.'

'The one your mother used to play doctor with? Go ahead...'

'First, ew, and yes. He basically said I need to really evaluate what is happening with my business, and all my employees are big boys and girls and can take care of themselves'.

'Seems like sound advice to me. I know you are the proverbial caregiver, you love your motley crew. Things will unfold like they are supposed to, just keep those rose colored glasses off, or least take them off once in a while. Ready to head home?'

'Yep, our first new home is coming in tomorrow, I need to be on my A game.'

♦♦♦

# Chapter 16

Toby can barely contain himself. 'Oh my god, oh my god, oh my god!' he squeals, 'This is the day! I have been sitting on the side of I-95 since 6 o'clock this morning waiting to see the new house come down the road in all its new home glory!'

I am barely on my way to the Fort Lauderdale office, and not nearly ready for all of this enthusiasm. 'Is Uncle Larry coming in?' I ask.

'Thankfully, no. I am sorry, how rude of me, how was the reunion? I wish I could have been a fly on the wall.'

'That, my friend, is a topic of conversation for the Infusion Bar, but bottom line is that it went well. Call me when you have connected with the trucks and I'll meet you at the site with a check.'

Toby's zeal seems to be contagious. I am not even out of my car yet I can feel multiple sets of employee eyes are on me. 'Not yet,' I answer the unanswered question as I walk through the door. 'Toby will call me as soon as he has the new home in his sight.' Sheesh, you would think it was the second coming.

'Uncle Larry wants me to call him as soon as the house is spotted,' June informs me.

'You do that, in the meantime, don't you all have other things to do?'

Mike and Diane fight to get through the door to my office, sibling rivalry. 'I have a buyer,' they both announce, loudly.

'Okay, you two, we are using this house as a model, take your buyers through the house as soon as it is set up, and we can order exactly what they want.' With that I shoo them out of my office just as my phone rings.

'I tried to stop them.' It's Sandy, and this doesn't sound good. 'Penny and Mable are on their way down to see the new house.'

'It's not even here yet,' I say in frustration. I never have all the sales people in one office. The only time we are all together is for the Christmas party, which involves lots of alcohol and things I don't want to acknowledge. Competition is stiff between the offices, this will not be pretty. I need to think fast.

'June, come in my office please.' I have hatched a plan.

'Yes Lana,' June quickly appears in my door way.

'Code Red, the West Palm sales people are on their way down, we need a diversion. Arrange for lunch at the new house, NO ALCOHOL. Invite the community managers, mix it up. Go, go, go!'

Next up, Tedi. 'Hey, where are you? We have a code red!'

'What are you talking about?' Tedi responds, 'I am in the middle of a flying lesson.'

'Yeah, okay, get your head out of the clouds and get to the new home staging site. The Palm Beach sales gals are on their way down to see the new house being delivered!'

'Oh crap! I am on my way,' she exclaims. I am positive I do not want to know the explanation of the flying lesson.

June is on the phone and gives me the thumbs up that things well under control. The Lauderdale office must have caught wind of the Palm Beach office headed our way as they are nowhere to be seen and I assume headed to the community to wait on the new house. Worlds will collide.

Tapping June on the shoulder, 'I am headed to meet Toby and follow the new house into the community. As soon as you can, wrap up, forward the phones, and meet us there. And you might want to put on a black and white shirt, and bring your whistle.'

With that I am out at a full sprint. No sooner I am in the car, then my cell rings.

'It's here, it's here, *it's here!*' Toby squeals with delight, then a bit more subdued, 'I think I just pee peed a little.'

'I'm on my way, I'll just meet you at the entrance to the community. You know the saying, 'not my circus, not my monkeys?' Well, it is my circus and they are my monkeys. All of the sales people are en route to the community to watch the house come in.'

'Weee! Now we're having fun! See you in a few,' and he hangs up. Oh good grief, nothing like feeding into the madness, I will apparently be the sole source of sanity.

Traffic is thankfully light, allowing me to get to the entrance in record time. I don't even want to go near the site yet, plenty of time to be in the middle of that mayhem. I'm not here even five minutes, and here comes Toby, leading the trucks pulling the two halves of the house. It is a sight to behold, and suddenly I am unwittingly caught up in the excitement. It's a banner day for my company. What the hell, let's celebrate it.

All I can see in Toby's car is a huge grin as he parades by. I know this will be a process, so I decide to head to the community manager's office and make sure they will be joining us for the impromptu party. They are just piling into their golf cart as I pull up.

'June called us,' Madge says. Madge and I have had a few *lunches* together, we are on the same page. 'Exciting day for you, congratulations. And I hear I finally get to meet the Palm Beach bunch, should be a hoot.'

'Well, that's one way of putting it, I'll see you at the site.'

And what a sight it is. The first half is in place already, and Toby is standing on the hitch at the front, arms spread wide, like he is on the bow of the Titanic.

'I'm king of the world!' Toby shouts, his pretend hair blowing in the imaginary wind.

'Yes, and I'm Queen of the F'in Universe,' retorts Penny. 'Now get down so they can set the home and we can get in. I have buyers ready to go.' Let the games begin.

With a roar, and a blast of Billy Joel, Tedi joins us. 'Did I miss anything?' she asks, running toward me, out of breath.

'No, and nice wings, they match the set you got on the flight to the reunion. Flying lessons my ass,' I respond. Tedi gives me her *so whats it to ya* look. 'Whatev,' I say, thinking, so what if she gets all the action.

Where the hell is June? I'm getting nervous, the Fort Lauderdale and West Palm crews are in a stare down. As if on cue, we hear a truck horn, 'Ahhh oooo gah, Ahhh oooo gah!' June is riding shotgun on a catering truck, brilliant. And the name says it all, *Cluck In A Truck*; slogan – *Big Breasts, Fresh Buns* – should be a hit with this crowd.

'Okay everyone, why don't we all get a bite to eat and let the set up crew do its job,' I announce. The truck chef takes the orders and everyone is silent for a few beats while they stuff their faces. Wow, excellent sandwich, wonder what this is costing me?

Praising June, I say, 'Great job June, this is a hit, you really pulled this together in no time.'

'Thanks Lana,' she replies. 'Should I go ahead and get Uncle Larry on the phone? I can actually face time him.' Oh goody.

'Sure, he deserves to be in on the fun.'

'I have him, here, you talk to him, wait, let me wipe the lipstick off.'

At this point I wish I had a rubber glove. 'Hey Larry, we have touch down, let me scan the camera around so you can see the new home.' I give Larry the five minute

130

video tour of the home, which, even though it's not completely put together, looks fantastic. 'We are all very excited, all of the sales reps have buyers they will bring through in the next week, and we'll hopefully start taking orders.'

From what I can tell through the smeared screen, Larry looks pleased. 'Excellent, Lana. I'll be in for the next house coming into West Palm. Tell the sales gals I look forward to seeing them.'

'I'll have Toby call you and confirm the date it's coming in. Let me give you a call later, it's somewhat of a zoo here.' Hanging up, I gingerly hand June's phone back to her, ew. 'Anyone have any hand sanitizer?'

'Okay everyone, let's all head back to the offices so the set up crew can do their thing,' I need to break this up before we have an incident and this celebration goes south. Reluctantly everyone heads to their cars, but I can hear the excitement in their voices as they talk about possible buyers. I get the nod of approval from the community managers as they head back to their own office. As for me, a sigh of contentment escapes, new home, pumped sales people, and best of all, no incidents.

'We need to celebrate,' shockingly says Toby. 'Let's all go to Comfortable Shoes tonight for an adult beverage or two.'

'Works for me,' agrees Tedi, 'and it's not karaoke night, so we'll be able to hear our conversation.'

'I'm in,' I agree. 'Toby, why don't you stay at my place tonight and we'll take a cab. Tedi, might as well make it a slumber party.'

Done, done and done.


The parking lot is busy, but not packed as we pull into Comfortable Shoes. We spot three seats together at the bar, and wait for the bartender to take our order. Teresa is at her regular spot, wine glass in hand.

'Hey gang, I don't see all three of you here very often, what gives?' she asks.

'We had our first new home come in today, it's an event worth celebrating,' Tedi explains.

'I'll drink to that,' Teresa lifts her, then notices her glass is empty. 'Fill me up and I will celebrate with you.'

'Sure, why not,' I give the nod to Candy, who is busy making martinis for us. Cocktails in hand, we raise our glasses to toast, 'To many more days of bringing in homes, salude.' Clink, clink, clink.

Excitedly, we discuss all the possibilities ahead with the ability to purchase new homes. Toby, finally coming down from his high of earlier today, tells us about the set crew and sub-contractors he has lined up in both counties. All of the community managers we deal with are on board to give us free lot rent for any model houses we bring in. Life is good, and we may find a way to stay out of the red. I also recognize that I have mixed feelings about the outcome.

'Pssst, don't look now, but there is your red headed friend,' Toby discretely nods to his right.

Across the bar, sure enough, there is Sherri, staring into her drink.

'Wonder what's up with her,' asks Tedi. 'Usually once she spots you, she makes a bee line over.' I just shrug, thankful she is staying put on her bar stool.

'Okay, ladies, and Tedi I use the term loosely, do tell about the reunion,' requests Toby.

Tedi and I look at each other, and she begins at the beginning, the flight there. When she gets to the part about both of us joining the Mile High Club at the same time, Toby claps with glee.

'Oh you both make me sooooo proud! I couldn't have done it better myself! Please do go on, can't wait to hear the rest of the tale. Tell me about Evita.' Toby just loves Evita, and the feeling is mutual. 'What was she wearing?'

'She showed up in a long floral print peasant skirt and top, very loud colors of course, and a cowboy hat,' my turn to pick up the tale of events. I continue on and describe the quest for chowder, beer, and little oyster crackers. Toby is hanging on my every word, Tedi piping in at intervals, especially when I get to the part about her measuring her height at the Science Museum.

'I don't know what happened,' she whines, 'one minute it was working, the next it wasn't.' Toby just looks at me rolling my eyes.

Continuing through our tale, Toby actually spits out some of his martini, laughing about our taxi, non-taxi ride after we left Legal Seafood. Magically, without us even noticing, all of our glasses are refilled by Candy. Onward we go, describing the bus trip and dinner, with insinuations of Evita's escapades.

Toby raises his glass once again, toasting the success of the reunion.

'Hey, my glass is empty,' we hear from Teresa's corner. 'How am I supposed to toast?' I nod to Candy once again, what the hell, the more the merrier.

Someone begins to sing, '*When you meet a girl….that you like a lot…*'

'Hey, I thought you said this wasn't karaoke night?' I ask Tedi. Not only is someone singing, but they are singing Cher, what's up with that?

Looking up at the stage, we see Sherri with the microphone, this cannot be good.

'*And you fall in love, but she loves you not… if a flame should start, when you hold her near, better keep your heart out of danger dear…*'

'She is staring right at you, Lana,' Toby says. I gulp, afraid of what is coming next.

*'For the way of love, is the way of woe... and the day may come, when you see her go...'*

'Is she crying?' exclaims Tedi in disbelief.

*'Then what will you do, when she sets you free... just the way that you, said goodbye to me...'*

Wait... what?!?! I never even said hello, not technically. Everyone is the bar is turning my way, nasty looks on all their faces. Sherri has lasered in on me.

She begins the verse again, in full voice, tears slowly sliding down her cheeks. I am frightened and confused. More and more of the patrons are turning and giving me the stink eye. Sherrie is their goddess. Tedi and Toby look from me to Sherri, from Sherri to me in ping pong fashion, like watching a train wreck, totally transfixed.

'Wow,' says Teresa, 'you really hurt her. How about another drink?'

'I didn't do anything, I swear, I never led her on,' I plead.

'Tall, hot drag queen alert,' warns Tedi with a poke to my ribs.

Before I even have a chance to react, splash! A drink is thrown in my face by Sherri's not boyfriend – girlfriend. 'Damn you Lisa! I told you to stay away from Sherri!'

'Geeeez, if she is going to throw a drink in my face, at least she could get my name right!'

Sherri is wrapping up the song, now at full volume, *'Just the way that you, said good bye to meeeeee... The way of looooooooooove.'*

If looks could kill, I would be dead ten times over. Tedi and Toby each grab an arm, propelling me toward the door. Toby shouting, 'The villagers are ready to arm themselves with torches and pitchforks, let's get the hell out of here.'

Afraid to look back, the last thing we hear as we push through the door, 'I'll drink to that,' Teresa can make a celebration out of anything, bless her little drunk heart.

Safely in the back of a taxi, we all let loose a sigh of relief.

Toby just looks at me, 'Never a dull moment with you Lana, never a dull moment.'

## Chapter 17

Things have been relatively calm for the last couple of weeks, but the second house arrives today in West Palm, and I am hoping against all hope that not as much fan fair is needed. Thankfully, the Fort Lauderdale crew is too busy showing the house down there to join the festivities. But, to add to the already banner day, Uncle Larry is coming in, whoopeee.

Walking through the door to the West Palm office, Penny and Mable are alert and seem to be on their best behavior. Sandy is status quo, wiping the moisture off her hands. 'So....what time does Uncle Larry get here? What time is the house arriving? Is Toby going to be obnoxious?' Penny asks.

'Should be any minute, waiting on a call from Toby, and yes, he probably will be,' is my rapid fire answer.

Penny and Mable's coloring may be similar, blond hair and ghostly white, but that's where it ends. Mable has a figure like an ironing board, Penny has an overabundance of curves. Mable is quiet and sweet, even after a few adult beverages, Penny is loud and aggressive, no cocktails needed. Not sure why Mable wears orange lipstick, have never bothered to ask. Penny is sporting a fresh slathering of fire engine red lipstick, no need to ask.

'I'll call Toby and see if we have an ETA.' I head into my office.

'I'll call June and ask about Uncle Larry,' Sandy says. Huh, more aware of her surroundings than I thought.

'Lanaluu! Just got a call from the lead truck, they're about two hours out, I'm headed into the West Palm office to hang out and take the opportunity to annoy Penny,' rattles Toby and promptly hangs up before I have a chance to respond.

'Two hours out,' I tell the gals, neglecting to inform them that Toby is on his way. It's really just Penny that he annoys. Toby and Mable worked together before, and as I mentioned, she is the quiet type, easy to get along with.

'Uncle Larry update, should be here about fifteen minutes,' Sandy reports.

Flustered, Penny jumps up, 'I'd better freshen up!

'If she puts on any more lipstick, her lips will go through the door five minutes before the rest of her,' quips Mable. Well, well, look who's coming out of her shell. I give her a nod of approval, then draw a mark in the air for her. Okay, back to my office to get the final moments of peace.

'How are my two favorite sales people,' booms a male voice. I sure as hell know it's not Toby. Herald the arrival of Uncle Larry, the dead baby bird.

I walk out just as Penny is bringing Larry in for a bear hug. Toby has come in right behind Larry, making gagging motions. What a fun day this is going to be!

'Release, Penny,' I command, 'Larry, how are you? How was the flight?'

Being a smart business man, Larry heads for Mable, giving her equal time with a soft embrace, then turns to me. 'Excellent as always and the trip was smooth. Exciting day isn't it. Toby, when does the house arrive?' Larry and I just shake hands, I've learned to wisely keep my distance.

'In about an hour and a half,' he replies.

Again, being the diplomat, Larry heads to Sandy's desk, and pulls out a gift box. Immediately, Penny dons her pout face. A surprised Sandy, mumbles thanks and gingerly opens the box. Curious, I take a step closer.

To Sandy's absolute delight, it's a large cereal bowl with a built in straw, I think she is misty eyed. 'Thank you Larry,' she manages.

'My pleasure,' he certainly knows how to score points. 'Lana, Toby, I have a few things to discuss, can we go in your office? And, if it's alright with you, I'd like to take the girls to lunch after we see the house?'

I glance over at Penny, who somehow is showing more cleavage than two minutes ago. 'I am sure they would be delighted. Shall we?' I lead the way to my office.

'Lana, I want to know what else we can do together, business wise,' Larry starts. 'Do you have any connections with the lenders? Maybe we can buy repossessed homes?'

This is Toby's forte, so he jumps right in. 'Funny you should ask Larry, I have been talking to the lenders and getting their inventory. Both of the big lenders are over in Tampa.'

'Excellent, what say we make a trip over, I rented a Cadillac this time.'

Toby and I just look at each other, and scream at the same time, 'Road trip!'

'Then I take it that's a yes?' Larry asks.

'I'll call my contacts right now and arrange everything,' Toby says. Enthusiastically, he runs out of the office to the conference room.

Just as he leaves, my cell rings, it's Sal. Somehow I feel I am caught cheating, I want to swipe Sal to voicemail, but I know that's a bad idea. 'Hello, give me just one minute,' I give Larry the 'excuse me' look, and head out of the office and outside.

'Nice to hear from you Sal, what can I do for you,' I am wiping sweat from my brow, thinking how ridiculous it is to feel this way.

'I just wanted to remind you of our dinner engagement Saturday night, my wife is looking forward to meeting you and Tedi.'

'Yes, we'll be there, looking forward to it.' I am hoping he is paying, but being old school Italian, I think I am safe.

'Saturday, seven o'clock, we'll meet you at the bar. And have a safe trip to Tampa,' with that he hangs up.

Wait… what? I collect myself, head back into the office, looking around for cameras. Larry has joined Toby in the conference room. 'So, how did you make out?' I ask.

'Point Tree will see us tomorrow, we'll need to hit the road about nine, that gives you time to do anything you need to in the Lauderdale office,' Toby reports. My wheels are turning so fast smoke must be coming out of my ears. Yet another opportunity, almost too good to be true. I look up to see if there is a shoe ready to drop. Still, there's a feeling nagging deep down. Do I want this to work?

Toby's cell rings, he looks at me and gives me the thumbs up. 'Okay, we'll meet you at the entrance to the community.' Then to us, 'Let's roll.'

Penny and Mable have been watching us intently through the conference room window like puppies. Larry turns to smile at them, steps out onto the sales floor. 'Come on gals, I'll take you in my Cadillac.'

Penny jumps out of her seat before Larry has finished his sentence. Is it possible she is showing even more cleavage? Toby looks at me, does a head slap, grabbing me by the arm, 'Come on Lanalu, you're with me.'

Glancing at Sandy, who is staring lovingly at her new cereal bowl, most likely dreaming of endless Cocoa Puffs, I ask, 'Would you like to join us?'

'What? Oh, no that's fine, take pictures, and if you go out to lunch, just bring me back tater tots.'

And out the door we go.

Originally from Detroit, Toby is a serious car aficionado, his tastes running to the old classics. His latest obsession is his 1959 baby blue convertible Plymouth Fury, retrofitted with a CD player of course so we can listen to Cher. His manta on cars, anything with big fins, I think that's code for something else.

'Shall we solve the world's problems on the way,' Toby asks. With a nod of my head, Cher starts to sing, '*Not enough, love and understand, we could use some love, to ease these troubled times*'. Right on Cher, she is so deep. Singing at the top of our lungs, I am sure we have perfect pitch because the car next to us gives us the thumbs up.

Just as we arrive at the community, the trucks arrive pulling our second new home. Not quite the same high as the first one, it's still exciting. Larry and the gals are bringing up the rear, all smiles. The community managers are also waiting in their golf cart, pleased to have a new home coming in.

It's like a parade! And being in a festive mood, I jump into the back, and sit on the back of the seat, my hand mimicking the Queen's wave. Off to the site we go, the halves of the home quickly in place. Our set-up crew is there and makes quick work of marrying the two sides. Once safe, we all file in to take a quick tour.

The home is surprisingly large and open, four good size bedrooms, counter tops that look like granite, tile in the kitchen and bathrooms. We all agree it's a winner, a great home to use as a model. Tour over, we exit to let the set up crew finish their job.

'How long before you can actually let potential homeowners take a gander?' asks Larry.

'We'll have it show ready in two days,' responds Toby.

'I have three customers lined up to bring through Larry,' coos Penny. Don't get me wrong, I am thrilled that Penny has three people, but the sucking up is making me throw up a little.

'I have four!' shouts Mable, just a little too loud.

I look at Toby, and mouth, 'what's up with her?' Toby makes the gesture of knocking back a cocktail. Oh great.

'Well, ladies, what say I treat you to a long lunch,' Larry invites, oozing charm.

I am not hurt we are not invited, I probably would have developed a headache from all of the eye rolling and head slapping anyway. But it is a bit scary thinking of the three of them on the loose together. Toby and I head back to the office, I want to be there when they get back just in case anyone needs a ride home.

The smell of chocolate assaults us as soon as we step into the office. It seems Sandy was anxious, her new bowl is full of chocolate milk made from Cocoa Puffs. With a smile on her face, she is using to straw to drink it down. Looking up at me, she says, 'I'm getting full, rain check on the tater tots?' Done.

Two hours later, Toby and I watch with amusement as Larry and the girls exit the Cadillac, all three arm in arm, giggling. Larry has orange lipstick on one cheek, red on the other, and who knows on the lower set. I shudder.

Purely for Toby's benefit, Penny slurs, 'Oh Larry, that was the best sushi ever! I don't know how to thank you.'

'I see you didn't finish all of yours,' observes Toby. 'But I must say, I have never seen anyone use cleavage as a doggy bag.' Seeing the location of what looks to be a partial California roll, Mable guffaws loudly, Toby giggles, I am thinking I have lost control. Then I laugh to myself... like I ever really had any control.

Momentarily bright red, Penny quickly recovers, 'Maybe I am saving it for a nosh later...' smiling sickeningly at Larry. Again, I throw up a little.

My look that can kill quickly shuts down any further foreplay. 'Sandy, why don't you drive Penny and Mable home and pick them up in the morning.'

'What,' Sandy is still under the spell of her straw bowl.

'Take the girls… home, pick them up… in the morning,' I repeat.

'Do I have to come back today?'

'No.'

'Cool,' and with that she picks up her Cocoa Puffs and bowl, shoos the girls out the door.

I turn to Larry, 'Where are you staying tonight, and should I drive you?'

'No, I am fine, drank ice tea. Staying in Lauderdale at the Hilton on the beach.' Seeing my look he adds, 'by myself, I swear.'

'Fine, we'll meet at the Lauderdale office about nine tomorrow morning. I assume we'll stay overnight so we are not rushed.'

Toby chimes in, 'I made us reservations at the Beach Comber, their restaurant has a great lobster dinner.' Score one Toby, lobster trumps sushi in my book.

'See you then,' and with a salute, he is out the door. I feel like I am in the middle of a bad sitcom.

'That was a nauseating display by Penny, and Mable was drunk early today,' Toby noted.

'Sometimes I wonder what kind of business I am running, and certainly how effectively I am running it. I am a nut magnet, present company excluded of course.'

'Yes but it works, craziness and all. Our sales people, even though they do not fit into the round hole, can sell ice to the proverbial Eskimo, with work ethics second to none. Besides, I doubt they could get jobs anywhere else.'

And there is my quandary, once again these people need me. I feel obligated have to find a way to stay open, and maybe these new opportunities are the answer.

◆ ◆ ◆

## Chapter 18

*What the hell is she doing?* I am thinking to myself as I look at the contraption on June's desk. 'I am not sure I want to know, but what are you doing,' I ask anyway.

With a silly grin on her face, June squeals, 'Look what Larry brought me! Snails! I'm fattening them up with corn meal, can't wait til they are fat enough so I can make escargot in herb butter!'

Good grief, just what I want to deal with at eight am. 'Do you have to have them on your desk? You know what, never mind, Larry should be here momentarily and we're headed to Tampa. But I suppose you already know that. I'll be in my office.'

'Okay, Lana,' June replies sheepishly.

Hiding in my office, I hear the front door open, then Toby appears at my office door with his shock face on, 'Did you see…'

I cut him off before he finishes, just shaking my head. 'Let's just wait out front for Larry, no need for him to come in here and have any further interaction with June.'

As we pass by, June has one of the snails in her hand watching it eat the corn meal; there is something twisted about the whole scene. 'We're leaving as soon as Larry gets here. Tedi is in the West Palm office if you need anything. We should be back tomorrow noonish,' I inform her.

'Buon appetito,' Toby adds while I just roll my eyes. One of these days my eyes are just going to stay in the back of my head.

Larry's shiny, spiffy white Cadillac comes into view just as we step outside. Getting out, he asks, 'Which one of you wants to drive?' Nearly knocking me over, Toby, aka Mr. Detroit Car Guy, is in the driver seat. Fine with me, I take the passenger side and Larry gets in the back seat hoping to rest his bloodshot eyes. Our not so scenic route takes us across the bottom of the state via Alligator Alley, through the Florida Everglades. And yes, chances are we will see an alligator or two lounging in the sun. Maybe we should stop and get one for June to feed and skewer.

As the sun climbs further into the sky, the car interior temperature is also climbing. I am notoriously cold by nature, body temp wise, no comments please. Toby on the other hand, runs hot, and so it begins. He reaches over to the AC controls, cranking up the fan. My turn, I turn them off. Now his turn, back up. I slap his hand, he slaps mine.

'I'm freezing!'

'I'm sweating!'

'Probably the alcohol you drank last night!'

'Just put on your shawl, old lady!'

Peaceful slumber interrupted, Larry jolts up, 'Seriously? There are two sets of controls, use them, stop bickering!' We just glare at each other, like siblings, whatev.

The rest of the trip is quiet. Toby and I can't have our usual chatter, it's not anything we would want to share with Uncle Larry. Fifteen minutes away from Tampa, I reach back and gently shake Larry, 'Almost here, do you want to stop and freshen up? Get a coffee or anything?'

'Starbucks much?' Toby retorts.

'Well, my phone app does say there is one about two blocks from here. We can sit and go over our game plan,' I smile sweetly at Larry. Toby looks nauseous, good.

As usual, the seating at Starbucks includes comfy, overstuffed chairs. Lattes in hand, we settle in and get down to brass tacks. 'I suppose we should have discussed this first, but how much money are you willing to invest?' I ask Larry.

'Well, we can invest up to $500,000, once we have

proved the profitability of buying and fixing repos. Let's do a beta test with $100,000.'

Shocked by the amount, never realizing Larry et al had such deep pockets, my wheels naturally spin. 'We need to see the inventory for Palm Beach and Broward counties, moving homes is too expensive and will have too much of an impact on the bottom profit line.'

Toby interjects, 'Right now there are about ten homes that they have on their inventory sheet. After the meeting, Tedi and I will do the analysis on the available homes. The key will be for us to be able to also have access to and buy from the homes that are not on the books, that's where Lana comes in.'

Okay, Toby is back in my good graces, Larry just looks at me with a raised eyebrow. Toby continues, 'Lana just has a way, you'll see when we are in the meeting.' And with that, we are ready.

The waiting area at Point Tree Lending is nondescript, a plain-jane area, vinyl padded green chairs from the seventies, white laminate reception kiosk, mortgage magazines. We let the receptionist know who we are, who we came to see, and take an uncomfortable seat to wait for the powers that be. Our wait, thankfully, is not long, a man and a woman, both in inexpensive suits, approach us with smiles and outstretched hands.

Taking the lead – are you surprised – I stand and move to greet them. 'Good afternoon, I'm Lana Turner, these are my associates, Larry Kraft and Toby Gile.'

'Pleasure meeting you all. My name Jack Hoff, assistant repo manager, and my associate Jill Ribble, repo manager. Follow us to the conference room and let's see how we can do business.' Okay. Jack & Jill? Toby and I just glance at each other, saving the jokes for later.

'I understand you are looking to purchase our repossessed homes, possibly in bulk?' Jill starts.

'We have your current inventory, but would like to see what other homes you may have, focusing on Broward and Palm Beach counties,' Toby's says, taking his turn. Larry is oddly looking out the window seemingly not paying attention.

'Of course,' says Jack. 'Do you have an amount you are looking to invest?'

Toby and I look at Larry, who seems to be deferring to me. What the heck is going on? 'We have the resources to acquire a good portion of your inventory, depending on how well its discounted.' How's that for saying something without really saying a damn thing.

'We have prepared a list,' Jill passes out copies to us. 'Let's review and see what will interest you.'

The list is longer than we could possibly have hoped for, I can see a multitude of possibilities. Going through the list, we discuss the condition of the homes, the communities where they are located, how to deal with back rents, and so on. All in all, the meeting seems productive. Larry finally participates, but minimally. Toby senses like I do that there is something askew. The meeting continues down the list, all of us making notes.

'The game plan for us will be to view the homes, and come back with an offer. We would be willing to take several of the less desirable homes off your hands as part of the package. Give us a week or so and we'll submit a proposal,' I conclude.

Standing, we all shake hands, appreciating each other's time, looking forward to speaking again soon, blah, blah, blah. As soon as we are in the elevator, I whirl around to Larry, 'Okay mister, spill, what is the back story?'

'Well, I know Jack from California. We were involved in a business transaction that did not end well. His wife was not happy.'

146

'Okay, sometimes happens. Why wasn't his wife happy?' I ask.

'Well Jack worked for Point Tree Lending in California, I met him when I was trying to buy a few of their repos. He put together a list for me, was very accommodating, if you know what I mean.' Toby looks like he just threw up a little. 'Somehow he got the impression that if he slept with me, I would buy more homes.' Somehow? Sheesh.

'But this should have nothing to do with our business at hand, that was then. There must be more to the story, did you buy any homes?'

'Well, Jill was his wife, and she divorced Jack after that, but now apparently they are married again.'

'And how did you did not know this??' I am flummoxed. 'Is this a wasted trip?'

'Look Lana, I had no idea that Jack and Jill are now in the Tampa office, or I would not have joined you on this trip. I am truly sorry. Let's go have a cocktail or two, then a nice lobster dinner, all on me.'

Crap, my wheels are spinning on how to do damage control, it's still just business, we can all be professional, I hope. Toby is watching me closely, waiting for me to fix the situation. Silence fills the car as we head for the hotel, this is definitely a buzz kill. We agree to settle into our rooms and meet at the lobby bar in thirty minutes.

'Knock Knock.' Toby is at my door.

'What the freak,' is my disgusted reaction.

'Larry is just the investor, Lana. Point Tree will be dealing with you, not him.'

'Yes, but we need the best pricing to really make this work,' I answer.

'All is far from lost Lana, worst case scenario if they decline, we are in the same position we were before the trip. We still have the new homes, Larry still finances bad

147

credit, and we still have Sal…' He is valiantly trying to make me feel better.

'Yes, I know it's not the end of the world, we still have options. I just want to take advantage of every option we can. Come on, let's go run up Larry's credit card.'

Eyeing the most expensive things on the menu, we start with Grey Goose martinis and jumbo shrimp cocktails at the bar. Larry is in a very accommodating mood, as well he should be. The conversation stays light and positive, he even offers to call Jack and Jill to see if he can do anything to sway them, I let him know in no uncertain terms that it's a bad idea. Toby, my cheerleader, tells Larry that if anyone can keep this deal on track, I can. I agree, toot toot, yes that's me tooting my own horn.

Onward to the restaurant literally on the beach, Toby did great with this spot. The tables are on wooden platforms in the sand, surrounded by candles and Tiki torches. The linens are crisp white with a sensational tropical floral centerpiece.

My brain begins to relax. My mentality is such that if I expect to make a deal, that's what is going to happen, no ifs, ands, or buts. But I make peace with the situation, knowing that once I put the offer in on the repos, the real negotiation will begin and I have no qualms about going over Jack and Jill's head. There must be a pun in there somewhere referencing the children's poem, but the martinis have me too mellow.

'Anyone up for dessert?' asks Larry. 'It doesn't have to be the high calorie variety, in fact, we can actually burn calories.' Toby looks like his is going to lose his dinner.

Just in the nick of time, Billy Joel comes out of my phone, singing *Uptown Girl,* its Tedi. 'Excuse me won't you, I need to take this.' Toby's eyes plead with me to stay, I just shrug my shoulders, oh well, gotta go.

'You have a letter here from the Governor's office in

Puerto Rico. I was hesitant to call you, but figured you would be anxious to know what it says. Do you want me to open it?' Tedi asks.

'Shoot, I never did call Robert, okay, I hope its good news. We may have crashed and burned here,' I answer.

'Why? What happened?'

'Larry happened. At some point in his sordid past, he lead the once eager underling at Point Tree, now assistant repo manager, to believe that for sex he would buy oodles of repos, resulting in no homes and the poor guy's divorce. Now the guy's ex-wife who is now his wife again, is the new repo manager and she was not happy about it.'

'What?'

'I'll give you the details when we get back, hopefully all is not lost and we can convince them they will only deal with us, that Larry is just the silent investor. So let's see what the letter says.'

I hear the envelope being ripped open, then silence. 'Maybe I should have waited until you were back.'

Yippee, must be more good news. 'This day is already a bust, go ahead, give me the gist of it.'

'The Governor's office thanks you, blah blah blah, appreciates your proposal, blah blah blah, however finds your solution is not suitable. Lana? Lana? Are you there?'

Tedi's voice is in my ear, but my eyes are searching for the beach bar. I knew it was a long shot, but damn, this sucks. I can never comprehend when business does not go my way. 'Yeah, yeah, thanks Tedi, see you tomorrow.' Another martini is calling my name.

'Barkeep! Belvedere martini, please. And by any chance do you have blue cheese stuffed olives?'

'Why yes we do, it's your lucky day,' she replies.

Lucky, yeah. Martini in hand, I am careful not to spill any, as I walk towards the beach. Needing to regroup, I mentally list the items in my pro column. Toby is right, we still have great options. Mmmm, this is a good martini. Make the most of what we have, that's all we need to do, stay focused, continue to look for more options. Huh, empty glass, how did that happen.

I wander into a beautiful garden area of lush greenery surrounds the pool just off the beach. A crowd of people have gathered in front of a camera mounted on a pole. The sign says *Your Friends Can See You on the Web! Stand Here. Have Them Log onto Www.Seemeonthebeach.Com.* Cool!

Rikki answers my speed dial, 'Hey Lana, thought you were in Tampa.'

'I am! Have the kids log onto *www.seemeonthebeach.com*, I want to wave and say hi!'

'Neato, stand by!' Rikki screams for the kids, 'Bring the laptop! Okay Aunt Lana, we are all here, we can see you! You may want to put that glass down.'

'Hey Gang! Watch this!' Usually not a dancer, I am feeling the rhythm! A little bit of the swim, next some Soulja Boy, some Gangnam style.

'Mom, make her stop! Is she doing the Worm!' Sadie cries. 'Can everyone in the world see her?'

Suddenly, I am rudely yanked to my feet, putting a halt to my epic dance moves by Toby. 'Hey! Come on, join me,' I say, moving his arms, trying to get him to dance.

'Ohhh noooo, Lady Gaga, your show is done for the night. Say good night to your family.'

Spoil sport, whatev. 'Good night, love you guys, you've been a great audience.' Close curtain…

# Chapter 19

'My children are permanently scarred, *Aunt Lana!*' It's my Saturday morning family calls, and obviously my sister Rikki is not happy with my impressive web dance moves while I was in Tampa.

'Well, I'm sorry about that,' I apologize. 'But it can't be any worse than when the kids found the newspaper article with the picture of you Jello wrestling.'

'Nobody even does the worm anymore. So what prompted the dance meltdown?'

I'm reluctant to share the reasons for fear of another pitch by her to be a pie maker at the Pie Hole. 'Things just didn't go as planned with our investor, plus we got a *thanks but no thanks* letter from Puerto Rico. We knew the Puerto Rico deal was a long shot, but it still stung.'

'No lecture from me about your pie options; I'm sure you will just focus on your other possibilities,' Rikki says.

It takes me a moment to recover from the fact there is no lecture, 'Thanks Sis, I appreciate it. So what's happening in your world?'

We talk for a while about the fun we had during the reunion, how The Pie Hole is doing, and her trials and tribulations with her kids. About five minutes into our conversation, we are interrupted by a impatient Sadie.

'Aunt Lana! I have a concert is in two weeks, and I'm not even famous yet! You gotta be there, you just gotta!' she screams into the phone, possibly puncturing my eardrum.

'Slow down, pumpkin, I am sure I can be there.'

'And it's free, I told my teacher I wanted to charge people, at least to see me, but she say the school would frown upon it. This does not make me happy, but I have a solo, so you just gotta be here!'

'Okay, Okay, sweepea. Put mommy on and I will get the details.'

'Yay! Love you Aunt Lana!'

Rikki gets back on the phone, 'Are you really coming up?'

'Sure, why not, I have been wanting to come up and see your brood anyway. So tell me about this concert.'

'It's just a first grade concert, not really a big deal. But she does have the solo, she's decided on *You Are My Sunshine* after her teacher nixed *Me and Bobby McGee*. Not sure where she even heard that song. Anyway, its two weeks from Friday.'

'Should be fun, I'll take a look at flights later today and call you with my itinerary. Love you.'

'Love you back,' end conversation.

Time for another cup of coffee before the call to Evita, going to be a busy day. Once I make my calls, I'll head to the gym with Jillian, then off to get my hair cut, and last but not least, the big dinner with Sal and his wife. Tedi being invited definitely takes some of the stress out of the event. Safety in numbers and all that.

My cell rings, expecting to see a picture of Evita, I am pleasantly surprised to see it's my brother, Max. 'Hey stranger,' I answer.

'Hey yourself, just called to make sure you are still sane after the family reunion.'

'Missed having you there, but yes, I seem to still have all my faculties. This is a pleasant surprise, what's new with you?'

Max is a workaholic, he not only is teacher at a school for homeless kids in Atlanta, Georgia, but he spends his spare time coaching little leagues, and planting community gardens. It's almost do-gooder overload. He was always my hero growing up; still is.

'Nothing much, just saving the world.' Did I mention modest? 'So how much crazy did I miss?' he asks.

'How much time do you have?' And with that I give him the speed version of events.

'By the way,' he says, 'Patrick called but I did not buy into the whole business going under thing and the two of you getting married. Want to give me the real scoop?'

'He is such a pain in my ass! Truth be told, we could be doing better, and sometimes I think about doing something else. But bottom line, we are holding our own.'

'Good to hear, I don't want to see you resort to making pies. Gotta run, we are planting zucchini today, love you lots.'

'Back attacha big bro,' I say with affection.

Next up, Evita. 'Hey Mom.'

'Leebee! Can't wait to see you, so nice of Toby to put me up, the cruise is going to be a hoot, and don't worry, I have my own cabin. Kiss Sadie and the kids for me, I'll miss the concert because of the cruise.' She takes a breath.

Jumping in before she can start again, 'What cruise, and why would you stay with Toby and not me?' Seems I have missed something.

'You are never going to believe this! On the ride back with Melvin from the reunion, we were listening to the radio and they were having a singing contest right on the air! I was stunned when I was one of the callers that got through. Anyway, I sang Harper Valley PTA, and got the most votes! Free cruise to the Bahamas, plus spending money! Of course I am taking Melvin, it was his car.'

'Okay, that's cool. But the still doesn't explain why you are staying with Toby.'

'First off honey, he is way more fun than you, no offense; plus he is closer to the port and he promised to take me to the Philling Station,' she explains.

Again, Oy. 'Have you already spoken to Toby?' And why did I not know about this?'

'Now don't get your thong in a twist, of course I did, just before you called. And it's only for one night. I assume you will come down?'

That was not a convincing invitation. 'If you want me to?' I think my lower lip is out.

'Oh for God's sake Lana, buck up, of course I want you to.'

Before I have a chance to respond, I hear a blood curdling shriek coming from the direction of Jillian's house.

'Gotta run mom, I think that's Jillian, call you next week, love you!' Flying out the door, I spot Jillian in her front yard totally freaked out. Looking around, it's easy to see why. Signs litter her yard, and they're all of her ex with his new girlfriend, having sex! Bile starts to rise in my throat. The caption on all of the signs is, 'He *loves me now, not you.*'

'Are you freakin kidding me,' yells Jillian. 'My eyes are burning!'

'Go inside, I'll get rid of these. Go!' Grabbing a pair of yard gloves from my shed, not looking at the pictures, I grab all of the signs and stash them around the opposite side of my house. Jillian may need these for evidence.

'Freakin whack job! That's what she is! I have no idea what to do, should I call the police or just go kick her ass?' she sounds exasperated.

'Let's not do anything rash,' I say, hoping to keep things calm and avert violence. 'Why don't we go work out as planned, and then sort this out.'

154

'Good idea, think I'll do some kick boxing.'

Off we go, power walking to the gym. Even my long legs have a hard time keeping up with Jillian, she is definitely on a mission. At the gym, I do my usual work out with Martini-with-a-Twist, frightened each time I glance over at Jillian beating the crap out of the heavy bag. All done, we leave the gym and walk back toward our houses. No surprise on our route, we see Patrick at Starbucks. However to my utter surprise, Jillian actually accepts his invitation to join us.

'So Patrick, I want your legal advice, and don't even think about charging me,' Jillian, always direct to the point.

Patrick looks at me, as if to say, *is this a trick question?* I just shrug. 'Sure Jillian, shoot.'

She explains what she found in her yard this morning, and asks what if anything, the police can and will do. In her eyes, I see a devious plan forming.

'Honestly... trespassing, harassment, but nothing that will put her behind bars, which I don't think is your intent anyway. If it were me, I think I would do an eye for an eye, something that will shut her down.'

'Patrick!' I yell, I can't believe Mr. Straight and Narrow just said that. Jillian doesn't need that kind of advice.

A sneaky smile creeps on her face, 'My thoughts exactly. I suddenly have things to do, catch you later Lana? Thanks Patrick, you're not as bad as I say.' And away she goes to hatch her diabolical plan.

'What did you just do!' I hit him in the arm for emphasis. 'And get me an iced mocha!'

Returning with my iced mocha, he says, 'Sorry I missed you doing the worm.'

'How'd you hear about that?' Knowing damn well it could be anyone from my family. Traitors.

'Actually, it was Toby, saw him last night when I was out to dinner.'

Nice, guess it was just too juicy to hold in. 'I was just having fun, wanted to entertain Rikki's kids.'

'Yeah, okay. But seriously, that sucks about Puerto Rico. You had a good plan, Lana. I reached out to a contact I have there, the real reason for the turn is they want to give the contract to a business on the island.'

Sighing, I know that makes sense. 'Whatev, I knew it was a long shot.'

'How about if I make you dinner tonight,' he suggests. 'We can discuss income options that don't include sex addicts like Larry.'

Pompous ass. 'Sorry, I have a dinner engagement.' With a mobster, sheesh, what I do to keep my business going.

◆◆◆

# Chapter 20

It's true what they say about hairdressers being therapists, mine is also my bartender, which should not be a shock. I have been going to Amela at Spa by the Sea for, well let's just say lots of years. When she sees my name in her appointment book, she checks to make sure she has a bottle of Grey Goose. Haircuts are such *me* time, truly an escape, and I am sure today will be no exception, for which I am thankful.

'Lana! My favorite client!' Amela as usual has a warm greeting for me, and I really don't care if it's true or not. She looks gorgeous as always, tight, short black dress, no idea how she stands in those spike heels all day. She hails from Croatia, with an accent that is her perfect accessory. Long, flowing deep red, almost maroon hair, crazy in all the right spots finishes her look.

'You look fabulous as always,' I go in for the two cheek kiss.

'Emilio, bring Lana a cocktail.' Emilio is her brother, also gorgeous, and a kept man by a part time local, part time New York socialite. Perfect arm candy. He helps Amela out at the salon out of boredom, and love. Toby is sure he is... wishful thinking he is gay. I don't care as he gives the best head massage while shampooing. Out he comes carrying a martini with, I think, sprig of broccoli. This is a new twist.

Amela reads my expression. 'We are trying to be healthier.' Not sure how that works, but okay. 'What are we doing today my dear?'

'I guess the usual,' I respond.

'You look like shit today, what's going on?'

'Thank you. Just the usual work drama. I have a big

dinner date with an investor and his wife at Tuesdays tonight, so I have to look smashing.'

Amela, looks at me, moves around the chair, taking in all sides. 'Let's shake it up a bit, do some shocking blond chunks of highlights,' she suggests.

'What the hell, go for it,' mmm, broccoli is not bad with vodka.

And so she begins the strategically placing of foil and color in my hair. All the while I catch her up on the reunion, Larry, Tedi, and my web dance performance. Even if I am not her favorite client, I most likely am her most entertaining.

'Okay, my lijep' – Croation for beautiful – 'come sit under the dryer while the color works its magic.'

I nod okay, nibbling on my broccoli. I now have thirty minutes in which to totally veg – no pun intended,well maybe – and not think about anything. Emilio takes my glass for a refill, but I decline, too early for that second martini, especially since I have dinner plans.

Far too soon, the egg timer dings summoning Emilio, who guides me to his wash station, the best part of the visit. Once he has the foils out, he starts the head massage, slowly, perfectly. I let out a low moan, not caring if any of the other patrons hear me, they all understand and are anxiously anticipating their turn. Amela smiles, her brother is good for business, he gives the proverbial good head.

Sadly, it's is over, and I seat myself in Amela's magical chair, knowing the end result will be a knock out. A snip snip here, and a clip clip there, she spins me around to see the final product, and I am over the moon happy, I look faaaabulous! 'You have out done yourself! I absolutely love it!' I exclaim.

Beaming, Amela, gives me the kiss kiss and sends me merrily on my way. Walking home, I am positive everyone is staring at my incredible new doo.

Of all of the descriptions I have heard, none do the central bar area of Tuesday's any justice, it's a fairytale land. Royal palm trees soaring overhead accented by short pineapple palms, birds of paradise, all highlighted by twinkling white lights. I am mesmerized.

'Hey, Spacecase! Eyes down before you run into something,' Tedi shakes me from my euphoria.

'And Happy Saturday to you as well, princess,' I retort.

'Well, well, look at the new doo, pretty snazzy,' she admires my highlights. 'How many martinis did Amela have to serve to get you to agree to that.'

'She didn't have to twist my arm, and only one, with broccoli.'

'Not going to ask. So what do you think is on Sal's agenda? No one has ever met him but you. Maybe he's going to make us an offer we can't refuse.'

I groan, 'Seriously? Please don't make any mafia jokes. Did you order us drinks? I think it's a good idea to take the edge off.'

And viola, shots arrive. Eyeing Tedi, she explains. 'It's called the Mafia's Kiss,' with that she picks her shot up, holding it for me to clink, 'Fredo, I saw what you did.' This is going to be a long night.

'Salute,' and down the hatch. Yowzer, that'll put hair on my chest.

As soon as I am able to refocus my eyes, I spot Sal and his wife, Concetta approaching. Then I am blinded by the rocks in her ears, holy camole, that's a bunch of carats.

Sal takes the lead, 'Lana, lovely to see you, and Tedi, a delight to meet you finally. This is my lovely wife, Concetta,' and the introductions are done, now what.

'Signor, your table awaits you,' the maitre'd sweeps us off to our table, Concetta in the lead, Sal bringing up the rear. With a flourish, the maitre'd opens our napkins and gently places them on our lap. The table is adorned with crystal and silver, probably enough that if I hocked it, I could buy a new car. Just as swiftly, fresh baked, still warm bread is placed on the table with individual baths of extra virgin olive oil infused with fresh herbs. I am in heaven.

Concetta starts the table conversation, 'Lana, my husband has told me all about you, and he is having so much fun doing business with you. I don't remember a time when he smiled so often.'

Wait... what? I have never seen him smile. 'I also enjoy doing business with him.' I hope she is not getting the wrong idea, like maybe we are having an affair, nah.

As if reading my mind, Concetta reaches over, lightly places her hand on mine, 'Lana, I am not worried about Sal having an affair. Our marriage is solid as a rock. Did he ever tell you how we met? He was actually working for my father, in well, let's say in a certain capacity. My father brought him into the family business, they are very close.'

By now I have endured five kicks from Tedi, Sal is simply enjoying the fresh, warm bread. I am not really sure what to say, so I eat bread, we all eat bread.

Prices on the menu are outrageous, maybe I should just go with a side salad. However, both surf and turf are calling my name. The server recites the list of specials, drool invoking specials. I opt for the Five Spice braised short ribs, maple smashed yams, and grilled asparagus. Tedi, knowing me, and that I will want to taste her dinner, went with the cedar plank salmon with cream dill sauce. Are you salivating yet?

Our conversations weave through a cross section of topics, from real estate, to recipes, to family life. Sal and Concetta's two boys are grown and living in New York, one is saving the world a single house at a time with

Habitat for Humanity, the other is taking Wall Street by storm. They are proud parents.

The meal is absolutely divine, heaven on a fork. Tedi and I swap plates about half way through, and the comfortable banter continues as we clean our plates.

'So Sal...' Tedi starts. I am nervous, she is on her second martini. Please, please, please don't let it be a wise guy joke. 'Thanks again for inviting us to dinner, I assume this lovely evening is to *cement* our relationship.' She kicks me as the word *cement* comes out, ouch.

'Well, Tedi, we did not come here to measure for shoes,' says Sal. Did he make a funny? 'I see a bright future in us all working together, and I thought it would be nice to share a meal and get to know each other a bit better. And Lana, the gentleman at 12 o'clock has been looking your way for the last ten minutes, do you know him?'

Tedi rolls her eyes, 'Oh boy, this should be interesting.'

And as if on cue, the mystery man heads our way. 'Pepper?,' he looks around the table at everyone, 'Please excuse my interruption, but gosh Pepper, it's really good to see you.' He leans in and kisses my cheek, which by now is flaming red.

'I believe you have mistaken me for someone else,' I politely say.

'I don't blame you for saying that, Pepper. I know you and I should not have had sex in the linen closet at my wedding reception, and because we did, you lost your best friend Jen, and Jen and I were only married ninety-three minutes, which I guess I deserved. But there hasn't been a day that has gone by I haven't thought about you, would you consider going out with me?'

I am speechless. Sal is watching with one eyebrow raised, Concetta appears to be amused, Tedi steps up to the plate. 'I am sure this woman looks familiar, she seems to look familiar to everyone, but I can tell you with certainty that she is not Pepper. Now if you don't mind, we'd like to get back to our meal.'

'Oh, I get it,' he winks and backs away from the table. His thumb and pinky go out into the classic phone gesture, and he mouths, *call me*, with a wink.

'So the legend is true,' states Sal. 'How about if we end the evening under the stars at the outside bar with a nightcap?' Off we go into the balmy night air, my eyes trained forward, carefully avoiding the man who thinks I am Pepper. Cocktails under the stars, perfect end to a wonderful evening.

Tedi drops me at my house, declining to come in for a night cap. We both agree the evening was fruitful as well as enjoyable, and the opportunities with Sal and Concetta will be profitable for all. Sleep comes the instant my head hits the pillow.


Leave me alone, go away. Someone is shaking me from my slumber. 'Come on, you have to come with me!' It's Jillian, and it's still dark out, what the heck?

Wiping the crust from my eyes, and forcing them open, I gaze up at her, 'What's the emergency?' My clock reads five-thirty.

Enticing me, she waves coffee under my nose. 'We need to be there when they come out of the house, hurry up, just throw on some sweats.'

Barely dressed, Jillian drags me out and into her car. 'So are you going to tell me what's going on?' I ask.

'The less you know the better. Let's just say I prepared a surprise in the middle of the night for my ex and his whack job girlfriend. We need to be there when they head out this morning for their early tee time.'

'How are you going to get into his community, its guard gated.'

'I made a friend,' is all she says. I don't want to know.

Approaching the guard gate, Jillian simply blinks her headlights twice, and the gate magically opens. Stealthily, we park just down the street from the ex's house, close enough for a good view, far enough away to hopefully not get noticed.

'Oh My God, Jillian! What did you do?!?!' I exclaim. All of the pictures that were posted in her yard by the whack job, are now staked in her ex's yard, with a couple of minor changes. Jillian pasted pictures of pig heads where her ex's were, and cow heads where the crazy girlfriends heads were. Should I laugh or be frightened?

'Here they come, get down,' she hisses. The Barbie and Ken dolls emerge from the mansion, not a hair out of place, ready to conquer the social world. But alas, the world is quickly shattered as Barbie, the lunatic girlfriend, spots the lawn signs.

'What the...' is followed by an ear piercing scream. I don't have to look at Jillian to know she is smiling ear to ear. Barbie is running like a mad woman, grabbing all the signs as her neighbors come out to see what the screaming is all about. I think a few less party invitations will be in their mailbox this year.

Smoke coming out of her ears, Barbie whack job spots our car and makes a rapid bee line.

'Oh shit,' Jillian slams the car into gear, we leave tire on the road as we haul ass down the street. I can see Barbie and Ken in the rear view mirror, shaking their fists, coming full steam at us and I assume they are shouting obscenities. Blowing by the guard, Jillian rolls the window down giving the guard a quick wave and, wait, did she really just boob flash him?

'So, is it too early for a Bloody Mary?' she asks.

◆◆◆

## Chapter 21

Wham! Toby opens my door with such force, he almost puts a hole in the wall. It's way too early on a Monday morning for this.

'Cha Ching!' he yells. 'I got you the freakin deal of the century, the century I tell you!'

'Okay, so tell me,' I reply.

'Two bedroom, one bath, carport, eat off the floor immaculate, fully furnished down to the salt in the salt shaker. Guess how much, come on, guess.'

'Let's see, $2000, yes $2000, that's my final answer.'

'Hah! Try $500!'

'Wow, you did get the deal of the century, what community is it in?' I ask.

'Whispering Palms, no back space rent, nothin!' He seems to still be on his deal high.

'Cool, so who owns it now, the community?'

'Here's the scoop. A little old lady, who is now headed for the old ladies home, gave it to her grandkids, who want nothing to do with it. So Mindy, the park manager, called me, and said the grandkids would take $500 for it. You just have to come see it.'

'And I will, but here is your counter offer. Tell them you will take it off their hands so they do not have to pay any lot rent which is $425 a month, plus of course water and electric, and lawn maintenance.'

'Damn! Why didn't I think of that? Couldn't you have let me bask in my glory for at least ten minutes?' Poor Toby is crushed.

'Oh, you would have thought of it. Let's go take a look. I'll drive.'

'Only if we can go topless,' Toby says.

'It's the only way to drive.' We head out the door, letting the girls know we'll be back in thirty. Their looks convey doubt, and in their defense, Toby and I have been known to play hooky.

Whispering Palms is a short five minute jaunt from the office, but still time for us to do our own rendition of Cher's greatest hits. Wow, the home looks like a gingerbread cottage. It's evident that Toby indeed has hit a home run with this deal, too bad he doesn't know what a home run is. So sue me for stereo typing.

Inside, the furniture is pristine, even though it's a bit dated. The kitchen table is solid blond wood, the chair pads a sunny yellow, and yes, salt in the salt shaker. We tour the entire house, all of the furniture is quality and in great condition.

'And the best part, Lana, is that you don't need any partners, there is nothing to be done but sell it. I have looked at comparable homes, they go for $6000 or better, unfurnished. This will so help your bottom line this month.'

'Do you think we should offer to just take it off the grandkids hands,' I ask.

Toby taps his forehead lightly with his forefinger, eyes closed, his thinking mode. 'Well, if it was the old lady, I would pay the $500, but since it's the grandkids, I say we unburden them. I'll handle it from here, I got this.'

'I know you do, okay, let's head back to the office and we can wrap this up and get it on the market,' and away we go, singing Cher's greatest hits part deux. We scurry right back into my office, ignoring the questioning looks from the girls. Toby hops on the phone to close the deal.

'Hi, this is Toby from Florida Manufactured Homes, we spoke earlier about your grandmother's place in Whispering Palms. Yes, we took another look at it, yes, it is immaculate, very nice. The issue is that it's a bit dated for today's buyer. Yes, I agree, it's a classic look.' Toby is now rolling his eyes. 'We feel we can sell the home, but it may take a bit of time to find the right buyer. In the meantime, if you want to hold onto it, take care of the utilities, lot rent, and lawn care, we'll keep trying to find a buyer. How much? Probably about six hundred a month, and you'll want to have it cleaned every three weeks or so... right... to keep it in mint condition. Yes, everything is due on the first of the month, yes, tomorrow. Options? Well, we may be willing to take on the responsibility of the upkeep, if you are willing to simply sign the home over to us. But of course I have to check with our owner to see if she would agree, we like to help where we can, we understand your situation. How soon? Let me see if I can reach Lana, I will try to get back to you before the end of the day. Yes, you are quite welcome.'

And high five! "Well done!' I exclaim.

'I say we let him stew for an hour or so,' Toby replies.

'Well, at least fifteen minutes, I want to wrap this up and get it to the troops to sell.'

'Knock, Knock, Lana, are you busy?' It's Mable, little Miss Polite and Timid.

'Oh come on in Cindy Lou Who,' says Toby. I respond with my usual eye roll. To me he says, 'Guess she has not imbibed yet today.'

'Well Mr. Grinch, the day is young, and I after being in your company, a vodka on the rocks will be a welcome sight,' Mable counters.

'Ohhhh, you have on your big girl pants today, good for you,' Toby counters.

Mable answers back, 'And I see you have on yours as well'

'Mable, I do believe you have the makings of a smart ass, wonderful,' Toby is impressed.

At this point, my neck is starting to hurt from watching the zinger volleys. 'Okay then, Mable I assume there is a point to your visit?'

She takes a seat across from me, and gets a serious look on her face. 'Yes Lana, I do. I have been speaking with a woman, a single mom, trying to figure out how to help her. She is a victim of spousal abuse, she finally left her husband, and has nowhere to go.'

'Okay, so what is her credit situation? Does she have any money down? What is her budget?' I ask the standard questions.

'Here is where it gets tricky. She left about a week ago with not much more than the clothes on her back. Right now, she and her son are living in the airport, sleeping on the benches, washing up in the bathrooms. She takes her son to school, heads off to work, then picks him up and back to the airport they go.'

I can feel my heart breaking for this woman.

'She has no money Lana, her credit is not good enough for a loan, but she has a decent job. We just have to do something for her!' Poor Mable is almost in tears, and I am getting a bit misty myself.

'Mable, let me work on this, I think I have an idea.' Toby shoots me a look, he knows what is coming.

Mable smiles, 'I knew you would Lana, I just knew you would!' She closes the door behind her with one last smile.

'No No No Lana! This deal we are getting will help to keep you in the black, don't do it!' But Toby knows his words are lost on me.

'Toby, we have to, the woman is living in the airport. We'll make money on the next deal. Wrap up the deal with the heirs, let's give this woman a home.'

'Oh alright, I guess it's good karma, but I still don't like it.'

'And why don't you share the good news with Mable, it's your deal.'

'Yeah, because that's me, the giving compassionate type, a regular Mother Theresa,' he grumbles as he leaves my office. I can't help but smile, because contrary to his belief, he is a kind soul.

'Oh My God! I could just kiss you!' Mable screams. She comes running into my office. 'Thank you, thank you Lana!'

'It's not a done deal yet, she still needs to pass muster to live in the community,' We pass a knowing look, hopefully I won't have to take the manager to 'lunch.'

Toby walks in five minutes later, orange lipstick on his cheek. Unsuccessfully, I try not to smile. 'Shut up,' he grumbles as he is wiping the lipstick with the back of his hand. 'Okay, it's settled with the grandkids. The title is at the community office waiting for us. I still say this is a big mistake Lana, you could really use this money.'

'It's a mistake I am willing to make. Thanks for being concerned, but I'll find some way to make it up. Speaking of making money, what's the story with the list from Point Tree on the repos? Have you evaluated all of them and do you have a list of what we should put an offer on?'

'Why yes Lana, to both, Tedi and I should have the list ready soon. And can I be the one to tell her the exciting news about you giving the house away?'

'What exciting news and what house did we *give* away?' As usual, Tedi's timing is impeccable.

'You are going to be soooo proud about what we did,' I say.

'Ohhh nooo, this was all you Lana,' Toby adds.

'Come on already, spill it,' Tedi demands.

I give Toby a sideways, *shut it* glance, I need to be able to spin this so Tedi sees the merit in giving away $6000.

Here goes, 'You know how we are always saying we need to give back? Today we were presented with the perfect opportunity.'

'Uh huh, go on.'

'Mable has a battered wife who narrowly escaped the bastard husband with her life and her son's life. Miraculously, Toby came in to me today with a free house in Whispering Palms. A cute little thing, but possibly a tough sell.'

'Oh brother,' exclaims Toby.

After shooting him another *stay out of it* look, I continue, 'The woman has a decent job, a car that runs, just no money and not so good credit. We just had to do it, Tedi, she was living in the airport!' I conclude.

'Seems like a no brainer to me, Lana. That's awesome, it will come back to us tenfold, karma and all that.'

'Insanity runs in your family,' is the only response from Toby.

In unison, Tedi and I say, 'You have no idea.'

169

# Chapter 22

'Now what?' I am staring into June's long face, this can't be good.

'There is an unemployment attorney on the phone for you, it's about that guy that wanted to work here that used to sell pot.'

'This should be interesting.' I answer the phone, 'This is Lana Turner, what can I do for you?'

'Ms. Turner, Perry Mason here, I represent Charles Stroker, we will be suing you for lost wages.'

'Guess your career was predestined,' I wait but no laugh, 'And exactly how did Mr. Stroker lose wages if he never worked for me?'

'Mr. Stroker was in an automobile accident after he left your office, his car was totaled and now he cannot seek employment.'

Scratching my head, I wonder if I should just hang up now, 'You know your argument defies all logic, don't you?'

'We'll see about that Ms Turner, we can also throw in the cost of the car repair and Mr. Stroker's head injury.'

'Okay, well, I am thinking his head was injured long before the accident. So, good luck with all that. Any further communication needs to be directed to my attorney, Patrick Callahan,' Not waiting for a response, I hang up. Maybe I should call Patrick and give him a heads up... nah.

Unbeknownst to me, Tedi and Toby have been my audience. 'Pot guy?' Tedi asks.

'Yes. Moving on, let's review the repo homes from Point Tree and finalize an offer. Uncle Larry will be available for a conference call in about an hour.'

Twelve homes in total are on our target list. They are spread out nicely throughout our favorite communities, each has a gross profit potential of at least ten thousand dollars. Total purchase is just under $45,000, should not be an issue for Larry and his partner, fits into their budget.

Tedi and Toby have done a bang up job with the package; pictures, detailed repair costs, after repair value. Larry has already been emailed a copy, so hopefully the conference call will be short.

'June? Please get Larry on the line for us, not sure if he is in his office or on his cell, thanks,' I yell into the front office.

'Hi Larry, Lana wants to speak with you. Me, too,' Giggle, giggle, then low voices so words cannot be understood. More giggles.

'Uh, June, do you want to transfer him so we can start our conference call?' Tedi asks.

June yells into the office, 'I am putting him on hold now,' then back to low tones, 'Of course I never would, silly. Hold what?' Burst of laughter.

Tedi, Toby and I just look at each other, ew.

'Hey Larry, I want to keep this a positive conversation, but you really must stop this, whatever it is with June. Now, on to business at hand,' I start, hearing a giggle now from Toby and Tedi.

'Yes, Lana, and how are you today? Are the musketeers with you?'

Together, Toby and Tedi, 'We're here!'

'Perfect,' he says. 'First I want to compliment you on the evaluation you sent me, very concise, makes decision making easy. Let's review each home briefly and get this offer nailed down.'

And so we begin. The review produced the results we were looking for, all seems in order and we agree on an offer amount. Tedi agrees to write the formal offer for submission, and we all whole heartedly agree to keep Larry's name off the paperwork for obvious reasons.

'My partner took a bit of convincing, but in the end he sees the logic. I just don't think he is as comfortable as I am doing business long distance,' Larry remarks.

'Maybe you should introduce him to June?' Nice smart ass remark from Toby, thank you.

I cut in, 'Larry, why don't you bring him on your next trip? And when will that be?'

'He's not much of a flyer, he is more of a nose to the books kinda guy. But I will tell him you extended the kind invitation. Right now I have a flight booked for three weeks from today.'

It's a wrap, we all agree this is a great opportunity and Larry will be copied on all correspondence. Larry's task is to send me the contract between our companies, spelling out responsibilities and profit splits. Done and done.

'Let's celebrate!' shouts Toby.

'Although this is certainly a valid reason, it is only ten o'clock in the morning, not that the hour has stopped us before,' I say.

'Spoil sport, maybe later? Happy hour?' he suggests.

'Let's revisit at the end of the day,' Tedi suggests.

The day continues, everyone handling their assigned tasks. Toby pokes his head in my office, ' I know this is probably not the best time, Lana, given the pot guy suing you and all, but you have an interview in about an hour for a new sales person. He's an old friend of mine from Detroit, Tom. And he has actually sales experience.'

'Isn't he the one who came to visit you last year? He got drunk, passed out, and you dressed him up in boas and floppy hats?' asks Tedi.

'Sounds like he'll fit right in,' I nod. 'Let me know when he's here,' and with that I shoo them out of my office.

Cher's *Strong Enough* erupts from my cell, it's Patrick. I debate myself on answering, knowing I have to. 'Patrick,' I answer.

'Lana,' he responds, the game is on. 'I just had an interesting call from Perry Mason.'

'From beyond the television graveyard?'

'Might have well as been, or possibly from the Twilight Zone. I told him in no uncertain terms that he was out of his mind, and any judge would throw him out of court. I don't mind you giving out my name as your attorney, but I would at least expect you to have dinner with me.'

Crap, I am trapped like a rat. 'I suppose you have a point, and I need you to review a rough draft contract we have with Larry on a repo package. I agree to dinner as long as it's at a restaurant, not your house.'

'Fair enough, how about Fra Diavolo's? Shall I pick you up?'

Not falling for that one. 'Nope, I think I can walk three blocks, see you at seven.' Click.

Toby is standing in my doorway. 'Don't you ever knock?' I ask.

'No. Guess our celebration is out. Tom is here, should I bring him in?'

'Sure.'

In a flash he is back in my doorway with a man that looks like an elf, a beardless elf. Not more than five foot two, he has rather large ears, rosy cheeks, silver gray hair, no pointy toe shoes though to my disappointment. Overall, a jolly looking fellow.

'Lana, Tom. Tom, Lana.'

I reach over my desk and shake his hand. 'Tom, pleasure to meet you. Toby tells me you have actual sales experience. What brings you to Florida from Detroit?'

'And Toby has told me wonderful things about you, Lana. Not sure if you are as bright as he says though if you are asking me why I came here from freezing cold Detroit.'

'Good, a smart ass. A point for you in the plus column. Tell me about yourself.'

'Being from Motor City, it's a given that I sold cars. Beyond that, I actually sold these trailers before they got all fancy. Originally they all had silver skins, that's why we called them Tin Cans. Used to hand out a can opener with every one that I sold.'

He seems like a keeper. 'First rule in this office Tom, if you want to work here, we don't use the T word, only manufactured home. If you're game, I am. Toby will set you up with a desk and a training manual so you can learn our methods. I'm sure you'll do well here.'

'Thanks Lana, it's much appreciated. By the way, I also indulge in adult beverages, Toby told me that's part of the hiring criteria.'

Eye roll directed at Toby. Okay, it's already three o'clock, where the hell did this day go. I am feeling a one and done celebration is in order.

'Toby? Tedi? Can I see you both a minute?' Instantly they appear. 'You're right, we should celebrate, but it has to be a one and done. I'm meeting Patrick for dinner tonight at Fra Diavolo at seven.'

'Hmmm, meeting the Fra Diavolo at Fra Diavolo. What's the occasion?' asks Tedi.

'He fielded the call from Perry Mason about Pot Guy, and I want him to review the contract with Larry. Might as well get a free meal, too. How about we head to Scallops

174

for a martini, see you there in an hour?' Nods from both, a quick good bye to the troops, and we are all out the door.

'These are the freakin biggest martinis *ever*, I love this place!' Toby is easily excited.

'Hence the one and done,' I say. 'And, if for some reason you should choose to continue, you can always walk back to my house and spend the night.'

'Nice to have options, cheers,' Tedi raises her glass.

Glasses clink, carefully so no liquid escapes. 'Feeling positive about the deal with Point Tree,' remarks Toby.

'Say what you want about Uncle Larry, but he is still a great investor. I just hope his, shall we say, indiscretions, don't put a damper on the deal.' I am still just a bit concerned about that.

'You never did give me the scoop, so spill,' Tedi is hungry for the sordid details.

Toby gives her the run down, with of course a bit of embellishment. He continues through the part where we order the most expensive items on the menu during the guilt dinner. Once he starts on my dance moves, I decide the story is over.

'Please, no sense rehashing my *So You Think You Can Dance* moment,' I plead. 'Not my finest moment, but unfortunately, not my worst.'

'Hahahaha, we certainly are an entertaining group,' adds Tedi. 'And speaking of entertaining, doesn't Evita land in a couple of days?'

'Yes, and it should be a treat. Why did you agree to have her stay at your place, Toby?' I ask.

'Oh come on, you know I love Evita, and it only makes sense, I am only fifteen minutes from the port. It'll be a hoot! I am assuming you will stay with me that night? Tedi, are you joining in the bon voyage festivities?'

'Wouldn't miss is it.'

Looking at my watch, I still have forty-five minutes to hang with my BFFs. Our conversation flows easily from one topic to the next, with laughter a constant interruption. Listening to my friends, I inhale the tropical air, drink in the warm surroundings. Uncharacteristically, we are responsible in our sips of our martinis. But after all, it is a school night.

'Alas my peeps, I must go and ready myself to meet Patrick. What did you guys decide to do?' I ask.

'Hmmm, Toby? You up for another round? We haven't had any one on one time in a while? We can compare dating stories.'

'That might be interesting, sure, I'm in!' agrees Toby.

'Then I will expect the both of you to stay over, you know where everything is, and you both have keys.' With that I slide off my stool.

'And should we expect you home this evening?' Tedi the smartass inquires, as they both giggle.

Eye roll and I am out the door. My brief walk home allows me to contemplate my attire for the evening; not business, not slutty, some skin, some cleavage. I should start a clothing line.

In the end, only a handful of clothes end up on my bed prior to my decision. Sleeveless silk blouse, subtle powder blue print, white linen shorts accentuating my long tan legs, flat leather sandals. Mirror check on the hair and makeup, good to go. Not sure why I am making such a fuss, it's just dinner with Patrick.

Being a gentleman, Patrick rises to meet me, kiss on the cheek, pulls out my chair, as Evita says, the days of

176

chivalry have not passed. We both agreed to dining outside on the patio, why wouldn't one want to be surrounded by palm trees and twinkling lights?

'You look ravishing tonight, Lana,' he begins.

'Don't start with me. I'm sure it's just the incredible, delicious smells emanating from the kitchen that has you salivating. And seriously, eyes up!'

The smells truthfully are driving me crazy, I didn't realize how famished I am. Fra Diavolo is, like all of the Delray restaurants, to die for. Authentic Northern Italian cuisine, emphasis on seafood. The server appears and pours us a glass of Pinot Grigio that has been chilling in the bucket next to the table. Fresh, warm bread is placed on the table, with an herb butter. It's amazing I am not as big as a house, extra cardio this weekend for sure.

'Do you have the contract you want me to look at, I prefer to get business out of the way so we can have relaxing dinner.' Patrick quickly and expertly goes page by page, nodding, making affirmative noises. 'This looks solid Lana, whoever Larry's attorney is did a great job, fair to both sides. Another glass of Pinot?'

Wait... what? No negativity? No slashes with a red Sharpie? This man across from me, with the tousled sandy blond hair, and soft lips, with a head so big you have to open both sides of a French door for him to enter, is okay with the contract? 'Who are you?' I ask. 'And yes, you may pour me another glass of wine.'

'It's a beautiful evening, my company is beautiful, and honestly, the contract is solid. You are an amazing woman... person, Lana. You always manage to land on your feet no matter what is thrown at you. There is no way I could handle the twists and turns of your business, all while caring for the people who work for you and buy from you. Here's to your success.' And with that he raises his glass to meet mine, smiling that million dollar smile.

177

What's his game? This appears to be the man I fell for not so long ago, but I know the other side. 'What's up with you tonight? Did you start early?'

'No, Lana. I just don't want to be the guy who misses what's right in front of him. You know I care about you, deeply. But let's not get all mushy, I hear Evita is coming to town, what are you two gals going to do while she is here?'

This may be an alternate universe, but what the hell, I'll play. I tell him about our loose plans, since Evita is only in for a night. Staying down at Toby's, probably dinner and then to the bar to sing a little karaoke. He smiles, nods, laughs, seems genuinely interested.

'How about you order for us tonight? You always know the right combinations,' he says.

'Alrighty,' I am liking this alternative universe Patrick. The server comes to the table, 'I think we'll skip the appetizers, a nice tossed salad with house balsamic vinaigrette. For the main course, we'll have the Cotoletta alla Valdostana along with the wild mushroom risotto. We'll share the main dishes, thanks. And bring another bottle of Pinot, please.' Patrick is smiling like the Cheshire cat.

'Too much?' I ask him. 'I was going to do light fare, but it's near impossible at this restaurant.'

Shaking his head, 'Nope, its perfect.' Now he is scaring me. 'Do you remember that little French cafe in the Bahamas? It overlooked the town square; Luciano's I think.'

'Yes! And the electric slide came on! Everyone joined in; the eighty year old couple, the kids on their bikes, people on skates, it was actually magical. What fun.' I look into Patrick's baby blues, remembering. I quickly look away, I feel my face go flush. What the hell?

'Didn't we go snorkeling that morning on the catamaran? I seem to remember the free Goombay

Smashes. When they asked if anyone wanted a life vest, we were the only ones that raised their hands.' he chuckles softly.

'It was the smart choice after three Goombay Smashes, they should have had a warning label.' My turn for a soft chuckle. Are we sharing a romantic moment? I hope Toby and Tedi don't find out, I'll never live it down.

Timing could not have been better as our food arrives. Just the smell makes me think I have died and gone to heaven. Our clever server, leaves the main dishes in the center, and places smaller dishes in front of us. '*Godere!*' he says, filling our wine glasses, again.

We laugh, we eat, we smile, we drink. Conversation stays to the pleasant and lighthearted. I try not to analyze, to contemplate any ulterior motive. Relaxed, I go with the flow, and just enjoy the moment.

'I am so full, I'll need my walk home to help digest,' I wish I could undo my top shorts button, but you know, not a good idea for at least two reasons.

'What? No Tiramisu? I know that's your favorite,' Patrick smiles. 'Let me get you some to go. And I insist on walking you home.'

Uh oh, here it comes. 'That's nice of you, Patrick. But I can get home by myself, it's only three blocks.'

'Please.'

'Okay, but understand you are not coming in.' I know I have a safety net, Toby and Tedi are there, I hope.

'Understood.'

Another balmy, starry night in Florida, with warm caressing sea breezes. Patrick suggests we detour down by the Intracoastal, to continue to walk off our dinner. To my surprise, I let him hold my hand. We sit on a bench, looking out over the water, the waves slapping against the yachts, neither of us saying a word.

A sigh escapes me, 'This has been a wonderful evening Patrick, thank you. I can walk by myself from here.'

With a look, I know Patrick will walk me all the way home. I hope I have the strength not to let him come in. At my door, I turn to him, 'Really, it was very nice.'

Without a word, he leans down and kisses me, and I mean kisses me. Sparks are flying in parts of my body I had no idea existed. Literally, my knees go weak.

'Goodnight, Lana,' And with a kiss on my cheek he turns and walks away, hands in his pockets, whistling. Sonofabitch.

Turning back to open my door, I see two wide eyed faces peering out. 'Oh My God! Seriously!' I yell as I walk into my house. 'You two are stalkers!'

'Now Lana, did you really expect us not to watch? If it had gone beyond a kiss, we would have turned away, probably,' Toby says.

Tedi does not mince words, 'Spill, cousin of mine.'

'It was like being in Bizzaro World. Patrick was nice, funny, charming. It was very confusing.'

Tedi eyes the bag in my hand that I had totally forgotten about. 'Most importantly, what's in the bag?'

'Tiramisu.'

'Okay, Toby, get three forks, I'll pour us a nice glass of wine. Lana, get your suit on and we'll all meet in the jacuzzi for a debriefing.'

Five minutes later, we were all surrounded by hot bubbles, digging into the Tiramisu. Gone in sixty seconds.

Settling back against the head rests, I start, 'It was like the Patrick of old. We had a fabulous dinner, he let me order. We reminisced, he was funny, his ego was in check. I saw tonight what I first saw in him, make sense?'

'Yes, but you know all too well there is another side, Lana. The side that makes you want to slap him senseless.' Tedi as usual is trying to be the voice of wisdom.

'Still… being with him could make life easier. I love you guys, and the business, but it's taking its toll. I worry about everybody, I don't want to let anyone down. I constantly have to reinvent, to look for more sources of income. Larry and Sal are great, but I worry about relying on them. Enough about my evening, tell me about yours.'

Tedi starts, Toby interjects, Tedi passes the baton, sounds like it was a rollicking evening. Watching their synergy gives me confidence that whatever happens to the business, we will always be in each other's lives.

'And then, Tedi challenged me. Well, you know me,' Toby finishes the story with flourish, 'I stood right up on that bar stool and sang.' Tedi is laughing so hard, wine starts to come out her nose.

And so the night went, and so went two more bottle s of wine. Finally I ask the time. 'It's one,' answers Toby.

'In the morning!' I am incredulous. 'We have to work tomorrow, everyone out and get to bed.'

Toby states the obvious, 'We are so not good at the *One and Done.*'

# *Chapter 23*

'Am I dreaming? If so, don't wake me up,' standing at my bedroom door, I am salivating, the smell of coffee and bacon assaulting my senses. Toby is in chef mode, I like it. 'Oh my God! It's eight-thirty,' I shout as I look at the clock.

Enjoying my panic, Toby calmly says, 'Yes, and I have already called both June and Sandy, told them that the three of us are doing a last look see at the repos. So sit yourself down and eat.' Bless him.

'Works for me!' Tedi joins us, looking famished.

It's quite a spread; waffles, scrambled eggs with scallions and peppers, scones – where the heck did he get those – fresh strawberries with whipped cream, yummo. Without another word, we all dig in until our plates are clean. Pushing back from the breakfast bar with some struggle, I pour another cup of coffee.

'Anyone else,' two cups go into the air. 'And where did you get the scones?'

'Ran down to the School House Bakery, its only two blocks,' Toby replies.

'Not sure where you got the energy Toby, but thank you, thank you,' says Tedi gratefully. 'If you weren't gay and I wasn't a lesbian, I would totally ask you out.'

We slowly saunter out onto the lanai, one by one plopping down on the chaise lounges. Sucks that we have to work today, sighs all around. Silently, I wish for an endless cup of coffee so I don't have to move, but alas, the cup is empty and it's time to motivate.

Begrudgingly I say, 'Reality calls, come on gang, let's get moving. Tedi, you're with me in the Palm Beach office? Toby, what's on your agenda?'

'After I go home and shower so I don't smell like I took a wine Jacuzzi, I'll follow up on the repo offer. I'm also going to go look at a couple of homes in The Gardens that management wants to give us. They seem like Sal deals.'

'Cool beans, now off with the both of you, I am sure we will chat later.'

Something is up at the West Palm office; the gang is all scurrying, trying to hide something from me. Hmm, it's not my birthday. Standing in the doorway, I scan the room, giving each of them the evil eye. Someone will crack, who will it be?

Then it dawns on me, 'Okay, get the white board out, I'm in. Does anyone have sailor hat yet?'

Evita's visit always means a hat pool. Everyone in both offices throws five bucks into the pool, betting on which hat will adorn her head. For some reason, the crew thinks the pool will upset me, isn't that silly?

Toby and I are the last ones to make our selection, and sailor hat is already taken by Mike. 'I choose fedora!' I shout.

'Too late, Mable has it,' Sandy informs me.

'Poop, okay then, doo rag, that's a hat, right?'

'Done,' Tedi enters my choice.

The phone rings, 'It's Toby, the hat he is throwing in the ring is the Vagabond, seems fitting,' Sandy announces, smiling at her own cleverness. Nice.

'So, when is Evita supposed to be here?' asks Mable. 'I only ask because I think that's her getting out of that cab.'

I spin around so quickly I get dizzy. Once I focus, sure enough, it's Evita in all of her glory. What the heck is she doing here today? I'm positive it's supposed to be tomorrow, I am certain of it. But no, it's her. She flies through the front door, leaving the cabbie to get her many suitcases out of his trunk.

'Hail, Hail the gang's all here,' she bellows. 'Anyone have Peach Basket, cause that's what's on my head! Lana, sweepea! Pay the cabbie please and grab my luggage like the favorite daughter you are. You all look *fabulous*, group hug!'

Without a word, Sandy goes into petty cash and extracts the cab fare. Tedi joins her to get the luggage, the rest are busy hugging. Tedi and Sandy join in once back in the office.

'Soooo, Mom, what brings you a day early?' I inquire.

'Well, pumpkin, you sounded so disappointed when I said I was staying at Toby's so I thought I would cheer you up and stay a night with you.' Oh yippee.

'Great,' forced smile, 'I do have to work, but I can have Sandy take you to my house so you can relax.'

'I have a better idea, I'll chit chat with the girls, you do what you have to do, and we'll bug out about noon, spend some quality time. So let's see the white board, did anyone guess peach basket?'

This battle will not be won, I turn and head into my office, leaving behind lots of giggles. I don't really have much on my plate today, just tie down the repo purchase. I could actually leave now… nah. I decide my desk needs to be cleaned.

'Penny for your thoughts,' Tedi is standing in my doorway, smiling.

'So did anyone guess peach basket?' I ask.

'Nope, so Evita wins the pool, should I dig into petty cash and get the $45? You know she is going to ask for it.'

Sighing, 'I'll make sure she gets it before we leave.'

'Why don't you just leave now? I've got it all covered, spend some time with your mom. Its sweet she came early.'

'Maybe you're right, will you join us tonight?' I'm thinking there is safety in numbers.

'There's nothing to be afraid of, Lana, you'll be fine. I'm going to join you tomorrow night, at Toby's.'

I know she is right, my mom is a character for sure, but she loves me fiercely, probably will not be as bad as I am imagining. What the heck, I'm going to leave now, do some bonding.

The troops are hysterical laughing at one of Evita's stories when I walk out, I can't help but smile. 'Want to let me in on what's so funny?' As that came out of my mouth, I know I am going to be sorry.

Still laughing, Evita says, 'Just telling the girls about the time we were in the liquor store, and that guy stole the cheap bottle of wine. Remember? The store owner was a friend of ours, and I sent you chasing the culprit. There you were at thirteen years old, chasing a drunk thief through the streets of Washington, DC. You had on that old black velvet cape of mine, it was flying in the wind. I'll bet you thought you were some kind of caped crusader.' More laughter.

'Yes, very nice, you sent your daughter possibly to her death for a five dollar bottle of wine.' This story is not as funny to me.

'Oh lighten up, sweepea, all's well that ends well. You never even came close to catching him.' More laughter.

'What do you say we get leave now, Mom. We'll get you settled at my place and take a walk down the avenue in Delray, get a bite to eat.' Sooner the better, I truly do not need my employees hearing tales from my dysfunctional childhood. 'And here's the forty-five for winning the hat pool... again.'

Evita promptly tucks the cash into her cleavage. 'Sounds like a plan, dearheart. Girls, it was lovely seeing you again. Mable, don't ever change the color of your lipstick, really brings out your eyes. Penny, keep the travel log coming of your sexual romps; Sandy, next time I am in, I want to see that bowl with the built-in straw, awesome. Tedi, how about helping your dear old aunt with her luggage?'

And out the door we go, no reason to be scared, right? Tedi gives hugs and kisses, promises to see Evita tomorrow night. The top goes down on the Spyder, and I decide to take the scenic route down A1A.

Spectacular. No matter how many times I make this drive, I am in awe. The ocean is a sparkling turquoise, waves are rising and rolling over into white foam. The beach dotted with colorful beach towels, people baking in the warm sun… paradise. Evita is soaking in the ride, her head back against the seat, big smile, eyes closed.

Evita opens her eyes as we pull into my driveway, 'You sure live in a wonderful area, Lana, it suits you.'

'Thanks, Mom, let's get your stuff inside.'

She enters my house, running her hands along pieces of my furniture, gracefully, thoughtfully. Her eyes scan as she moves, taking in her surroundings, nodding.

'I don't know if I have said this lately, Lana, but you have a beautiful home. It feels like you, I love it.'

Even though she is not one for displays of affections, she allows me to hug her. 'You say that every time you are here, but I can't hear it enough. Love you, Mom, glad you came in a day early. How about if we just relax by the pool for a bit, I'll get us some peach tea in honor of your peach basket hat.'

I take a few minutes to change, and by the time I get outside, she is snoozing. Seems like a good idea, especially after last night. It's not long before I am asleep, too.

'Heellllooooo!'

'What the hell is that?' Evita wakes with a start.

Jillian comes crashing through my palms, all smiles. 'Evita! I heard a rumor you were in town, you look fabulous! Love the peach basket hat!'

'Jillian, you ho bag you! You look scrumptious! I can't wait to hear about your sex life, you know I live vicariously through you.' Something creepy about that since I also live vicariously through Jillian's sex life.

'How about if I whip us up a light lunch, we can go on the avenue for dinner,' I offer. Both nod in agreement, wave me off, and start to catch up.

As I go into the house, I hear Evita encourage Jillian, 'I want to hear all about you getting your crepe stuffed!' Oy.

Let's see, what have I got hiding in my fridge? Assessing my inventory, I'm able to make chili lime shrimp, panzanella salad, an array of fresh fruits including strawberries and kiwi, that should do it.

Rejoining the girls on the patio, I am in time to hear Evita squeal with delight, 'No! You actually posted those pictures on their lawn! High five girl, you rock!' Another tale that probably should not be retold.

'Lunch is served, ladies,' I interrupt.

Evita digs right in, 'Looks yummy, Lana. I don't know where you learned to cook, it certainly wasn't from me.' How right she is, I remember her trying to make mashed potatoes from a box, always turned into potato soup.

'Delish, Lana, as always,' Jillian compliments. 'So, what are your plans for the rest of the day, besides a stroll down the avenue?'

'I'm thinking some mother daughter bonding on the beach, what do you think, Lana? You game?' Evita asks.

Glancing at Jillian, I hope I don't look as frightened as I feel. 'Sure Mom, that sounds like fun.'

'You are so full of shit,' Evita calls me on it.

'And with that, I am out,' Jillian announces. 'Have fun girls!' Oh please don't go.

'Join us tonight, Ho Bag!' invites Evita, hard to refuse such an eloquent invitation.

Jillian again looks at me, taking pity, 'Of course, should be a hoot.'

It doesn't take us long to throw the towels and beach chairs into the car. Normally I would walk, but Evita's beach bag looks like it weighs fifty pounds. At the last minute, she grabs a bottle of Pinot Grigio. I'm not sure if that's a good idea, but after I think about it for two seconds, taking the edge off probably is good idea. Plus, maybe it will make her sleepy.

The beach has a fair amount of sun worshippers, but we score a nice spot close to the waves. In a flash, our towels are spread and our chairs are ready to plop into, which we do. Ahhh, heaven, the sun warming my skin, sounds of the ocean.

Evita wastes no time pouring the wine into red plastic cups, she even brought ice. 'Here pumpkin, salud!' we bump cups. I can tell there is something on her mind and me taking out my Nook is not going to stop her.

'Okay Mom, go ahead.'

'Like I need your permission,' she says smiling. 'Lana, I think you are amazing. You have a wonderful life here. As Ava Gardner once said '*When I am old and gray, I want to live in a house by the sea. With lots of wonderful chums, good music, and booze around. And a damn fine kitchen to cook in.*' You are far from old and you have all of those things. But, you knew there would be a but, you feel personally responsible for the happiness of those around you. They are grownups, Lana, they can take care of themselves. I know you are killing yourself trying to keep this business profitable, not so much for you, but your employees. It's a noble endeavor, but not a weight you have to carry. I promise you, everyone will survive, and they will still be your chums if you decide to close up shop and take another path.'

'Thanks Mom, for kind your words, and your words of wisdom and concern. I have been wondering if I should simplify my life, be responsible for less people. I just feel like I owe it to my employees, and especially Toby and Tedi, to keep the business going.'

'I understand Lana, but there was life before you and there will be life after. Toby and Tedi are permanent fixtures in your movie. I just don't want you worrying so much about everyone else that your life passes you by.'

'You're right, I am going to give this serious thought. I am feeling stressed about it. Thanks.'

'Always got your back, Leebee. Now, let's have some more wine.'

We sit in silence for the next hour, just enjoying our surroundings. Evita may be right about scaling back, less responsibility is certainly tempting. But what can I do that will make me good money, and I will love doing? Cher already has a manager, so that's out. My cup is empty, it's a good time to nod off.

Slap, Evita rudely wakes me up. 'Come on, Pumpkin, you're getting as red as a lobster.' She starts to pack up.

Out of nowhere, 'When the hell did you get out of prison, Smokey! I had hoped they threw away the key, you rat!' A very threatening looking woman with lots of tattoos is towering over me.

'Hi, my name is not Smokey, I believe you have mistaken me for someone else.'

'Of course it's not Smokey, no mom would name their kid Smokey, well maybe. It's Madeline, which is of course why you changed it.'

'Um, this is my mother, she will tell you that my name is Lana, and I have never gone by the name Smokey.' I look to Evita for backup, she casually looks the other way. Really?

'Ramrod is looking for you, if I tells him where you are, you are dead meat.'

Oh great. 'Miss, are there any distinguishing features that would help you identify this Smokey?,' Logic dictates she probably has tattoos.

'Take off your sun glasses,' I comply. 'Hmm, okay both your eyes are the same color. But I'll be watching you!' She stomps off, motioning with two fingers, my eyes to her eyes.

'Way to have my back, Mom.'

Our walk to the car is silent. I'm not really thinking about the wrong identity incident, more about what Evita said about reducing stress from my life. Sensing my distraction, Evita leaves me in my own world. Even when we get back to the house, we go about the business of getting ready for the evening without conversation.

Jillian is here when I emerge from my room, more silence. I decide to break the ice, 'Okay ladies, let's go out and enjoy the evening,' All bubbly and smiling.

Evita and Jillian exchange glances. 'Guess what,' Jillian announces, 'It's Jazz on the Ave!' Every third Thursday, Delray closes down the main drag and the streets are lined with jazz bands and wonderful art. The restaurants go over the top, even bringing samples into the street.

'Perfect!' I agree, thinking this is a great distraction from pondering my life's direction. Arm in arm, the three of us set out to enjoy yet another balmy, tropical evening.

Strolling down the crowded ave, we periodically stop and sample tapas, order a Pinot Grigio from the street wine vendor, and even sway to the smooth jazz. We find an empty bench and people-watch for a while, sipping wine from plastic cups. As usual, dogs are accompanying the people enjoying the evening, even a few in special doggy knapsacks, gotta love it – keeps us entertained for a while.

'Come on!' Evita shouts, 'They are starting a line dance!'

Jillian jumps to join her, but I seem to have slipped back into thinking about my future. Before I can react, Jillian and Evita, grab my arms and yank me to the dance area.

'When in doubt, dance it out,' yells Evita. 'Jump in with your two big left feet.'

What the hell, I can think about my future tomorrow. Shake it to the left, shake it to the right, put your hands in the air like you just don't care.

◆◆◆

# Chapter 24

'Soooo, how was your day of bonding with Evita?' Toby is standing in my doorway, waiting for an answer.

'Well, I'm here and not in jail. What's the update on the contract with Point Tree?'

'Point Tree has signed off and is sending over the contract for your signature. Larry has signed and now we're waiting for his partner to sign, which he assures me will be done soon. It's all pretty exciting, we'll be busy rehabbing. All the sales people are going to take a look at the homes next week and start to market them to their buyers. This can really help keep you in the black, Lana.'

My response is a simple smile. Toby returns to his office to continue his day, I am left to ponder the next move. If all goes according to plan, we should be fine financially, I won't feel pressured to make any kind of decision, at least not yet.

Toby reappears, 'Almost forgot, what's the plan for tonight?'

'Tedi is going to pick up Evita, bring her here about three. She wants to do a last minute shop for cruise wear, then we'll meet you at your place, say seven?'

His eyes light up with mischief, 'I have a surprise for all of you.'

I hate surprises, 'How worried do I need to be?'

'Very.'

Yay. 'Can you please bring me the final figures for rehab and expected profit for the Point Tree portfolio? I am thinking it's a good idea to do some budget planning.'

'Novel idea.' Smart ass.

The rest of the day I am engrossed in paperwork. Rehab costs; can we improve them, are they enough? Are the proposed sale prices right? Will they sell fast at these prices? Are we leaving money on the table?

About one thirty, June pops her head in. 'Lana, can I get you something to eat?'

Bless her whacky soul, she does take care of me. 'I lost track of time, thanks. How about something simple, turkey sandwich?'

'I just happen to have one right here,' she reads minds, too.

Growling stomach satiated, I put my nose back to the grindstone. If we perform as expected with these homes, I can put extra money into buying more without Larry and his partner, keeping more of the profit. The sales people should be doing quite well also if we sell all of these homes in three months like we are anticipating. And… or, it may certainly be a good time just to hang on to the profits and look for my next career adventure, hmm.

'Earth to Lana, yoo hoo.' Enter Toby. 'I am going to take off shortly, do you need anything else from me?'

'Nope, I am good to go; we'll see you in a couple of hours.'

'Ohhhh yes,' Toby's smile is devilish, another interesting night in store.

A half hour later, the front door bangs open, 'Come on Lana, time's a wasting, need to find a dress with feathers.' Who else could that be but Evita. Chuckles emanate from the crew. Evita makes her rounds, hugs and kisses for everyone.

I take the time to close up the books, shutting my office door behind me.

'Too fast Evita,' Diane whines. 'No time for stories? The West Palm crew got to hear about the cape caper.'

It's nice that my employees all enjoy my mother's visits, but I know that also means one more exposed embarrassing episode of my life is shared.

Alas, I am too late. 'Hey Lana, tell them the T shirt story, it's a doosie,' Evita insists.

I look around for my dignity, but it's nowhere to be found. The only solace is that it's Friday and I will not have to see anyone for a couple of days.

So I begin, 'Not too far in the distant past, when I was still full of wonder for the world...'

'Oh for God's sake Lana, get to it, you'll put these poor people to sleep and they'll miss Happy Hour.' Looks of amusement all the way around, nice.

'Okay, I was in a bar, had a couple of drinks. Lively crowd, loud music. A young girl comes up to me, looking at my T-shirt, she says, *Hey! I went to that prep school! What year did you graduate?*

Still being naive to the ways of the world, I answered, *Funny story, my mom was house sitting for some locals, the Shermans while they were on vacation, and took this T-shirt for me from their house. So, I have no idea even where this school is.* Big smile on my face, even let out a laugh. At which point she says, *Really? I'm Jane Sherman, and that's my shirt!* No smile in her face. Thanks again, Mom.'

Evita et. al. find the humor once again in my humiliation. Happy to be of service.

'Have a great weekend everyone,' Evita waves goodbye, I am already out the door, Tedi close behind.

Stifling a giggle, Tedi adds, 'That one never gets old.' I just shake my head in disagreement.

Finding a gown with feathers was surprisingly easy, making the mall stop a quick one. We pull into Toby's driveway, grab our stuff and head in, no knocking necessary.

'Evita, you are a vision as always!' Toby wastes no time crossing to the door and giving her a tight hug.

'What have you got on tap, Toby? I can't wait to get to The Philling Station, ready to sing like a bird.' as usual, Evita is raring to go.

Three blindfolds are in Toby's hands, oh my. Evita squeals with delight. Toby ties the blindfolds, spins us around, and leads us through his sliding glass door to his pool area.

'On three, remove the blindfolds,' he is so dramatic, 'Three!'

'Toby! You have outdone yourself!' Evita screams.

Wowzer! Toby has indeed outdone himself. Amid his tropical pool setting, Toby has placed a martini bar complete with blue cheese stuffed olives, six other types of olives, cocktail onions, and lemon twists. The adjoining table is tapas heaven; jumbo shrimp, king crab legs, barbecue spare ribs and fried pork dumplings. I think I feel a little drool slipping down my chin.

'Nothing in a jar,' notes Tedi.

'And now for the *piece-de-resistance*,' he heads over to a mystery pile, covered with a sheet. 'Viola! Who needs The Philling Station?'

Underneath the sheet is a full set of Rock Band equipment; drums, two guitars, two microphones on stands. He has also moved his fifty two inch TV onto the deck.

'Brilliant,' I say, applauding. Now I do not have to endure the possible and probable humiliation of Evita in full swing in public.

'I love it! And I love you,' Evita crosses to Toby, giving him a fond hug.

'Where to start, where to start,' muses Tedi.

A damn good question. Toby starts shaking martinis, everyone decorating their glass with their favorite accompaniment. I choose blue cheese olives, of course, Tedi seems to have everything but, Evita opts for a twist. The food is a no-brainer, one of everything to start. Yummo.

'So let's see the play list,' Evita says to Toby. 'I am ready to let loose.'

Toby grabs Evita by the hand, 'I have a song just perfect for you, come on. Lana, you and Tedi play guitar, I'm on drums. And now, for your listening pleasure, straight from her cruise winning performance, the fabulous Evita!'

Evita approaches the microphone, we all assume our positions. Five, six, seven eight…

Prelude, Evita starts, '*Sweet dreams are made of this, who am I to disagree, I travel the world in the seven seas, every body's looking for something.*' She looks the part of a tiki bar singer, windblown wisps of silver hair in her face, her left hand grasping her gypsy skirt, waving it to the beat.

I am pleasantly surprised by her voice, I mean I have heard her sing before, she's not half bad. Neither is my fake guitar playing. I glance over at Tedi and Toby, heads banging to the beat, playing their fake instruments, all of us grinning ear to ear.

'*Some of them want to use you, some of them want to get used by you, some of them want to abuse you, some of them want to be abused,*' Evita pretends to crack a whip. We are all just a little frightened.

'*Hold your head up.*'

'*Movin on,*' Toby, Tedi and I join in.

'*Keep your head up.*'

'*Movin on.*'

And so it goes until the end of the song, at which point Evita gives us a sweeping bow and we all applaud.

'Round two for tapas?' asks Tedi. We head back to the tapas bar for another wonderful nosh. One of those, one of these, one of those…

Evita starts, 'So how come I am the only one in this group with a love life? It's a good looking group. Tedi, what's the scoop with that stewardess? Toby I just think you hang out with these girls too much. Lana, I don't know what to think about you, Mr. Button Up always chasing you, and some red headed lesbian stalking you. You got me face to face if any of you want my advice to the love lorn.'

We all glance at each other, who will be the first to respond. Toby shakes his head, no help there.

Tedi sighs, 'It's not *stewardess* anymore, Evita, it's *flight attendant*. She's an old flame from high school. I don't know where it's going, but at least I am having sex… unlike Lana.'

Oh, nice, thump thump, the bus just ran over me. Evita is watching me expectantly. 'Mom… Evita… I am not having this discussion with you, but thank you for your concern.'

'Toby said even he wouldn't throw the red head out of his bed, live a little, Lana. Did I ever tell you about…?'

I see the fear in Tedi and Toby's eyes, I cut her off right there. 'I have the perfect song, come on Toby, let's do an old Cher song.'

'Like I didn't see that coming.', replies Toby as he takes his place at the microphone. Evita on drums, Tedi on guitar.

Prelude, and we're swaying, I start, *'They say we're young and we don't know, won't find out until-il-il we grow.'*

Toby's turn, *'Well, I don't know, if all that's true, but you got me and baby I got you.'*

197

All together, '*Babe, I got you Babe.*' Hmm, maybe we should take our act on the road?

Seems we are only capable of one song before we need a set break. We head back to the tapas bar, filling our plates and settling into the lounge chairs. All is silent for a few minutes as we again stuff our faces. Apparently, singing makes you hungry.

'Who's ready for another martini? I'll do the shaking,' offers Evita. We all raise our hands. She does make a mean martini, one of her many marketable skills.

'Mmm, excellent Evita, thanks,' says Tedi. 'Okay, my turn at the microphone, let's go.' Evita on guitar, Toby on backup singer, I'm on drums.

Cue music, five six seven eight, '*Our day will come, and we'll have everything,*' hips are moving,' *we'll share the joy, falling in love can bring. No one can tell me I'm too young to know.*'

Enter Toby, '*too young to know.*'

'*I love you so.*'

'*love you so.*'

'*And you love me. Our day will come, if we just wait a while. No tears for us ...*' And on she goes, just the right mix, a little Ruby, a little Amy. I glance at Evita, she is totally lost in the song. Kudos to Toby for this inspired idea.

Once again, we head back to the lounge chairs and our waiting martinis. I steer the conversation to the non-controversial by asking Evita about the cruise ports of call. She is animated in her description of the events of the cruise. I wonder if the other passengers on board will ever be the same.

We all take a breather, enjoy the sounds of the night, breezes through the palms, turn our eyes to the stars in the sky. But I should know better, silence in this group is a prelude. All eyes dart from me to each other. They are up to something.

'Spill,' I demand, glaring at Tedi. She is the weak link.

Evita gives her a nod, this should be good. 'So…
well… we just… you know… well, you know how much
we all love you, right?'

'Seriously!' I am annoyed. 'Please don't start on the
whole thing about getting rid of the business, you are all
big boys and girls. I love you all, but let me breathe and do
my own thinking about this. Thanks for caring, but I know
my options.'

'It was Evita's idea for the intervention,' Toby adds.

'Geeze, I'll never rob a bank with you, Toby,' Evita
rolls her eyes, it's in the genes. 'Dime dropper.'

'The night is still young, let's break the rules and have a
third martini. I'll even shake.' I need to lighten the mood.

Toby steps up, 'I'll do the honors, I make them the
best anyway. You want yours dirty, right Evita?' Hah! We
all get a laugh from that one.

Third martini in hand, we chat about anything that is
not serious; hats, sunburns, boating, and favorite foods. Of
course all interspersed with guffaws and chortles and ear to
ear smiles. Much better.

Evita is suddenly inspired, 'Okay! One more song, one
that will bring the house down. This is an all sing, Toby
and I will share a microphone, Lana and Tedi on the
other,.

Prelude, clear throats, Evita begins, *I've paid my dues,
time after time.*

Toby, *I've done my sentence, but committed no crime.*

Tedi, *And bad mistakes, I've made a few.*

Me, *I've had my share of sand kicked in my face but I've come
through.*

All together now, *We are the champions, my friend. And
we'll keep on fighting til the end. We are the champions, we are the
champions,* we all exchange looks, *No time for losers, cause we*

*are the champions, of the fucking world!* I am now rethinking the wisdom of the forbidden third martini.

Not sure that waking up to a Bloody Mary bar is the best solution to last night, or... or, I can go with a hair of the dog.

Toby is in the lounge chair, sunglasses shielding his eyes. 'Do you think Evita would mind taking a cab to the port? I think I'm still drunk.'

'Hah! Lightweight!' Evita appears, looking totally refreshed. Unbelievable. 'Of course I won't mind. And look what the cat dragged in,' Tedi is right behind her, looking worse for the wear.

Toby gets up to make us all a Bloody Mary. Surprisingly, it does make me feel human again. Evita goes back inside to get her luggage ready, the three of us veg on the lounges, in the baking sun, with hopes of drying up the excess alcohol.

'I say you two hang with me today, get some sun, splash in the pool a bit. I'll throw meat on the grill later.' A trip to Toby's is never complete without a meatfest. Tedi and I just nod our heads and put on our sunglasses.

Beep Beep! The cab arrives, and with many kisses and hugs, Evita is on her way. Promises to see each other soon are made. Whew, love to see her come, love to see her go.

Resettled, I address Toby, 'And when you pick her up at the end of the cruise, take her directly to the airport, do not let her go to either of the offices, do not take her to the casino. I don't think she has time anyway, her flight home is only a few hours after her return.'

'Yep.'

◆ ◆ ◆

# Chapter 25

'Hey Mike, UPS is here with a really long box for you,' yells Diane. 'Maybe it's your new inflatable girlfriend.'

I hear Mike emerge from the little boy's room. 'Don't touch it!' he screams.

This should be good, I come out of my office and join the rest of the crew, anxious to see what's in the box.

'Well, open it,' I say.

He's transfixed by the box, glancing up to meet every one's eyes, as we all focus on the mystery box. Come on already. Slowing, he cuts through the tape. Whatever is in there must be fragile. Now, he pulls out the brown paper packing material, carefully, delicately. What the hell can this be? We are all on the edge of our seats.

Yikes! We are blinded! It's long and shiny! It's a leg! A gleaming, silver leg.!

Mike's beaming smile almost outshines his new leg. He gently cradles his new leg, kissing it, 'Titanium.'

'Geeze, get a room,' Diane says with disgusted look on her face.

'Alrighty, everyone, back to work, nothing more to see here.' I return to my office. Lots to do, I am getting on a plane to North Carolina in four hours. I still don't have the signed contract from Uncle Larry, and Point Tree is pushing me for my signature on the contract for the homes. Unfortunately, without Uncle Larry, I can't pull it off.

'Knock, knock.'

Mike has appeared at my door. 'Come on in' He is still hugging his new leg.

'I just wanted to thank you. Without your help making money in this crazy business, I would never have been able to afford the leg of my dreams. Do you want to touch it? Do you have clean surgical gloves?'

'Not with me, but I'll bring some when I get back from North Carolina. And you are quite welcome, you are a pleasure to work with.' That was a bit creepy.

Toby, which it seems he like is always doing, is hanging in my doorway as soon as Mike leaves. 'Yep, a bit creepy,' and he again seems reads my mind.

'What's up with the contract from Uncle Larry?' I ask him. 'It's making me a bit nervous. Let's take the bull by the horns. Hey June? Please get Larry for me? Try his cell.'

Now June is in my doorway, 'Uh, I can but he is in Greece at the snail festival.'

'What? Why didn't I know this? I need that contract signed and back here asap. He promised me that his partner would sign a couple of days ago! Can you get his partner on the phone for me?' I not excited about speaking to his partner, but this needs to get done.

June reappears, 'His partner is out of the office until Monday.'

Oh great, I hate leaving here with loose ends. 'Toby, you are going to have to stall Point Tree. I am getting a bad feeling about this.'

'Don't get your panties in a twist. I'll handle things here and keep you in the loop. Just enjoy your time with your family in North Carolina. Speaking of leaving, what time is Tedi picking you up?'

As if on cue, we hear Mike, 'Look Tedi! My leg finally came in! It's titanium!'

'Wow, it sure is shiny,' Tedi is now in my doorway, maybe I should make it bigger. 'Phew, glad I still had my sunglasses on. Are you ready, Lana?'

'Yep, bit of drama with Larry and Point Tree, I'll fill you in on the ride. Toby, don't forget what I said about taking Evita right to the airport from the cruise ship, no stops.'

'Yeah, yeah, yeah. Go, go, go. Tedi and I have everything under control.' Famous last words.

'So, what's the drama,' asks Tedi.

'Well, seems Uncle Larry is in Greece at the annual Snail Festival. And, his partner has not signed the contract for funding the Point Tree homes yet.'

'First, ew, second, crap. Okay, let's think positive thoughts, don't let this overshadow your trip to see Rikki. And please give hugs and kisses to the whole brood for me. Take lots of pics and record Sadie, she is such a pip. And don't talk to strangers!'

'Will do. I am going to email Larry as soon as I get checked in, I'm sure he is not totally incommunicado. Love you, thanks for the lift, see you Monday morning.' Hugs and kisses and I am on my way.

The lines are not too bad, I am able to get through the checkpoint in reasonable amount of time. In fact, time to spare, might as well start my mini vacation with a one and done at the airport bar. Martini in front of me, I keep my head down and fire off an email to Larry. If I don't make eye contact with anyone, I should be able to stay out of trouble.

'Lana Turner to the check in desk, please,' blares over the loud speaker. Crap, I know I didn't do anything wrong.

'Hi, I'm Lana Turner, what's wrong?'

'Why nothing at all, we just wanted to inform you that you have been upgraded to first class. You'll be able to board momentarily.'

Wait, what? Ooooh, thank you Tedi, keep on dating the flight attendant. I head back to the bar, down the rest of my martini. Careful still not to make any eye contact with the other patrons.

'Excuse me?' Damn, almost got away.

'Sorry, gotta go, planes leaving,' I try to hurry back to the gate.

'Excuse me, Miss,' crap, he is following me.

'Look, I don't know you, I just have a face that looks familiar.'

'You left your phone,' he says as he hands it to me, 'Sheesh, weirdo.'

'Oops, sorry, thanks, that was kind of you!' I am a jaded person. But a jaded person that is flying first class!

'Good afternoon, can I get you a drink?' It's Karen.

'Hey, how are you? Two questions, how long is the flight and can you make a Belvedere martini?'

'Two hours and yes.'

Hmm, half hour to drink the martini, an hour nap, the math works. 'Then by all means, I will have a martini.'

And presto, I have a martini complete with blue cheese stuffed olives. Before the plane hatch is bolted shut, I text Tedi – *thanks, this doesn't suck.*

The flight is uneventful, the best kind. Thanking Karen again with a hug, I step off the plane and head for the pick-up area. Takes me just a moment to spot Rikki, she is waving a large, orange foam finger. Like I wouldn't be able to see her six foot frame in this small crowd of people.

Big squeeze, 'I came sans kids, thought we could have some sister time. In fact, the kids don't think you are getting here until later tonight. Sadie is a bit frazzled, she wants to make sure you are bright eyed and bushy tailed, her exact words, for the concert tomorrow. I think she spends too much time talking to Mom.'

'So what do you have up your sleeve?' I ask.

'I know how much you like Starbucks, let's head there and relax... chat. Then maybe we'll pick up something for dinner and you can reconnect with the kids.'

We whisk off in her giant black Suburban like the covert government agents drive, and arrive at Starbucks unscathed. However, my knuckles are white from gripping the arm rests, and my ears ringing from listening to her scream at bad drivers, but we are in one piece.

'I have no idea what to get, the only time I am here is with you. Suggestions,' she asks.

'Go sit down, grab the comfy chairs, I'll bring something you'll like.'

As the drinks are being made, I glance over at Rikki, she looks verklempt. It's certainly understandable with five kids and helping her husband run a successful business. Boggles my mind, I could never do it.

'Here, just drink it, promise you'll like it,' I saying handing her an iced vanilla coffee. 'So give me the scoop.'

'The pie maker wants to open another store, in Charlotte. Mmmm, this is good. Anyway, it's a two edged sword. The best edge is that he will spend a good part of the week away, because if he doesn't, I will probably stab him.'

'And the bad part?'

'Five kids, one mom.'

'But PJ must be of some help at nineteen, and Adam is driving isn't he?' Adam is the seventeen years old.

'Yes, but PJ will have to run the pie shop here. He is actually quite the pie maker. He makes a Nutter Butter pie that people stand in line for.'

'Well, what about Adam, he's seventeen now. Can't he help drive the others?'

'Mr. Jock? We actually got him his own car so we wouldn't have to spend every afternoon driving him to some type of practice. Jonah does help with the younger ones. Look, we'll work it out. Once Peter gets Pie Hole Two up and running, PJ will probably move to Charlotte and manage it. In the meantime, it will give Peter and me a much needed break. I don't suppose you want to move in with me for a while?'

I feel bad, but that isn't going to happen, and Rikki knows it. 'Is everything okay with you and Peter except the needing a break thing?'

'We still have sex at least once a day, so I am thinking yes. We've learned to be very creative, especially at the Pie Hole. What the customer doesn't know won't hurt them.'

'Ew, I don't want to know. Hang on, I just got an email from Uncle Larry, my investor. He's in Greece at a snail festival.' I read the email, Larry says he will be back Monday, and make sure everything is signed. Whew, now I can enjoy myself and not have my stay overshadowed.

'All is well?' Rikki asks. 'I haven't even had a chance to ask about what is happening with you. How was Mom's visit?'

I proceed to tell her about buying the repossessed homes from Point Tree, the incredible dinner with Sal & his wife, and karaoke with Evita. At one point while I was describing our singing, I think vanilla iced coffee came out her nose. We talk about my own challenges, and the possibility of my life taking yet another career tack.

'Well, the gang is right, everyone that works for you is a grown up, you need to do what's right for you. You'll know when the time comes. Look at Peter, he was an engineer, clocking in day in and day out. Now we are getting ready to open our second pie store, who woulda thunk it.'

'What do you say we head out and grab dinner for your gaggle?' I suggest. I am excited to see everyone, it's been six months.

Ribs and chicken tenders are on the menu, with loads of baked beans and coleslaw. Dessert has been taken care of by the kids, apparently made by their own little hands.

We are barely in the driveway when the gang comes rushing out of the house, screaming *Aunt Lana, Aunt Lana*! Nice to be loved. Of course I am sure they are expecting presents.

After a group hug that almost topples everyone, we head in and set the table for a casual meal. I love her farm table, gorgeous distressed dark oak, big enough for her brood plus some. Peter arrives just as we finish laying out the food.

'Hello Lana,' he says warmly, follows up with a kiss to my cheek. 'Really sweet of you to make the trip.'

'Of course she did Peter,' retorts Sadie. 'She would never have forgiven herself if she missed my first concert. Would you, Aunt Lana? And by the way, did you bring me a present?'

'No, I would never be able to live with myself, and I thought I would take you and Jacob to the toy store and the other boys to the sports store. Get you all a little something.' Jacob is the quiet eight year old, I think he just gets lost in all the turmoil.

'Brilliant idea!' and with that Sadie digs into the ribs, seconds later her face is covered in barbecue sauce. Rikki just shakes her head. We all dig in until there are no leftovers.

Only bones left, Rikki stands and barks commands, 'Hop to gang, get this table cleaned up. The grownups are going to relax on the back deck, we'll have your special dessert in a half hour or so.' They all jump up and start to clear like a well-oiled machine. Damn, she's good.

'Impressive,' I say.

'I threatened them with death if they did not behave while you are here. Sweetened or unsweetened tea?'

'Sweetened, please,' I reply. Rikki's back deck and yard are magical. The deck hosts a large picnic table on one side, to the other side is a rocking bench, and several overstuffed lounge chairs. The colors and fabric blend with mother nature perfectly. The railing that rings the deck is adorned with long pots of herbs, everything you can imagine; lemon thyme, sweet basil, chocolate mint, Greek oregano, mmm ... an olfactory high.

Down the deck stairs, a wandering flagstone walkway leads to four paths, each with their own theme; one to a fairytale butterfly and hummingbird garden, one to a gazebo sporting twinkling lights and a jacuzzi, one to a large firepit surrounded by eight different color Montauk chairs, and, lastly, one leading to a two story, every kids dream, tree house. If I lived here, I would never be inside.

Rikki joins Peter and me, all of us stretching out in lounge chairs. PJ joins us as well, sporting a look that says, *what, I'm a grown up too.*

'So PJ, I hear your Nutter Butter pie is to die for and has customers lined up out the door,' I say.

Beaming with pride, he responds, 'That's just the tip of the iceberg, I have ideas that'll knock your socks off!'

Paternal pride is evident on Peter's face, who chimes in, 'Yep, he's a chip off the old block. We have big plans, Lana, expansion. We're even talking about maybe opening a Pie Hole down your way in Delray Beach, we think it would be the perfect venue. If we could only think of someone to manage it for us.'

Oh boy, the pie pitch. Rikki is shooting daggers at Peter, PJ is oblivious. 'Capital idea Peter, it's foodie heaven down there. If I can think of anyone that could fill the manager shoes, I'll let you know,' I respond hoping to shut the subject down.

'I was thinking, Lana, since…' Peter starts, but quickly stops after seeing the death stare from Rikki.

'It's very sweet of you, Peter, really. And if I ever want to make pies, I couldn't be in better company. But for now, and the foreseeable future, I am going to stick with manufactured homes.' Pie making, schmie making, just not my scene.

The rest of the gang comes clamoring out the sliding glass door with a very lopsided but delicious fifteen layer carrot cake. Slices are passed around and amazingly, silence rules as we scoff the cake.

Sadie is in my lap. 'I know this is your favorite, Aunt Lana, just like me,' she schmoozes, topping it off with an icing kiss, yum.

## Chapter 26

The big day has arrived. 'Are you nervous, pumpkin,' I ask. She just looks cute as a button. Her silky blond hair is pin straight ending just at her shoulders, bangs just above her eyebrows. Yellow is her favorite color, hence the yellow daisy print sun dress. I could just gobble her up.

'No butterflies for me Aunt Lana, anyway that would be gross to have them flying around your stomach. Plus, I think they would get bored being in the same place all the time.' Makes sense to me.

'Okay Peter, Lana and I are leaving so we get Sadie there early. See you in twenty minutes, and I mean twenty minutes, Peter.' Rikki, large and in charge.

Since Peter has the job of bringing the majority of the crew, we take his smaller SUV, but the ride is the same, white knuckle. Sadie is used to the NASCAR style driving and seems unfazed, doing vocal warm ups. Thankfully the trip is short, and we scoot Sadie in to get ready for her big debut.

Rikki does a superb job saving seats for Peter and the boys, no one dares sit in the entire first row. A simple death stare from Rikki encourages parents to seek other chairs. I am sure she is a welcome addition to the PTA.

'Welcome families to this year's first grade graduating class. Our children have worked and played hard this year, we are so proud of all of them, as I am sure you are,' begins the principal. 'We'd like to start our program with a short concert starting with Sadie Baker singing…

Uh oh, Sadie is tugging at her dress. Being so close we can hear her whisper something about being the *headliner*. The principal carefully extracts her with the famous spatula move.

'Sadie will start our show with *You are my Sunshine*.'

'Thank you Mrs. Shippley, and thank you all for coming to see me. I'd like to dedicate this song to my Mother and my Aunt Lana. Also, please hold all applause until the end, the song will be available to download after the show.'

Oh boy. With the voice of an angel, she begins:

> *You are my sunshine, my only sunshine*
> *You make me Happeeeeeee, when skies are gray*
> *You'll never know babe, how much I love you*
> *Please don't take…my sunshine… Awaaaaaaaaaay!*

With that, she bows, then blows kisses to Rikki and me. I look over at Rikki, her eyes moist, 'Are you crying?' She never shows emotion.

'No! Are you?' she responds.

'Absolutely not,' as I wipe my eyes.

The rest of the concert and presentations are a blur, not much interest in Miss and Mister Congeniality in first grade. Once it's over, I have a dozen roses for Sadie, who excepts them like the star she knows she is. She suggests that we slip out the side door, to avoid the throngs that will probably want her autograph. Rikki just takes her hand and heads for the car.

'How about if I treat everyone to lunch,' I suggest.

'What are you, crazy? I have four boys. Peter will take care of the boys, let's just have a girls' lunch. Okay with you Sadie?'

'Of course mother, sounds delightful.' Rikki and I just exchange glances, yikes, she has her hands full.

The restaurant Rikki picks is perfect, of course, everything is fresh from the decor to the food. Sadie orders with the flourish of a well-seasoned foodie, offers to place my order as well. Sure why not.

After lunch we head back to the house. Peter and PJ have gone back to the Pie Hole, the other boys are engrossed in some crazy video game. My eye is on the hammock in the butterfly garden, Rikki looks like she could use a nap as well.

'What do you say we all have some quiet time, then we can decide what to do about dinner,' says Rikki.

'I agree, mother, my concert was so exhausting. I have to be careful not to overdo. Love you. Aunt Lana, how exciting for you to see my first concert.'

We all go our separate ways to refuel and re-energize. I carefully hoist myself into the hammock, stretching out and gazing at the trees and blue sky above. Butterflies are fascinating, they seem to just float, vibrant oranges and yellows... zzzzzzzz.


Wow, I awake with a start, almost throwing myself out of the hammock. Takes me a minute to remember where I am. Ahh, relaxing in nature. I think I'll check on my Florida crew.

'Hey Sandy, who's in the office today? Tedi or Toby.'

'Who is this,' Sandy replies.

After my eye roll, 'It's Lana, Sandy. I'm looking for either Tedi or Toby.'

'I thought you were in North Carolina?' Sandy seems confused, what else is new.

'I am, but I just thought I would check in and see how everything is at the office.'

'It's fine, thanks for asking.' Click. Remind me why I keep her?

Let's try another way, I call Tedi, 'So how's the pie making brood,' she answers. 'And why are you calling, you've only been gone a day.'

'Just wanted to let you and Toby know that I got an email from Uncle Larry, he'll be back on Monday and promises the signed contract.'

'Bullshit, you're bored.'

'Fine, I am going to hang up and go spend quality bonding time with my sister and her large family.' Click.

The house is buzzing when I walk in, the boys are arguing, Rikki is yelling, Sadie is tapping her little foot. When they realize I am standing in the doorway, everyone stops talking, all eyes on me.

'As you were,' I say.

Immediately, the boys start arguing again, Rikki starts yelling. Looking for quiet space, Sadie comes over for a hug. Rikki wins the battle of the lungs, the boys go to their separate spaces grumbling.

'Just another day in paradise,' remarks Rikki. 'Let's go out onto the deck, I'll grab some iced tea.'

'You and Sadie go ahead, I want to spend time with the boys.' Yes, I am brave.

With all of them in separate spaces, I am hoping to get a chance for a good chat with each one. First up is Adam, he stops doing whatever it is kids do on their phones when he sees me approaching. We chat about school, what's next for him and about girls. I find out that he thinks high school relationships are silly, they are just going to end anyway. That he is applying to six Ivy League schools, wants to be an attorney, he is sure his family will need one. Probably right.

Next, Jacob, who never takes his eyes off the screen, his hands feverishly working the gaming controller. He does not like dinosaurs anymore, he does like girls, but not too many like him. He is the best shortstop ever and will absolutely play for the Chicago Cubs. I promise to be at his first major league game.

Last, but certainly not least, Jonah, the rebel. He is watching YouTube videos of skateboard tricks, tells me that he can do most of them. I promise to come outside later to see for myself. Next he shows me the skateboard graphic designs he is working on, I'm impressed. He even has sold a few to his friends, with hopes of having his own graphic design company. Wow.

'Your kids are incredible,' I join Rikki and Sadie on the deck.

'They're not bad for boys,' says Sadie.

Eye roll from Rikki, she must do that a lot, too. 'Why don't you go inside sweepea. I know you and the boys have volunteered to make dinner tonight.'

Off she goes. Rikki and I sit in silence, enjoying the sounds of nature without loud voices. Just as I am about to doze off again, the sliding glass door opens. It's Peter with a chilled bottle of Pinot and glasses. I could get used to this, I can't figure out why Rikki calls him an a-hole.

'I bought rib eyes to grill this evening, the kids are doing the sides, could be anything,' he says. With that he fills our glasses and leaves the bottle.

Nodding my approval, 'I think he may be a keeper.'

'Like the kids, he is on his best behavior, but yes, most of the time he is a keeper,' Rikki replies.

Mellow is the theme for the rest of the evening. PJ does a great job on the steaks, using a yummy blackened seasoning. Expecting macaroni and cheese for the side, I am pleasantly surprised with balsamic glazed grilled vegetables and caprese salad. The conversation is easy and filled with humor, all of the kids interjecting, no one shy. Almost makes me think about taking Peter up on the pie making, almost.

'Pssst, Aunt Lana, are you up? Aunt Lana?' Sadie fails at whispering. She is snuggled in bed next to me. 'I am not saying you have to get up now, but when do you think you'll get up and we'll go to the toy store?'

'Get out,' Rikki screams at Sadie. If I wasn't up before, I sure am now.

Eyes mostly closed, I head for the kitchen in search of coffee. I don't have to go far, Rikki is standing in the kitchen with an outstretched arm, mug in hand. Bless her.

'Thanks. What's the schedule today?'

'Slow roll morning, Peter took Adam and Jacob to their baseball games. How about we do the toy store after brunch?' Rikki then looks at Sadie who apparently does not agree. 'You'll live, go clean your room to keep yourself busy.'

The kitchen island is filled with a breakfast smorgasbord; fresh strawberries and blackberries, vanilla Greek yogurt, croissants, and homemade peach preserves, and last but not least, spinach sausage quiche. I'll need to pace myself.

Peter drops the boys home at noon, and we pile into the suburban. First stop is the toy store, then we'll move onto the sporting goods store for the older boys. They scatter like ants as soon as we go through the door.

Looking around, I spot pogo sticks. 'Hey Rikki! Remember these? Remember the time I pogo sticked on Max's finger? He still has the scar!'

Rikki comes around the corner, amused as I climb on the stick and start to jump. Alas, I don't have the balance I did when I was seven, and start to fall backwards. Note to self – do not attempt to pogo stick in flip flops. Unable to catch myself, I fall backwards into a shelf of volleyballs, which then, like a domino, falls backwards into a shelf of basketballs.

Another customer comes flying around the corner to see what has happened, he looks at me incredulously, 'Were you trying to pogo stick? Are you alright?' Rikki and Sadie are too busy laughing to help me up. Gotta love family.

'I am fine, thanks. It was the flips flops.'

Finally Rikki catches her breath, 'Anything bruised besides your ego?'

'Ha… Ha, can we check out now,' I answer. With a brave face on, we head to the cashier, I take note that my ass hurts.

Thankfully, Jonah and Adam are quick in the sports store. Adam picking up a new lacrosse stick, Jonah new skateboarding shoes.

The kids scatter again once we get home, Rikki and I head for the deck. 'Go ahead,' she says, 'be there in a minute.' Gingerly, I situate myself on the lounge chair, favoring my left cheek.

'Here,' Rikki hands me a tall glass with a promising looking liquid, and two pills.

'What am I drinking and taking?,' I ask.

'Moscow Mule and two ibuprofen.'

'Perfect.'

'You know, you didn't have to do that.'

'Yes, but the temptation to pogo stick was just too great,' I reply.

'I meant buying the kids presents, a-hole. I'll count the pogo stick incident as my gift.'

Peter, with excellent timing, comes through the sliding glass door, with a large wooden basket. 'Guess what my customer brought us!' Whatever it is, he is very excited about. Sensing we are not going to guess, he spills his guts, 'A bushel of Maryland Blue Claw crabs!'

Rikki and I look at each other, 'score,' we say simultaneously. Peter retreats into the house to start steaming.

Before long, the kids come out and cover the picnic table with newspaper, passing out bibs and mallets. Peter dumps the crabs in the middle, and the clan goes to town, grabbing the crabs and smacking. Quite a sight to behold, watching the bibbed clan, mallets in hand, crab shell flying. When in Rome... whack!

'Did your Mom ever tell you about the bloody mallet incident?' I ask the kids. From their faces, I think not. 'Well, your mom used to think it was funny to hide, then jump out and smack me with a wooden mallet, just like the ones you are using. One time, we were taking a family trip, Uncle Max was driving, Evita in the front, and your mom and me had to squish in the back. As soon as we got on the highway, your mom pulled out a mallet that she had spattered with ketchup to look like blood, and whacked me in the knee. Needless to say Evita was not happy, we pulled over, she smacked both of us with the mallet, then threw it as far as she could into the woods. And that was the end of the mallet wars.'

'How old were you?' asks Jacob.

'Your mom was twenty-three and I was nineteen.'

Adam rolls his eyes, 'I see. This is one for the leverage bank when I am asked to be more mature.'

'Thanks Aunt Lana,' drips with Rikki sarcasm. 'Be sure that I will return the favor.'


'Shhh!' Sadie the whisperer is at it again, trying to keep the boys quiet. Mornings come early in this household.

I limp out into the kitchen, 'Good Morning all, coffee?' This time it's PJ standing with a full mug ready. 'Thanks sweety.' I reward him with a peck on the top of his head. 'Where's mom? And how come you are not at the bakery?'

'She's on the deck. I'm done already, I was baking at four-thirty this morning. Are you really thinking of making pies with us?' He looks at me, hopeful, bless his heart.

'The four-thirty am thing may be a deal breaker, but you never know.' I take my coffee and head for the deck.

Rikki seems deep in thought, looks up as I come through the door. 'Hey sis,' she starts. 'I heard PJ, I know you don't want to make pies but it sure would be nice having you closer.'

I decide to share the lounge chair with her, 'I know, I know, but if I lived here, we would both be busy and probably not see much of each other. Visiting gives us better chunks of quality time. Plus, you get to visit me, all by yourself.'

'True dat, always nice to have time away sans kids.' We clink coffee cups.

'Hello sleepy head,' it's Peter, once more coming through the door bearing gifts. 'I know it may be a bit early, but I thought you would enjoy a Bloody Mary.'

Early schmearly! Wow! The Bloody Mary is a feast in itself; shrimp, pepper jack cheese cubes, pepperoncinis, I probably put on five pounds this visit. I look at Rikki, 'I think, though, I should visit more often.'

The rest of the day involves more eating and lounging, perfect combo. We watch a movie with the kids, and I say goodnight, with kisses and hugs since I leave at the crack of dawn tomorrow. Sadie fights tears, I lay with her until she falls asleep.

At the airport the next morning, it's my turn to fight tears as I hug Rikki goodbye. 'Oh buck up,' she says. 'I'll come down and visit soon. Keep me in the loop about what you are going to do with the business. And remember, do what is right for you.'

On the plane, my brain kicks into work mode. Being on California time, I'll have to wait for Larry to get the signed contract to me, I am hoping by noon Florida time. The flight is smooth, I grab my bag and almost sprint through the terminal, knowing Toby will be waiting in the arrival zone.

'Hey,' I greet him as I jump into his car. Uh oh, the expression on his face is not good.

'Good trip?' he asks.

'Oh no, I can tell something is wrong, spill it mister.'

'Uncle Larry is dead.'

◆◆◆

# Chapter 27

'What?' I scream. 'This is just a terrible joke right?'

'Sorry, Lana, but it's true,' replies Toby.

'It can't be! What the hell happened?'

'He choked on a snail, they couldn't dislodge it in time.'

'Okay, now I know you are kidding, you must be. He was at a festival, there must have been medical staff around, a doctor, a nurse, someone.' I am in utter disbelief.

'Well, he wasn't exactly at the festival. He was actually on a boat just offshore... in a threesome.'

Oh, this just keeps getting better. I am too stunned to continue the conversation, this can be disastrous. What about the contract to fund Point Tree for the repos? Will Larry's partner still sign? What about my contract with Point Tree? Thank God I didn't send it yet.

'Lana? Are you okay' Toby watching me with worry written all over his face.

My mind is racing, the best I can do is nod my head. Crap. Well, one of my first calls will be to Patrick. I just hope he won't say the dreaded, *told you so*. Toby does not even get the car in park before I open the door and sprint full speed into the office.

Flying by June's desk, I come to a screech to a dead stop. What the hell? June is all dressed in black, with a black lace veil covering her face. Geez. And wait, what? She has a friggin black veil on the snail! I know I should be sympathetic, but no time. I give her a quick pat on the back, plus a mumbled sorry. Nothing for the snail.

As soon as I am in my office, Tedi and Toby come in, closing the door behind them.

We all exchange looks. I blurt, 'This is a fucking disaster,' their heads bobbing in agreement.

Toby begins, 'Larry's partner called me late Friday on my cell with the news. He wants you to call him asap. I didn't think it was appropriate to ask him if he signed the contract. He seems the business type, no sense of humor.'

'What! Why am I just finding out now?'

Toby and Tedi exchange sideways glances, Toby says sheepishly, 'We didn't want to ruin your weekend?'

I just shake my head, I couldn't have done anything anyway.

'I think June is going to be useless today, probably all week. Why don't I send her home, so you don't have to deal with it,' Tedi offers.

'Okay, then come right back in here, I am going to call the partner, put him on speaker phone. Do we even know his name?'

'Fred,' answers Toby.

Tedi is kind with her words to June, who gratefully accepts the time off. This is twisted, I think to myself, she was not even supposed to be seeing him. Wrong on so many levels. Whatever, water under the bridge.

Tedi steps back into my office, closing the door. 'I'll have to deal with the other employees later, right now I need to know what Fred is thinking. I don't have a good feeling about this though.' I have a lump in my throat as I dial. If ever I needed to step up my game, this is the time.

Fred Fredd speaking.' Seriously? I look at Toby and Tedi, they just shrug their shoulders.

'Fred, its Lana Turner. First let me extend my condolences, and the condolences of my staff on the loss of your partner. We were all very fond of Larry.'

'He was a putz, but a likeable one, thank you. No surprise how he died. When he described to me, on more than one occasion mind you, the sexual positions he would get in during a three way, I'm surprised he lived as long as he did. I warned him about eating during those threesomes. Moving on, we need to talk about how we move forward.'

Ew and ew. 'Well Fred, I am hoping we can continue our profitable relationship. All of our streams of income are running smoothly, and the new venture with the repo purchase promises to be highly successful.'

'Your operation was Larry's baby, he was the proverbial boots on the ground. Quite frankly, I don't need the money, I kept Larry around for entertainment. I suppose if I were a traveling man, and not happily married, I would enjoy the trips to see you. It mystifies me that every one of you had sex with him, even the lesbian.'

Tedi catapults from her chair, 'That sir, is not true!'

I glare at her, doing the slicing motion across the throat. 'Fred, Larry made a verbal agreement with us regarding the Point Tree repos, we'd like to at least finish the project.'

'I don't see that happening, Lana. Sorry, but without someone making regular trips to check on progress, I have no way to hold you and your company accountable. Please send me a status on the two new homes we financed, hopefully they will be sold quickly and we can conclude our business. Good day.' Click.

Three jaws hit the floor. 'What the freak happened?' I can only shake my head.

'What now?' Toby asks.

'I call Patrick and do damage control. Don't worry, I'll figure everything out.' I hope.

Patrick listens intently on the other end of the phone, he is deep in lawyer mode. I recap the projects we had working with Larry; financing those who can't get financed, financing new home models, and the Point Tree repos. His assessment is not what I want to hear. Without Fred's signature the verbal commitment doesn't mean squat. Luckily, I did not sign the agreement with Point Tree to purchase the repos, so I should be off that hook. Fallout being they will not readily work with me again. As far as the new home, just get them sold, and fast.

'Thanks, that's about what I expected,' I say, sadness in my voice.

'Lana, maybe now is they time to think seriously about closing the offices. I know this feels like defeat, but look at it like an opportunity.'

Blah, blah, I just hang up. I call in Tedi and Toby, give them the scoop. Now I have to put on my happy face and deal with the employees. When I go out on to the sales floor, you can hear a pin drop. Oh boy, this should be fun.

'Tedi, can you please get the West Palm office on speaker?'

I clear my throat and start, 'As everyone knows, we've lost a friend and a partner today. Sad as it is, we need to keep moving forward with our business. Toby will contact Point Tree and see how we can still rehab and sell the repos. I need you all to concentrate on getting the new homes sold yesterday. In the meantime, I will look for an alternative financing source for our buyers with not so good credit. Unless you have appointments, I suggest everyone take the rest of the day off, and let's regroup tomorrow with a strong game plan.'

Mumble, grumble, mumble, is the response in unison. Tedi and Toby join me back in my office. 'Tedi, go see the park managers where the new homes are, assure them everything is okay, we'll cover any site rent necessary. But see if they will continue to give us free lot rent as breathing room. Toby, call your contact at Point Tree, let them know the situation, and see if they will let us buy the homes one at a time, but at the bulk price. I am going to get a meeting with Sal, see where he can fit into a new game plan. I'll call you after the meeting.'

'I have been expecting this call, Lana. My condolences to you on losing your Texas partner, especially in such a tragic way. Snails can be very tricky,' Sal says. Creepy how he knows everything. 'Starbucks in twenty minutes.' Before I can even respond, click.

Exhaustion from all the drama is setting in, but this is no time for weakness. Everyone else has left the office, I lock the door on my way out. Top down, I hit random Cher play, need to clear my head.

*Every now and then I begin again*
*I've pushed the rock up the mountain*
*Though I'm learning slow, now I think I know*
*How to step aside when the rock begins to slide*

Oh Cher, how do you know me so well?

Sal is at our usual table, my iced mocha waiting for me. A chocolate martini might be a more welcoming site today. 'Sal, thank you for meeting with me on such short notice.'

'Lana, I want to preface this meeting by saying I have no desire to take the place of your dead investor, but I do have the desire to continue to do business.'

'So let's clarify, you would like to continue to rehab homes with us, finance the homes you rehab. No bulk buys, no new homes, everything status quo.'

'Yes, and I have no intention of sleeping with your administrative assistant, June.' Did I detect a slight smile a small upward turn at the edges?

'Good to know, I don't think it wise for anyone to cross Concetta.'

With a real smile, he responds, 'Truer words were never spoken.'

Back in the Spyder, I call Tedi and conference in Toby.

'Okay, we are on solid ground with Sal, but no expansion of projects. I'm actually okay with that, all the eggs in one basket, yada, yada.'

'Apparently good news travels fast,' Toby reports, 'Point Tree heard about Larry, aka our money, and they have the homes under contract with another investor.'

'Lovely, and how did you make out, Tedi?'

'The sharks are circling, they want to start charging site rent at the beginning of the month.' 'I am not going to panic,' I try to remain confident. 'I'll talk to you both in the morning.'

Like an egg in a hot pan, that's how fried my brain is. Casa Lana is a sight for sore eyes as I pull in the driveway. I just want to get on my comfies and veg by the pool. And hope a brilliant idea pops into my head. Wait, something is out of whack. Why do I hear music playing?

'Hey sweepea,' Evita is in the doorway to the patio.

'Mom! What are you doing here? I thought Toby put you on a plane last Saturday?'

'I was never getting on a plane Saturday, Toby and I had a night out planned. Once he told me about Larry, I decided to stick around, thinking you might need your dear old mom. Come on Leebee, I have wine chilling outside.'

As I pass by her in the door way, I turn into her, hugging her tightly. I don't want to cry, I'm tougher than that. Despite my efforts, tears fall.

'There, there pumpkin. You will figure this out, you always do, I have absolute faith in you. Now let's drink.'

◆ ◆ ◆

## Chapter 28

I awaken with a start, cold sweat beads on my forehead. Evita is sitting on the edge of my bed, fully dressed, peach basket hat adorning her head.

'Boat or elevators?' she wants to know.

'Boats this time'. The streets are rivers and I am in a boat trying to navigate turns and hills and intersections in a rocking, rolling boat. Another one of my reoccurring dreams that indicates my life is out of control.

She gently sweeps my bed head hair out of my eyes, 'I didn't want to wake you, I have an early flight, my cab is outside. You have an eye bugger.' With that she scoops in with her pinky nail and extracts the crusted sleep.

'OW! And ew.' That hurt.

Beep Beep! 'Gotta fly pumpkin, the cabbie is waiting. Remember, you are the queen of your fucking universe, rule your world!' Backwards wave, and out.

'Thanks for staying and being here for me last night. Love you Mom,' I shout after her.

'Back attacha, sweepea!'

Right, rule my world. My first call is to Tedi to confirm she is meeting me in the West Palm office to calm the restless natives. Next is Toby.

'So was I ever going to learn that you and my mother had clandestine plans?' I ask, annoyed.

'You know how Evita is. I picked her up at the ship and before I knew it, we were off and running. Her flight was never for the same day.

'Do I want to know about your adventure at the Philling Station?'

'No.'

'Okay then, let's move on. You have Fort Lauderdale covered, keeping the troops focused on work, not drama?' I ask.

'Of course, they'll be fine. In fact, June called me, she is coming in today, sans the black attire.'

'Cool, I'll talk to you after a while.'

The West Palm office is sober, I mean somber when I walk in. Freudian slip – like someone had died. Too soon? There is a mysterious shoe box on the reception desk, marked SOS with a slit cut in the cover. I raise my eyebrow, looking around to see who is going to explain.

Sandy volunteers, 'Save Our Snails, donation box.'

'Better than the Dead Baby Bird Foundation,' adds Penny, always the sympathetic one. She was the one that gave Uncle Larry that description.

'Okey Dokey, maybe we'll just send flowers. I'm sure everyone has deals to work on, let's get crackin.'

Tedi is already in my office when I walk in, 'I put in two dollars,' she says.

'Don't encourage them. Had the boat dream this morning, and Evita scooped a bugger out of my eye.'

'Signals it's going to be a banner day.'

'I think we need face to face time with the communities where we were going to buy the repos, do damage control. It shouldn't be that big of a deal, we have been working successfully with them for over two years.'

As we come out of my office, Penny confronts us, Mable and Sandy watching on, 'So is it true? Was it at the same time? If it was, that's really gross, you're cousins.'

'What the hell are you talking about?' Tedi asks.

'Don't play dumb. You two sleeping with Uncle Larry.'

Tedi and I just look at each other and head out the door, more ew.

The visits go well, the managers haven't lost in any confidence in our rehab and sales abilities. All extend their condolences. The question remains, are doing rehabs one at a time, even with Sal, enough to keep us afloat? And is that enough for me?

Toby checks in and lets us know that, although no one is jumping for joy today, they are indeed back to work. Point Tree is still talking to us, just on a different level. Back to where we started it seems, at least we aren't in a worse position.

Back in the office, the atmosphere seems to have regained its buzz, everyone on the phones. No one even looks up when we walk in, Tedi and I head into my office and shut the door.

'So, do you have a plan?' She wants to know.

'At this point, I think we just have to keep working with what we have, and wrap up our business with Fred Fredd. I need to take a hard look at the numbers and the inventory to make a decision for the future.'

'Sooo… speaking of the future,' Tedi looks hesitant, this can't be good. 'Karen knows some people that have this really cool ship that makes it into international waters in ten minutes. It's a casino ship. Karen told them they should talk to me about running their on board casino. I haven't talked to them yet, I wanted to talk to you first.'

Huh. Tedi was a dealer in Atlantic City and Las Vegas, she can deal any game and has the personality to pack a table. Her issue has always been with the corporate BS. Before she showed up at my door and started working with me, she was working in Atlantic City. And as I said before when I opened the door, she came in, mumbled something about being a dissident, and a hole in the wall of the casino manager's office from a door knob. I didn't ask any questions, she started working with me the next day. I try to not look too disappointed, I know how much she loves dealing.

'What are they offering you? Any idea?' I ask.

'I think I would be in charge of the whole casino, training and everything, but I won't know for sure until I talk to them. If I talk to them.'

'Tedi, you have to meet with them, this sounds like a great opportunity.'

'I was going to wait to see what you are going to do.'

'Go talk to them, Tedi, see what they have to offer.'

Hesitantly she says, 'Okay, thanks. Hey, by the way, what are we getting Toby for his birthday? It's Thursday.'

'We are forcing him to go to Key West, remember? I booked him into the Bed and Breakfast right in old town. We have to tell him that if he doesn't go, we lose all of our money. Guess we should actually tell him today, so he can plan.'

'Why don't we take him to dinner tonight?'

'Sure, why not, set it up, doesn't matter where,' I reply.

We decide to all meet at Sudsy's Room, in Delray of course. Even though it's a sports bar, Toby loves going there for the wings, best blue cheese dressing *ever*. And Delray works in case, just in case, we decide to have a cocktail or two, my house is always in walking distance.


Six o'clock on the dot, we are all locking our cars and walking into Sudsy's, perfect timing as usual.

'So, are we here to drown our sorrows or celebrate new beginnings,' inquires Toby.

Tedi gives him a sideways look, 'Neither my friend, let's order then we'll tell you.'

Sudsy's is your standard sports bar and grill. Lots of high top tables, wide open room, huge TV screens all with different sports. It's enough to make you dizzy. We head for our favorite high top, far from the center, close to the pool table and Pacman machine.

Kinda scary that wherever we go, our server says, 'The usual?' Here that means a large order of barbecue grilled wings, extra blue cheese and celery, side of fresh made potato chips. Coronas all around, extra limes.

In two shakes of a lamb's tail, our food and beverages arrive, tipping well is the key. 'Tedi, let's not try the thumb thing again,' I warn.

Toby smiles, 'Oh please do, I am so sorry I missed that. Okay you two, so what's up?'

'I know your birthday is not until Thursday, but this is a time sensitive gift,' I explain. 'And we will still go out on your actual day, so this is a twofer birthday.'

Tedi hands Toby a small, brightly colored gift bag. Gingerly, he pulls out the tissue paper, and unfolds the paper. 'Oh My God! I love Maxwell's Bed and Breakfast! Three nights! I'll look at my calendar and see when I can go right now.'

'No need,' Tedi explains. 'It's only good for this weekend. We already know you don't have any plans.'

Toby is by far one of the hardest working people that I know. There are mornings that he is in the office before six, but never later than six thirty. Never missed one day of work, will work night and weekends if I need him. He takes on jobs and tasks that I would normally hire a contractor for, without even a word to me, it's done. And on top of all that, he's an awesome friend. So this is the only way to get him to go, with an expiration date.

'What? But… oh what the hell, I'm going to Key West!' he shouts. Several of the other patrons, hoot and holler, raising their glasses in celebration. Happy hour is indeed happy tonight.

With that, we dig into our wings and potato chips with gusto. Soooo good, you would never know that I am basically a carb conscience, healthy eater. Really. Bellies full, we come up for air and order another round of Coronas.

'We going to talk about the elephant in the room?' Toby asks.

'Not tonight,' I answer. I'm actually sick of talking about the business, I need to look at the pros and cons, get off the fence, and make a decision, but on my own.

Tedi thrusts her bottle into the air, Toby and I follow suit. At the clink of the bottles, she cheers, 'To living life our way, Cin Cin.'

◆ ◆ ◆

# Chapter 29

The drama of earlier in the week seems to have died down, although mumblings and rumblings are still present. Sol is in from Phoenix, we have a lunch date scheduled. Spending time with him is like spending time with a wise old owl, he freely shares his nuggets of wisdom and insights into life. As a bonus, Sol genuinely seems to care about my success, and, of course, he always pays for lunch.

'Alright ladies, I am headed for my lunch date,' I announce, to no one that cares, nice.

The only head that looks up is Sandy. 'Leftovers please.'

Sol has chosen Dorothy's Dock, a casual seafood restaurant with a perfect touch of elegance, which in Florida simply means cloth instead of paper napkins. That's a big deal for lunch. The best part is the fact that it is right on the Intracoastal Waterway.

The hostess greets me, and seems to know who I am meeting, 'Right this way, your lunch companion is already seated.' She whisks me directly to the outside patio, where Sol is relaxing, watching the boats cruise by.

Seeing me approach, he stands like a gentleman to greet me. 'Lana, such a pleasure as always, you look absolutely wonderful.' And of course a kiss on my cheek.

'Sol… your visits are too few and far between,' I warmly reply. 'So what brings you to Florida?'

He reaches into the ice bucket next to the table and extracts an expensive bottle of Pinot Grigio, 'I hope I am not presumptuous in assuming you would join me in a glass of wine?' he fills my glass.

We both laugh, this is not our first rodeo together.

'My brother died,' he states. 'I am no spring chicken, I have decided to go ahead and sell my communities here, give myself more free time.'

'Oh Sol, I am so sorry about your brother, I know the two of you were close. And of course sorry that you will be selling your Florida businesses. I hope this does not mean the end of our friendship.'

'Not sure what you see in an old codger like me, but thank you. I would hope we will stay in touch. You know Lana, I'm aware of your, shall we say, your business challenges – and sadly our Puerto Rico venture did not come to pass. You should think about selling entire communities. You would make more in one sale than you do right now in a year. Food for thought, and speaking of food, let's order.'

Scanning the menu, I decide on grilled shrimp and crab salad, with the house feta vinaigrette. See, I told you can I eat healthy. Sol likes my choice, and orders the same.

'So is it true you had an affair with Dorothy,' I ask meaning *the* Dorothy of Dorothy's Dock.

Sol simply smiles ear to ear and pours me another glass of wine. A gentleman never tells.


Walking back into the office, I quietly deposit a white 'to go' bag on Sandy's desk, she looks up at me, questioning, 'Waffles?'

'Waffle fries,' I respond.

'Close enough,' she digs into the bag. 'Score, ketchup, too.'

Back in my office, I am feeling a bit melancholy.

'Why so glum Lana Banana?' Tedi is standing in the doorway of my office. There is always someone standing in the doorway of my office.

'Sol decided to sell his communities here.'

233

'Wow, that sucks, not for him, but us. He is terrific to work with.'

'I know, yet one more change to our world. Speaking of, when do you meet with the casino boat people?'

'Headed there now. You sure you are okay with this?' She is hesitant, but she knows my answer.

'Go! Are you kidding, this is an awesome opportunity! Call me after your meeting, can't wait to hear about it. And Tedi, they will love you.'

I have a meeting of my own. I set another appointment with Dr. Babs, didn't tell anyone because I don't want a lot of hoopla, just some help with clarity. Half an hour later, the pile on my desk a bit smaller, I let the crew know I am headed out. The drive is not too bad this time of day traffic wise, and as usual, Cher is willing to keep me company.

There is a small knot in my stomach as I get out of my car and head to Dr. Babs' office. Not like I have to make a final decision today, I say, chiding myself. Did I say that out loud? Hmm. The door to her inner sanctum is open, no other crazies waiting or leaving.

She glances up over her granny glasses, taking them off, she smiles at me. 'Lana, come in, close the door behind you.' Said the spider to the fly. 'Sit, get comfortable. Tell me what's going on.'

'Thanks. So, FYI, the family reunion went well. No more elevator dreams, but I did have one boat dream, the one where the roads are rivers? And I can't make the turns, and there are hills in the rivers? Maybe I forgot to tell you about that one.'

'Sounds like the same theme, you feel like you don't have control. What would you like to try and accomplish today?'

Good thing I have an hour. I describe the business, the ups, the downs, the sideways, how I gain one source of income just to lose another. It's exhausting just explaining, I realize I am tired from it all.

Dr. Babs looks at me. 'This is business Lana, this is how it goes, up and down. Deal with it or don't.' She must see the shock on my face, I was looking for a bit more sympathy. 'Do you enjoy what you do?'

'I'm good at it.'

'Do you have fun?'

'The people are fun.'

'Do you make a good living?'

'I support myself.'

'Are you afraid if you try something new you will fail?'

'No.'

'Are you afraid that your friends will desert you if you make a change?'

'No.'

'Then what the fuck are you waiting for? You are bored, Lana. Go, live life, take risks! I have heard you talk about the people in your life, they will continue to support you and love you. You know this is the decision you want to make, so strap a pair on and do it!'

Wait… what?? My kind of therapy! 'Alrighty then!' I jump up and head out the door feeling like I can conquer the world. Woot woot!

Walking to my car, I hear, 'Don't look this way, Betty. I won't tell anyone I saw you coming out of the shrink's office if you don't tell anyone you saw me.'

Just as I start to turn my head, she shouts, 'I said don't look!'

Snap, my head turns forward and I keep moving, nothing going to bother me today. Smiling all the way to my car, I am greeting by two more smiling faces, Toby and Tedi.

'Come on, we are all headed to my house,' Toby commands. Not even questioning how they knew I was here, I just get in my car and follow them to Toby's house. Dr. Babs certainly hit the nail on the head with regards to the people in my life, I hope she is just as accurate with her other insights.

Tedi plays bartender, Toby plays chef. Lickity split, we have martinis and a wonderful knosh in front of us.

'To new ventures, for all of us,' Tedi, lifts her glass into the air, Toby and I following suit.

'But how did you...' I start, then stop. Of course they know, they know me, and I know them.

# Chapter 30

I'm really doing it! My eyes pop wide open, today is the day I'm going to share my plans with the family on my usual Saturday morning calls. My family will have mixed reviews about my decision to shut down my business, but ultimately they will be supportive as always.

It's certainly not the first time they have heard this scenario from me, I have tacked and changed the direction of my career path more than once. There was the export business, the decorative wood burning business, the tee shirt business, the fitness shake business... you get the idea. I think I had a good run with The Manufactured Home Store, close to three years.

Needing a clear and concise brain, I brew an espresso, add a big dollop of cream to lower the temperature, and down it like a shot. Bam! That works, brain engaged. However, I am thinking since its early, I'll take a quick jog down to the Intracoastal and back, engage the whole body, the mind body connection, blah blah.

A quick mile, and I am back to the house, shaking out the muscles, head goes round and round to loosen the neck. It's like I am preparing for a heavy weight bout, float like a butterfly, sting like a bee. And for the final touch, I blend a fresh fruit protein shake. Let's get this party started, who should I call first?

Easy choice. 'Hey Max, surprised I caught you at home.'

'Hey Sis,' he greets, 'Yeah, I sprained my ankle so I am home taking it easy, well, until the Save Our Streams group comes over.' He'll never admit it, but his love for causes gene definitely comes from Evita.

'I have a bit of news, I am closing down the manufactured home business.'

Awkward silence, maybe I should have started with Evita. 'I see, any particular reason?'

'It's not a whim, Max. The business is just barely holding its own. The stress of keeping it going is to the point of not being worth it.'

'And what are your plans for the future, Lana? Do you any have any?'

Yikes, wrong choice, he is not exactly being Mr. Supportive. 'Yes Max, Toby and I are going to continue to rehab mobile homes and sell them. We have a money partner.'

'Uh huh, rehab being the operative word the way you two consume alcohol. In fact, I am willing to bet that you would have less stress and more money if you and your crew spent less time imbibing. And nice money partner, the mob guy, that's safe.'

Wow, judge much? Time to end this call and move onto the next one. 'Max, I have a plan, I am not doing this willy nilly. I'm going to hang up now and chalk this negative conversation up to your sprained ankle and pain meds, whatev. Love you.' Disconnect.

That did not go as expected. I jump up and down again, loosening up, should I do another espresso shot? Nah, I'm good, neither rain, nor sleet, nor bitchy brother will sway me from my decision.

So who's next? Eeny meeny miney mo, catch a supportive family member by the toe, if they judge me let them go, eeny meeny miney mo.

'Hey Sis! How's the family?' I ask Ricki.

'Ugh, Peter being in Charlotte so much has me exhausted, I actually am starting to miss him. What's up with you?'

'Well, I decided to close down my business,' I state confidently.

'Okay, okay, so what's your plan then? I know you worry about everyone that works with you. What's Tedi going to do?'

'Well, I need to wrap up what we still have on the table, I think thirty days should do it. It should also, hopefully, be enough time for everyone to make their own plans. As far as mine, well, when I talked to Max this morning, I told him Toby and I were going to do our own mobile home fix and flips. Not really true, but he was in one of his judgy moods, and I didn't want to deal with it. And, it looks like Tedi has a job with that casino ship, the Silver Cloud.'

'I hope you hung up on Max, he can be so negative sometimes. You know I support you, but I also worry about you. I just wish you would find something that can keep your attention for more than a couple of years, something you can really build on.'

'I know, I know, I just don't think it's in my genes. I have Evita's wanderlust, at least as far as careers go. It's not a bad idea for Toby and I to do the fix and flips, I'm going to talk to him about it.'

'So did he go to Key West for his birthday?' Rikki asks.

'Yep, he was really forced to with the expiration date on the bed and breakfast. Tedi and I just met him for a quick drink on his actual birthday, he was stressed about packing the right wardrobe. I'm sure he's having a blast.'

'Peter is serious about opening the Delray Beach Pie Hole, any chance you would think about, maybe, managing it?'

Oh boy. 'It's a really sweet offer, and if nothing else gels, I'll consider it. I'm sure it'll be a while before he can get serious about it. I still have to call Evita with the news, which will not be news to her. Love to the kids and Peter, I'll call you next week.'

'Love you back'

Next up, Evita, the best for last. I could tell her I want to feed fish to the whales at Sea World and she would be supportive and excited. Well, no, she would have to protest the incarceration of the whales. And I definitely get my job wanderlust from her, she has been an airline stewardess – yes, stewardess, that's how long ago – a proof reader, wedding planner, women's clothing store manager, museum curator, and who knows what else she has not told us.

'Morning Mom, what's on your agenda today?'

'Morning, Sweepea. Absolutely nothing, if you can believe that. So what's your big news, did you finally decide to throw caution to the wind?'

'Yep, I am going to tell the crew on Monday, the goal is to wrap things up in thirty days.'.

'Woot Woot! Good for you, any idea what's next?'

'Not really, but I have enough cash in the bank that I can take my time. I talked to Rikki, Peter is serious about a Pie Hole in Delray, she said again that I could manage it.'

I can literally hear Evita's eyes roll, 'Very nice, blah, blah, who doesn't love a good pie, but managing a pie shop is a whole nother ball of boring wax. I would say that you can come stay with me while you find yourself, again, but we both know I wouldn't mean it. Love ya pumpkin, but did my mommy time, need to be foot loose and fancy free.'

I have news for her, she never let kids slow her down. 'I'm good Mom, a weekend visit would be the max. Speaking of Max, I spoke with him this morning, he was very judgmental when I told him my plans.'

'Hang on a minute, let me go get my shocked face. That can't really have surprised you, he can be a real dick.'

So tell me how you really feel Evita. 'It's all good, I don't need his blessing to make changes in my life. Going to make this call short, I am headed to work out, then meet Patrick at Starbucks. He is going to help me close the business, all that legal crap.'

'Tell Mr. Anal I said hi, call me soon, love you!' Evita disconnects.

Still time for a workout before I have to meet Mr. Anal, I mean Patrick. It's a HHH day in sunny Delray; Hot, Hazy, Humid. My power walk to the gym counts as my warm up cardio, I'm drenched just walking the mile. No partner in crime today, Jillian is MIA, bummer, she is my motivator. But alas, she is in an undisclosed location after a sleepover with an undisclosed person, presumably of the male persuasion.

Martini with a Twist, puts me through my paces, which I attack with vigor. Finally making this decision has re-energized me, I am ready to take on the world. Workout done, I slug down a cold bottle of water, tempted to pour it over my head.

'Wow, maybe I need to change up your work out, it seemed too easy for you today,' Martine remarks.

'I'll let you know next week, but certainly a possibility.' I realize a big sweat bead just dripped off the tip of my nose. Wiping my face, I apologize, 'Ooops, that was a bit gross, but it's a tribute to your training skills. See you next week.' With that I am out the door.

It's going to be hard to cool down with this humidity today, I opt to walk on the shady side of the street. Taking my time, I window shop along the way. Gotta love these eclectic stores here in Delray, how many places do you find flip flops shaped like pineapples and bar stools in the shape of martini glasses. Hmm, may have to come back for a second look at those.

Patrick is waiting for me, at least he has the sense to get a table with an umbrella. He is classically dressed, white Ralph Lauren polo, khaki cargo shorts, dock shoes, hair appropriately mussed. I hate that he always looks so good. Wait, no mocha frappuccino?

'I know what you are thinking, but with the heat today, I wanted to make sure your mocha is frozen.' He pulls my chair out. 'Back in a sec.'

True to his word, he is back in a flash and I am slurping down the icy cold nectar, mmm, air conditioning from the inside out.

'So you are really doing this,' he asks.

'Yes,' slurp slurp.

'I thought this time maybe you would stick with it. Maybe you should just scale back to one office?'

'Nope,' slurp slurp. 'And no lectures! I have money in the bank, plus I will have even more as we sell off the inventory.'

'You would have more inventory if you hadn't given away that home to the woman living in the airport.'

'Did you just hear yourself?' I ask. 'Okay, so what do I have to do to shut the business down?'

'How much money do you have? How do you plan on making it last? Do you have a plan of any kind?' He lectures on…

Before I can stop them, my eyes roll. 'Did you not hear me say *No Lectures?*' Maybe if I offer to sleep with him, he'll shut up.

'Okay, it's really pretty simple, we dissolve the corporation and we have to do a final filing…'

My eyes glaze over, sleeping with him would definitely be less painful. I look at him over the top over of my frappuccino with my best bedroom eyes.

'Stop it, Lana' he warns. 'Well, not really, but this is stuff you need to do. Okay, never mind, I'll take care of it for you, sheesh.' Hah! Mission accomplished, he's so easy. 'I have another solution to your predicament...

Uh oh, Sherri at ten o'clock, headed this way, worlds will collide.

Patrick spots her as well, looks at me nervously. 'Lana, a very attractive woman is headed this way. Please know that I did not encourage this, I have been focused on you. This happens to me all the time, beautiful women approaching me. I will politely tell her that her advances are not welcome.'

Oh the ego of this man, this will be fun, sort of. Sherri is making a bee line for me in full sashay. She has on very short shorts, kind of like Toby's, and a white with sea foam green sleeveless linen blouse. Definitely brings out her green eyes, the white shorts accenting her long tan legs. Am I checking her out? Well, this is awkward.

'Lana, I seem to be running into you quite a bit lately, maybe it's Kismet,' her eyes boring into my very soul.

Recovering, I remember my manners, 'Sherri, this is Patrick, Patrick this is Sherri.'

Patrick is still trying to recover from the fact that he is not the target of her lust. I can't help it, a small, nervous giggle escapes me. 'Nice to meet you, would you like to join us?' he says. Wait... what? Is he crazy?

Sherri just tilts her head, smiles, looks at him, then turns her attention back to me. 'So this is my competition? Game on, see you soon I'm sure.' With that she takes my frappuccino, in one sip empties the cup. 'Mmmm, refreshing' and sashays off.

'I need another,' handing Patrick my empty cup.

'Me, too,' he replies.

Back at the table, he starts, 'As I was saying before, well before… anyway, I have another possible solution for you.'

Slurp slurp, 'And what would that be?'

'You can marry me.'


'Shut up!' Jillian screamed. 'What did you say to him?'

I just got home from Starbucks and Patrick's mind blowing proposal, Jillian was finally home from her sleepover, dirty stay out that she is.

'I was so shocked I spit my mocha frappuccino out all over his white Ralph Lauren polo shirt. You know how anal he is, he jumped up and ran to the bathroom to try and clean up. As soon as he was inside, I sprinted home.'

'Soooo sorry I missed that! So now what? That's a hellava elephant to leave in the room.'

'No shit, I guess avoid him as long as possible.'

'Sound plan.'

## Chapter 31

Just another manic Monday is an understatement, so much to do, so little time if I am going to stick to my thirty day goal to close down the offices. Toby and Tedi are in the Fort Lauderdale office with me, catching up on events.

'You go first, Lanalu,' says Toby.

'Okay, Patrick proposed, I spit my frappuccino all over his white polo shirt and then high tailed it out of there. Now you, Toby.'

With a shocked look on his face, he says, 'I met a gorgeous man in Key West and I'm in love! He's from New York, he is driving his U-haul down today and moving in tomorrow! Now you Tedi.'

Hoping to one up us, Tedi says, 'Karen and I are moving in together and we are going to have babies!'

No clear winner in round one. 'Okay then, details to be discussed later, clearly over cocktails. I need to tell the crew what's happening, do you think I can do a memo?'

Obviously, the answer was no. The tricky part was telling both offices without one leaking it to the other. There has to be a distraction to keep them from talking to each other. Got it. I'll tell the Fort Lauderdale office, treat them to lunch, ditch them, have Tedi babysit them keeping them off their phones. Then, I'll zip up to West Palm, telling them I'm treating them to lunch and meet me at the restaurant, with Toby doing the babysitting.

I share the details of my master plan, 'Everyone know the plan? Synchronize your watches, GO!' Toby heads up to the West Palm office, Tedi announces to the Fort Lauderdale crew that I am treating everyone to lunch. Free food works every time, no questions are asked.

Tedi and I spend the time before lunch to review the pending sales and inventory. If we stay focused, we can get everything sold and closed, and everyone should walk away with a comfortable cushion. And that includes Tedi, Toby and myself. Who says I don't have a plan?

'It's time,' Tedi is in my doorway, of course. 'Just let them order, including a cocktail, then rip it off like a band aide.' If adult beverages are going to be involved, I guess I better raid petty cash for the cab fare.

We decide on Los Amigos, they know us there and will hopefully be tolerant. As luck would have it our favorite bartender is working, and the place is fairly empty, the benefit of an early lunch. We decide on the large round table, the better to see everyone. The server takes every one's order; I opt out of the alcohol, I need to have a clear head.

Tedi clinks a knife on her Corona bottle, guess she is not abstaining. 'Hey guys, Lana has an announcement. Go ahead, Lana.'

Yikes, what if I wasn't ready? For good measure I give Tedi a swift kick under the table. We should all probably invest in shin guards. Smiling, I start, almost feeling like this is a press conference, 'Hey everyone, as you know, we have had a lot of ups and downs lately.' Server plops down drinks, good timing. 'We were hoping for Puerto Rico, but they stayed local. The new homes with Uncle Larry were certainly promising, but, unfortunately, he died. And with him also the large deals with Point Tree. We still have Sal, but he is limited in what he will do. Soooo...' drum roll please, ' I have decided that it's time to move on to new adventures and close down The Manufactured Home Store.'

Crickets chirping, blank stares, can you say awkward?

'You do know the wall in your office does not go all the way to the ceiling don't you?' Diane states. 'Most of the time you, Toby and Tedi are so boring we fall asleep, but we can hear you.'

'Huh, then I didn't need to buy you lunch?' I reply.

Mike chimes in, 'Of course you did. How long do we have?'

'I'd like to close in thirty days, time for everyone to finish their deals, clear the inventory, and put money in your pockets.'

'Cool,' says June. 'Can we have more than one drink?'

Poor Tom is just taking it all in. I feel badly, he didn't even really get started with us.

'I'm going to leave Tedi to chaperon, please remember she does have a budget. I need to head up to the West Palm office. Oh, and one last thing, if we get all the inventory sold, we'll have a big blow out at Adventure Island.'

Not sure they heard the last sentence. Diane seems to be calculating, 'if we're on a budget, maybe we shouldn't order food.'

I look at Tedi, 'Good luck with all that.'

She quips back, 'May the force be with you.'

I call Toby as soon as I am in my car. 'So how did it go,' he asks.

'They are probably going to blow the lunch budget on just cocktails, so pretty much as expected, seems they can hear us talk when we're in my office.'

'Duh, see you in thirty at the Coconut Hut.'

The lunch venue for the West Palm crew is obviously a tropical island setting, right on the Intracoastal, fashioned like a tiki hut, both inside and out. And of course, the prerequisite drinks in coconut shells with umbrellas. Your take would be that it's a tourist trap at first glance, but it's a locals place all the way. Reasonable prices, great burgers, and the best conch fritters with dipping sauce that has just the right amount of heat.

The gang is easy to spot, gathered around a large, round table. Deja vue? Except this one used to be a spool of some kind. The first round of adult beverages has been delivered. There is an empty seat which I presume is for me, with a ruby red grapefruit martini waiting. I wasn't going to drink, but what the heck, just one.

'Hey gang, thanks for meeting me for lunch. As you know, we have had a lot of ups and downs lately' -

'Blah, blah, June had Sandy on speaker phone. New adventures, yada yada, closing down, yada yada, thirty days. You are aware that Sandy has intercom to your office, aren't you?' Penny, always the delicate touch.

Toby steps up, 'Then let's drink a toast to new adventures!' Blank stares, crickets chirping. 'I have cab money if anyone needs it.'

'Barkeep, another round!' shouts Mable. I will miss her, she has grown and blossomed under my care. Salud!


Thirty days fly by, deals written and closed at the speed of light. All of the inventory including the new houses are sold and funded. Despite knowing that they will be out of a job, the crew maintains a chipper mood. I don't know any one's post Lana plans yet, but I've certainly heard rumblings, makes me happy and sad at the same time.

Sal of course is unfazed by the closing of my business, and of course he knew before I did. He assured me that this is not the end of our business relationship, I am too amusing. He has also hired Tom, something about having Detroit business acquaintances in common. Something else I don't want to know about.

Side note, I have managed to avoid a serious conversation with Patrick about the M word, citing being too focused on shutting down the business.

As promised, I have a big blowout planned at Adventure Island. Tedi and Toby voted against it, as it will cost a chunk of cash, but what the heck it's only money. And since I am paying, they promised not to tell Patrick.

Adventure Island is an adult water playground, tucked into a cove area of the Intracoastal in Boca Raton. Every water toy imaginable is at your disposal; jet skis, paddle boards, water trampoline, kayaks, water slides, and of course, several floating bars. Two rules for today, no motorized sports and keep your life vest on. To make sure everyone travels safely, I chartered two party buses to pick up and drop off. Let the fun begin!

As soon as the buses stop, the crew scatters like kids in a candy store. The brightly colored water toys are accented by the teal water against the turquoise sky. And as luck would have it, white puffy clouds only, no rain in the forecast.

Smiling at the scene, Toby and Tedi come stand next to me. 'Well,' I sagely remark, 'this should be a humdinger. What say we grab an adult beverage and mingle, find out every one's plans. Rendezvous in one hour?'

I'm going to do my best not to get mushy, so probably limiting my alcohol intake is a good idea. Mike is laying on a mat, just soaking in the sun. Good thing he did not wear his titanium leg, we'd have all been blinded. I am almost blinded anyway by his Casper the Ghost white skin.

'Hope you put on Sunblock,' I say.

'I have stuff I put on with a trowel, it's waterproof.' He answers.

'So what are your big plans?'

'I don't want to get sentimental, but thanks again, Lana. You allowed me to make enough money to realize my dream of becoming a dance teacher, and some day, competing. The new leg makes all the difference. And you have free lessons for life!'

I also have two left feet. 'That's awesome, and love the G-string swim suit.' Yikes.

Moving on, I take my time, swimming back stroke so I don't spill my drink. The crew all seem engaged, so I just enjoy the view. Toby is laughing with Penny and Mable, Tedi is chatting with Sandy. June and Diane are sleeping on water mats.

Seems like a good idea, I can just float and relax, turn my brain off. I must have drifted off, as I am rudely awakened by cold water dripping onto my face, its Sandy.

She rests her head in her hands on my mat. 'Hey Boss, well, ex-boss. This kinda sucks that you closed the business.'

My heart sank. 'I know, but the stress was no longer the good kind. Have you decided what you're going to do?'

'Going to live on a commune in New Mexico, they want me to be the cook. Probably will serve a lot of cereal.'

Okay. 'Don't they usually eat what they grow in communes?'

'If I planted Cheerios, then pretended to pick boxes, do you think they would buy into it?'

'Worth a shot,' I replied. I give her an A for creativity.

'Cool,' and she dog paddles away.

An ear piercing whistle gets my attention, Tedi and Toby are on the floating bar by the water slide. Time to compare notes.

'I'll start,' I say. 'Mike is going to be a dance instructor and I have free dance lessons for life.'

A nod of heads. Tedi's turn, 'Diane is going to be a phone sex person. Is there an official title for that? She just has to sit at her desk and talk slutty, so pretty much like she did at the office.'

Fitting, another nod of heads.

250

'I have a good one, June is going to move to Texas and be Fred Fredd's personal assistant!' Toby feels he got the scoop of the century.

Interesting. My turn again 'Sandy is going to be a cook in a commune, she is going to plant Cheerios.' Head nods.

'Here come the last two, can't wait to heat their plans,' Tedi says. Mable and June swim up to the bar, order lemon drops, down them and look at the three of us.

'Guess what we're going to do, go on guess, never mind, you never will.' Penny looks at Mable gleefully.

'You tell them Penny, I can't explain it like you do,' Mable defers to the stronger one.

'We are going to start an Internet business, selling sex lubricants!! The flavors will all be alcoholic drinks, like margaritas, slow gin fizz, mojito. How cool is that! Tell them the name Mable, go on!

'I'm going to spell it so you'll understand, LICKOR LUBES Get it! Come on Penny, let's go do the water slide.'

With a twirl, they are paddling away. With head nods, we look at each other and simultaneously say, 'Okay then.'

Watching Penny climb to the top of the slide is highly entertaining, she is not the most agile. In position, she hurls herself down the slide feet first, then for some reason unbeknownst to anyone in the entire universe, she flings her feet in the air.

Eyes wide, Toby notes, 'I always heard she likes to wear her feet for earrings.'

'I'll never be able to unsee that,' whines Tedi, rubbing her eyes.

'Another round?' I ask. Head nods.

## Chapter 32

The Saturday morning calls are kept to a minimum, just letting Rikki and Evita know the big bash at Adventure Island was a success. I don't bother with Max, as I am sure he will tell me what a colossal waste of money it was, blah blah. If I want to hear that lecture, I can just tell Patrick about the bash.

Rikki and Evita are both chomping at the bit to find out what paths the *ex*-employees decided on, so I promised I would call them both tomorrow. Right now, I have to get ready for Patrick, he's coming over to have me sign the few last papers for the business. Unfortunately, it's also time to face the music on his marriage proposal.

Bright yellow shorty nylon shorts, neon green sports bra, and multi colored tie dye tank top are the attire of the day, maybe I can distract Patrick by blinding him. To say I am anxious is a bit of an understatement, I definitely need to refrain from caffeine. Is it too early for a Bloody Mary? Probably.

Hearing his Corvette pull into my driveway, I do a last check in the mirror, good to go. 'Come on in, it's not locked,' I shout.

Damn, he looks yummy as always, Madras shorts, yellow polo shirt, blue blue eyes popping out of the tan face. 'Good Morning, brought you Starbucks, white mocha latte.'

Oh boy, he's bringing out the big guns. 'Thanks, so what do you have for me to sign?'

'What? No pleasantries?' He leans in and gives me a kiss on the cheek.

Mmmm, whatever cologne he has on is like the whip cream on top of the already perfect hot fudge sundae.

'Sure, how are you?'

'Why I'm fine, Lana. And you?'

'Good, thanks, now let's sign the papers,' before I give into temptation.

Sighing, he sits at my high top dining room table, breaks out his two-hundred dollar pen, and begins, 'Just sign everywhere indicated.'

'Do I need to read these?' Maybe I should make sure he didn't slip in a marriage application.

'Up to you.'

Nah, he knows he would pay dearly if he frigged anything up. Awkward silence, who will be the first to break it? What's the old adage? First one that talks loses?

Finally he speaks, 'Lana,' I hope he is not thinking of getting down on one knee. 'I hope you have been seriously considering my proposal, I did not make it hastily, you know how much I love you.'

What? Did he just say the L word? I need to derail this fast. 'Patrick, I know how much you care about me. And if ever I get to the point of in my life where I am considering marriage, and you are still around, I would consider marrying you. I am just not at the point right now.'

Shit, puppy dog eyes, are those tears? I walk over and take his face in my hands. 'You know I care about you as well… a lot.' Gulp. 'Let's just keep spending time together and see where it goes.' Then I give into temptation and put a lip lock on him, yummo!

Things heat up at the speed of light, madras and neon green are flying in the air! So glad I have plush oriental area rugs, tile is very hard. Something catches my eye on the back patio just as Patrick is doing something wonderful to my neck with his lips, Oh my god! It's Jillian! I frantically try to wave her away, but she just smiles, hands on hips. Bitch!

Out of breath, Patrick asks whats wrong, 'Big mosquito! Got it!' smacking him hard on the back, then give Jillian the finger. She sticks her tongue out at me and walks away in a huff.

Two hours later, Patrick is gone, and Jillian strolls back onto my patio. 'Damn girl, those work outs with Martine are working, and Patrick's booty ain't too bad either!'

Great, 'Let's never speak of this again. Thanks for not being you, and leaving.'

'You inspired me, I took a quick jog down the crepe store to indulge in the filling of the day.' Big smile on her face.

'Too much information, moving on, you're joining us tonight at Comfortable Shoes for the more intimate celebration of the Manufactured Home Store closing?'

'I have been waiting forever to go to Comfortable Shoes! Are you kidding! I have my outfit all picked out!' Oh boy…


The parking lot is jamming, but Jillian and I are able to snag a decent parking spot. 'Not as many trucks as I thought there would be,' Jillian remarks.

'You're thinking old school, most lesbians now are lipstick lesbians,' I remark with authority.

It's so packed inside we have to turn sideways to get through the crowd. Knowing Tedi, she is guarding our bar stools with her life. I can barely hear her screaming my name, but the arm waving frantically guides me.

'About time,' she yells at me. 'This was out and out war trying to keep these seats. Hey Jillian, you look fab, I see you brought the girls out to play.' No surprise that Jillian is showing off her cleavage, she should be popular tonight.

Candy is quick with two martinis. Sizing up Jillian, 'Any friend of Lana's probably drinks martinis. I'm Candy.'

Jillian returns the once over, 'Mmmm, Candy is Dandy, but liquor is quicker,' and with that she sucks down half of her drink.

'This evening will surely live up to my expectations,' says Toby, who came out of nowhere.

'Where were you hiding?' I ask.

'Dance floor, some of us actually have some moves.'

'A toast,' says Tedi, 'to new adventures, and to old friends. Salud!'

'Wait!' Teresa has somehow squeezed into our group. 'Candy, a glass of wine, please, and put it on Lana's tab.' How generous of me.

I ask, 'Where are Karen and Cristobal?' Tedi and Toby's now significant others.

They look at each other, Toby explains, 'We felt it better not to subject them to the crowds.' Translation, they wanted to let loose and not be on their best behavior.

'Speaking of crowds, Sherri at ten o'clock,' alerts Tedi.

The throngs seem to part for Sherri as she heads directly towards me, stopping with just inches between our faces. 'Lana,' then she leans in and speaks directly into my ear, her breath warm, 'I hope you're staying for karaoke, I've been practicing this song just for you.' Not waiting for an answer, she turns and walks away, parting the sea of worshiping lesbians.

'So that's Sherri, holy crap,' exclaims Jillian, the ego slightly bruised, 'And she didn't even look at me!'

'Her loss, no offense, Lana,' Candy is playing her cards right. Jillian pops open another button before she turns and thanks her. Another round appears on the bar before we can even ask. I may have to bring Jillian more often.

We spend the evening like we always do, laughing... a lot. More than once I find myself smiling, watching my friends interact. How lucky am I, and how silly of me to think this would ever change.

'Headed to the bathroom, if I'm not back in twenty minutes, send a search party,' I announce. It's for sure an obstacle course making my way to the ladies room, the line is out the door. Thankfully, it moves quickly, but it's still ten minutes of my life I won't get back.

Karaoke has started, that's going to make it harder to maneuver back to the bar. The crowd is manic, suddenly I am forced toward the stage. Now I can hear her clearly, its Sherri, singing Cher's *Take Me Home*. Wait… what? She has on a long black Cher wig, the curly one. I definitely need to avoid the stage, but the crowd is making it impossible.

I'm trapped! Front and center stage, the lesbians form a semicircle around me, blocking any escape, I'm doomed. Sherri is in all her glory, singing like there is no tomorrow.

*Take me home, take me home*
*Want to feel you close to me*
*Take me home, take me home*
*With you is where I wanna be*

She is down off the stage, I am looking around wildly, totally panicked, trying to get Tedi's attention. She is too busy watching the Candy-Jillian boob-fest. Sherri croons on, dancing dangerously close.

*One night with you*
*Lying here next to me*
*It's the right thing to do*
*It would be ecstasy*

Without warning, she has me in a lip lock, and oh my, what soft lips. Not thinking, I just react, tongues are touching, sparks are flying! Then just as suddenly, the spell is broken with the sound of a glass shattering. I look up to the silent crowd of wide eyes and slack jaws. Looking over at Tedi, I can see she was the one who dropped the glass, total look of shock on her face.

Candy comes to my rescue and starts the jukebox, slowly people start to move and talk again. Sherri is still next to me, staring. The best I can do is a nonsensical mumble and scurry away as quickly as I can back to the bar. Candy has a fresh martini waiting, bless her.

'So? How was it?' demands Toby.

'Well, it didn't taste like cherry chap stick, but I liked it.' Tedi salutes me with her martini. Jillian is observing all this with rapt attention, then looks over at Candy like she's a fresh filled crepe, oh boy.

The moment seems to have passed, we move onto to our usual silly conversations. However, I find myself glancing over my shoulder every few minutes, ready to bolt if I spot Sherri headed this way.

'Lana Turner, you're up next,' announces the DJ.

More surprised looks from my peeps, almost to the level of the kiss. 'What?' I ask. 'It's a banner evening, can't a girl sing to celebrate?' And off I go to the stage, ready or not. How bad can I be?

Gingerly, I take the microphone into my hands, and fortunately for me, no one seems to be paying much attention. Clearing my throat, I nod to the DJ, and I begin.

*That's life, that's what people say*

*You're riding high in April,*

*Shot down in May... But I know I'm gonna change that tune,*

*When I'm back on top, back on top in June*

One by one, the crowd is turning towards me, as you can imagine, Frank Sinatra is not one that they normally hear.

*I said, that's life, and as funny as it may seem*

*Some people get their kicks,*

*Stompin' on a dream... But I don't let it, let it get me down,*
*'Cause this fine old world it keeps spinnin' around*

I don't know if it's me or the song, but most of the bar patrons are swaying to the beat, drinks in hand. A few people mumbling the words along with me.

*That's life, I tell ya, I can't deny it,*
*I thought of quitting, baby*
*But my heart just ain't gonna buy it*
*And if I didn't think it was worth one single try,*
*I'd jump right on a big bird and then I'd fly*

Now everyone starts chiming in, full verse.

*I've been a puppet, a pauper, a pirate,*
*A poet, a pawn and a king*
*I've been up and down and over and out*
*And I know one thing:*
*Each time I find myself layin' flat on my face,*
*I just pick myself up and get back in the race*
*That's life, that's life... And I can't deny it*
*Many times I thought of cuttin' out but my heart won't buy it*
*But if there's nothing shakin' come here this July*
*I'm gonna roll myself up in a big ball and die*
*My, my*

End song, applause, applause, I drop my head in a bow. When I look up, the crew is giving me the martini salute. Sherri is front and center, staring at me, licking her lips, uh oh. I frantically look for an escape route.

Suddenly Candy is by my side, 'Come on, out the back way.' How very clandestine.

'But what about Jillian?' I ask as we reach the back door.

'Don't worry about her, I'll make sure she gets home safely.' How convenient.

One last look over to the bar, the peeps are laughing and enjoying themselves, nice. Out of the corner of my eye, I see a flash of red hair moving quickly this way.

'Go!' shouts Candy. 'I'll let the others know.'

Turning tail, I sprint to my car and peel out of the lot, wheels spinning, dirt flying. Oh, the intrigue, this night will be a story to tell over and over. As soon as I hit the first stop light, I take a breath, and put the top down. Cher, would you like to keep me company? Why yes Lana, I would. Wonderful, you choose the song.

*I've been brought down to my knees*
*And I've been pushed way past the point of breaking,*
*But I can take it. I'll be back -Back on my feet*
*This is far from over*
*You haven't seen the last of me.*


*There will be no fade-out*
*This is not the end*
*I'm down now.*
*But I'll be standing tall again.*
*Times are hard but*
*I was built tough.*
*I'm gonna show you all what I'm made of.*


And now for the duet

*I am far from over*
*You haven't seen the last of me.*


♦ ♦ ♦

CPSIA information can be obtained
at www.ICGtesting.com
Printed in the USA
LVOW01s1522140317
527180LV00010B/1034/P